Judy Astley was born in Blackburn, Lancashire and educated at Twickenham County School for girls. After taking a degree in English, she worked at the BBC for a while and then became a dressmaker and designer for Liberty's followed by several years as a painter and illustrator.

Judy Astley's previous novels, *Just For The Summer*, *Pleasant Vices*, *Seven for a Secret* and *Muddy Waters* are also published by Black Swan. She lives in Twickenham and Cornwall with her husband and two daughters.

Also by Judy Astley

JUST FOR THE SUMMER
PLEASANT VICES
SEVEN FOR A SECRET
MUDDY WATERS

and published by Black Swan

EVERY GOOD GIRL

Judy Astley

BLACK SWAN

EVERY GOOD GIRL
A BLACK SWAN BOOK : 0 552 99766 8

First publication in Great Britain

PRINTING HISTORY
Black Swan edition published 1998

Set in 11pt Melior by
County Typesetters, Margate, Kent

Black Swan Books are published by Transworld Publishers Ltd,
61–63 Uxbridge Road, London W5 5SA,
in Australia by Transworld Publishers (Australia) Pty Ltd,
15–25 Helles Avenue, Moorebank, NSW 2170,
and in New Zealand by Transworld Publishers (NZ) Ltd,
3 William Pickering Drive, Albany, Auckland.

Reproduced, printed and bound in Great Britain by
Cox & Wyman Ltd, Reading, Berks.

EVERY
GOOD GIRL

Chapter One

'Worm tablet. Don't forget the worm tablet.'

Monica Dyson, of meddlesome habit, stood at the kitchen doorway watching, ready to pounce with advice and criticism as her son decanted cat food from tin to bowl. One hand rested on the door handle for support, but the other, the one with all the silver bracelets, flicked and fluttered as if she was miming what her son's actions should be. Her tongue clicked little noises of impatience and she clung to the door handle to stop herself flying across the room and wresting the fork from his awkward, too-big fingers to dice the cat's supper herself. He was just mashing it about uselessly, in that hopeless way boys did, pulping it to a sodden thick mass instead of slicing it neatly crisscrossed to bite-sized shards the way she would have done it. Boys needed to be given jobs to do around the house, it made them feel important. Monica believed that men who weren't allowed to feel important made trouble for everyone, just to get themselves noticed. Her son-in-law for one. They had it in their hormones – something prehistoric about being allowed to think they were in charge of things. Any little thing would do, she'd come to realize over the years, just carrying a moderately heavy bag or being thanked for sweeping up a few leaves from the path. There wasn't a woman born who really couldn't change a plug.

'And cut it small otherwise she leaves half of it. Her

teeth aren't what they were.' Whose are? she thought to herself.

Monica's son Graham smiled down at the grey striped cat which purred and narrowed its sly orange eyes at him. He ignored his mother and concentrated on what he was doing. If he took his eyes off the cat she'd head-butt the bowl out of his hand and onto the black and white tiled floor and that would mean mess and trouble. He'd remembered the worm tablet (crushed and mixed in), he'd forked the food into a manageable mush and he knew there wouldn't be anything left in just ten minutes. The food was the cat's favourite – a foul-smelling mackerel mixture.

'It's all done, Mother, I did remember,' he told Monica patiently. He put the dish on the kitchen floor and the cat immediately started gobbling greedily at the food, still purring. She didn't care how neatly it was presented, she'd have wolfed it down straight from the tin like a greedy teenager home from a late night, foraging in the cupboard for spaghetti hoops.

'You'll choke,' he warned it, stroking the animal's ears.

'Don't fuss her while she's eating!' Monica scolded, reaching forward and smacking his wrist away from the cat. 'She'll only follow you for more attention and leave it all! She's got to get that tablet down. You'd know why if you'd seen what I saw in her litter tray this morning.'

Graham scowled but obediently left the cat to eat in peace, grumpily throwing the empty tin at the kitchen bin and missing. Flecks of processed mackerel scattered over the floor tiles and Monica gave an exaggerated gasp. 'Oh you are *such* a clumsy boy! Now look what you've done! Go and get a cloth, go on, and clear it up.'

Graham crouched at the under-sink cupboard, rooting through for a J-cloth and the Flash. He could hear his mother muttering furiously to herself as she went back to the TV in the sitting room. The sofa squeaked as she sat down heavily. 'Hopeless boy,' he heard her say. He smiled sadly to himself as he carefully swabbed down the floor. The 'boy' was thirty-nine.

The model's smile was sheer come-and-get-it, unsuitably so from among the virginal wisps of a white wedding veil. Barely deigning to touch the arm of her 'groom' as if to emphasize his lowly status as mere scenery, she strolled languidly along the shopping-mall catwalk, avoiding the meeting of eyes, the unprofessional temptation to be distracted from what she was doing. The simple dress clung to the full length of her body, with a curved split from ankle to thigh from which glimpses of one slim pale leg could be seen. It was the kind of dress that made it clear what marriage was really for.

Behind her, tiny and careful, watching the floor for where their satin-shod feet should be going, trailed a parade of six 'bridesmaids', in shades of pink and lilac, all net and silk roses, with baskets of daisies swaying precariously from their chubby fingers. The audience were bag-laden and weary but lingered to catch the end of the fashion show, careless of the approaching rush hour and the mounting car park charges. They sighed collectively at such a sight of pure prettiness and as the sleek couple reached the end of the catwalk, there was a spontaneous burst of applause. But when the model stopped to turn and pose and smile, the little train behind her continued walking, just as they had been told. No-one in the flustered, chaotic changing room had said anything about stopping. The girl felt them colliding together behind her and her paid-to-be-radiant smile faltered as they crashed into her and shoved her to a silky tangle three feet below the podium. There was an undignified scuffling of fabric, the rasp of ripping lace, and the pounding feet of the fleeing 'groom'.

'Mu-mmy!' wailed the model, clutching her tumbled veil and pushing her dress down to cover her mortifyingly exposed underwear. *'Mum-my!'* she roared, face scarlet and tears fast gathering. Lucy's mother Nina continued calmly folding clothes in the dressing area and assumed that she would be summoned if her daughter was truly hurt. If she wasn't, there was no point making a fuss − little mishaps like this would merely help Lucy on the stony road to independence. They'd laugh about it together later.

'Poor little thing. Where *is* her mum?' sympathized an onlooker, reaching across to help her back up onto the podium. 'Never mind dear, it was just an accident.' The reassurance attempt failed. The model gathered her crumpled skirt together, pushed her furious self past the sobbing remains of her baby retinue and fled. She was, after all, only ten years old.

Chapter Two

Nina Malone stood in front of her mirror and wished the bathroom lights weren't quite so ruthless. She was sure that under something less honest her face wouldn't look anything like as lived-in. She'd been a still-optimistic thirty-five when she and Joe had opted for the high-tech low-voltage lighting makeover. 'Then when you're old and your eyes have gone, you won't get lipstick all over your chin,' he'd joked at the time. At thirty-five, you were still a year or two from the end of thinking that was funny. Six years on, bloody Joe was no longer around to see (or care) where she smeared her make-up. She could be squinting into a powder-speckled hand mirror, or the reflection from the switched-off TV for all he knew.

'Oh what's the point?' she sighed, carelessly whisking blusher over her cheekbones. She placed her fingers each side of her jaw and eased the tiny amount of slack skin upwards. The years since the lights were installed disappeared, or at least she assumed they did, because that's what everyone who was slyly checking out the potential results of cosmetic surgery said. 'You've still got good bones, I'll say that for you,' her mother had told her a year or two ago. Monica had said it as if that was the only positive comment she was prepared to make, and then only grudgingly. Nina smiled at herself and forgave the brutal lights, because now they beamed down on the perfect gleaming teeth which had, many years before, got her the Pearl Girl toothpaste job, placing her grinning mouth on hoardings and magazine pages all over the country. 'So, you're a gob-model' had been Joe's bizarre first words to her.

'OK, so which earrings?' Nina turned and asked the man perched on the edge of the bath, watching her.

'Well it's only lunch,' Henry reminded Nina.

'I know. And it's only Joe,' she agreed. 'The pearl studs or the gold semi-quavers? What do you think?'

Henry inspected Nina by way of the mirror. He grinned at her, his weatherbeaten face corrugating. With the general unfairness of the ageing of the sexes, the light which was merciless to women made Henry look adventurous and interesting. He looked like an explorer, just back from discovering a new antipodean reptile. 'Huge great dangling diamond chandelier numbers, that would be my choice. Show the bastard that even without him – no, *especially* without him – you have *life*.'

Nina giggled. 'Oh *Henry*. You're completely useless. Joe knows quite well I'm perfectly happy, I don't have to prove anything. The semi-quavers, I think.'

She pinned them to her ears and rifled through her make-up bag for the right lipstick. Was the blue silk suit a bit *much,* she then wondered. It was new: Joe would comment, if only to find out how much it had cost. It was the kind of thing he thought he ought to know, now he was handing over alimony. He probably had a gaggle of friends who told him what to look out for in terms of overspending ex-wives, warning him she'd blow all the children's school lunch money in Harvey Nichols and leave them to forage on curled-up bread crusts and age-softened apples. She didn't want him to go thinking she'd made a special effort for him either. His vanity, especially since the delectable (and so *young*) Catherine had moved in with him, was thriving quite well enough without her accidentally feeding it. It was no good asking Henry's opinion, sweet and well-meaning as he was, he'd probably suggest an off-the-shoulder taffeta ballgown.

As she applied the lipstick she took a quick look at him. He sat observing her make-up process, just like the best of girlfriends waiting for gossip, picking up perfume bottles and taking interested sniffs at them and pulling faces. He was a cosy friend, she thought, so comfortably shabby, always wearing oversized shirts of soft, huggable fabrics, just like nightdresses back in childhood. He smelt of hand-rolled tobacco and oil paint and his newly greying hair looked as if he'd so long ago given up combing it that it no longer knew in which direction it was supposed to go. There weren't many people she'd feel so content to have draped over the bath edge while she got on with such personal going-out preparations.

Among the inhabitants of the Crescent where conversation of more than 'good morning' and some communal tut-tutting about what dogs had left on the pavement was seen as an assault on precious privacy, Henry's casual gregariousness was to be treasured. Unattached and uncommitted, he was always available for a drink, a grumble, a movie or a meal – no strings, no pay-offs required. The Perfect Man, Nina's friend Sally called him. Too close to home, Nina retorted, and anyway she wasn't looking.

Nina finished with the lipstick, put it into her handbag and leaned across to kiss his forehead. Henry recoiled, fending her off, laughing. 'You'll leave a big red mark!' he complained. 'I'll go all innocent into Mr Patel's for a paper and the whole neighbourhood will know that I'm the sort of sad old sod who can only get women to kiss me on the *head*!'

'OK then, no kiss, I promise,' Nina told him, picking up her bag and giving her back view a quick look in the mirror. 'By the way what was it you came round to borrow?' she asked him as they went down the stairs. 'Was it the stepladder, because if it was, I think you've already got it.'

'Can't remember,' Henry shrugged as they reached the hallway. 'No, I think, yes I'm sure it was the hedge trimmer thingy. I've had one of those notes from the Council; they're threatening to confiscate my privet if I don't stop it growing out over the pavement. Some small-minded sod in this miserable street must have reported me. They probably think it could put someone's eye out. My old mother was always saying that. Was yours?'

'Yes of course she was. They all were. There was that one and "If you pull that face and the wind changes." Probably still says them, on a good day. I'll have to ask Graham,' Nina said as she opened the door. 'The trimmer's in the shed, just help yourself. Key's in the padlock.'

'Thanks. Have a good lunch.' Henry strolled towards the side gate of the house and then looked back at her. 'Tell Joe from me that I still think he's mad. Oh, and run back upstairs and put the other earrings on. With his monstrous ego those little gold notes will have him thinking you're still hankering after the days when his so-called music filled the house. The *street*, even,' he added.

Nina hesitated on the doorstep as Henry disappeared round the corner towards the shed and the hedge trimmer. They're only earrings, for heaven's sake (only lunch, only Joe), she thought, hovering with her keys,

14

waiting to feel ready to leave. Joe was hardly likely to sit there over his *galette de tomates* or whatever wondering about the secret psychology of her jewellery. That was the sort of thing that happened at the beginning of relationships, not the end of them. She slammed the door shut and marched down the path. Fronds of stray wistaria reached out from the arch over the gate and brushed against her face. Perhaps Henry would notice, Nina thought, and give them a bit of a neighbourly clipping in return for use of the hedge trimmer.

Across the road, at number 26 (four bedrooms, late Victorian, period features) a man was attaching a SOLD sticker to the FOR SALE sign that had stood at the gatepost for only a couple of weeks. He looked up as Nina unlocked her car and whistled. She rewarded him with the full Pearl Girl power smile but he'd turned back to his hammering. Oh well, she thought.

In the car on the way to the restaurant, Nina felt the familiar rising nervousness that came over her every time she and Joe had this monthly so-civilized lunch date. It was an on-the-way-to-the-dentist feeling, dread and excitement and the certainty that real life was on hold till it was all over. It didn't have the same thrill as *dating*, but then it wouldn't with an ex-husband, but it came unnervingly close. This one would be the tenth lunch, all in different restaurants, just, as Joe had decided, for the pleasurable hell of it. They'd now covered all the seasons and were back to spring again, which made her wonder if she should be feeling new-startish, skin sloughed like a gleaming snake. 'The first Thursday of every month,' he'd suggested when their so-amicable separation had been agreed. 'Just you and me so we can talk about the girls and do all that family decision stuff without cutting into their time or having

15

silly misunderstandings over the phone.' He'd made it sound like a business meeting. She'd briefly imagined wearing a chalk-striped power suit and bringing along a file full of diary dates – doctors', orthodontists' and opticians' appointments, formalized lists of Emily's A-level grade predictions, what size Lucy's shoes were this week.

'Or so we can just have rows without feeling guilty about them overhearing us?' she'd countered wryly.

'We won't need to row, will we? Nothing to row about now that we've decided we don't live together any more,' he'd replied jovially. 'All that's in the past. We'll probably get on really well now.' How cheerful he'd sounded about it, as if this state of friendly separation, all the twenty years they'd been together, had been exactly what he'd been most looking forward to.

But although she and Joe were in the past, the girls weren't. You can't, Nina thought as the traffic crawled over Putney Bridge, you can't just have 'a nice clean break', as Joe had put it, when there were people involved who simply could not be broken from. She'd always thought that was a strange phrase anyway. Even with bones, a clean break meant just as many months of pain and difficulty as an untidy one.

Nina could see Joe arriving from the end of the street while she waited for a parking space to be vacated by a harassed woman loading a toddler into a Renault Espace. Joe was loping along as if he was walking for the fun of it, absorbed in his own thoughts and going nowhere in particular. He had a very loose way of walking, she'd always thought, like a lazily wandering lion. His legs were simply too long for staccato hurrying, so even when he was in a genuine rush he would give an irritating impression of leisurely pace. He was dressed in a smarter version of Henry-comfort, monochrome relaxed chic – white T-shirt (probably new, he bought at least four a month, unable to pass The Gap), loosely crumpled black jacket. His reddish-brown hair was, unlike Henry's, so expensively cut that it wouldn't dare think of being indecisive about which way it lay. He'd once said the secret of eternal youth was in a good haircut. And of course he'd got Catherine to bestow her mere twenty-nine years on him. Outside the restaurant Nina saw him stop abruptly as if the sight of its blue and white awning had suddenly reminded him why he was there, in that street at that time. What was he thinking so deeply about? she wondered as she backed her Polo, at last, into the parking space.

Graham sat in the weak sunshine on the steps of the Accident and Emergency department, neatly peeled the foil from the strip of gum and folded it carefully into his mouth. Three folds. Then he folded the silver foil (four folds) and tucked it into the top pocket of his shirt. He looked down and could just see it showing through, a little grubby greyish square outline against the white poly-cotton. He frowned. He didn't like the look of it but there was nowhere else for it to go. He couldn't put it in his trouser pocket in case of fluff. Though there wasn't likely to be fluff, he knew that. Mother always turned the pockets completely inside out before anything went to the cleaners. Clothes went into the washing machine with their pockets pulled right out too so nothing was ever lost, but nothing was ever hidden. Her hankies and stockings were washed inside one pillowcase and his underwear and socks in another one. She never lost socks like some people did. Nina, last time she'd come round to visit, had watched Mother pairing his up for putting away and had joked that her tumble dryer always seemed to eat them. She'd said there must be a secret place in every house where all the biros disappear to, and odd socks. 'Not in my house there isn't,' Mother had said, but she'd been smiling and he knew that was because she enjoyed Nina admitting there were things she couldn't do quite as well as Mother.

Behind Graham the swing door opened. 'Wheel-chair, cubicle three, straight up to X-ray,' a crisp voice ordered. There was a flash of white hat, and swish of dark blue skirt and the door banged shut again. 'No please, no thank you, no manners,' Graham muttered to himself. If he spoke like that at home, well it just wouldn't be on, wasn't something you thought of doing. But here, here it was jump whenever anyone ordered it, sometimes even *bloody* jump, and you just did it as if you didn't deserve manners.

He rose slowly to his feet, took the gum from his mouth, rolled it between his clean plump fingers into a perfect ball and wrapped it in the silver foil. This time it could go into his pocket because it was on its way to the bin, but he'd be careful not to forget and leave it there for Mother to find. Chewing gum, she always said, was a disgusting habit and tied your guts in knots. If it did, Graham thought as he went back into the bustling A & E with its smells of terror, blood and disinfectant, why didn't they see more cases in here? There should be ambulances full of kids clutching their stomachs, faces grey with pain and eyes wild. They should be squashed together on the shabby wipe-clean benches, groaning and pleading to be untangled inside as if they'd swallowed knitting with the needles still attached. He shook his head slowly as if settling his thoughts and made his way to cubicle three. There sat a plump old lady, with a badly cut and bruised leg, sausage curled sparse hair ashy grey just like Mother's. She wore a big pink knitted cardigan, patterned with holes and ribbons like a vast baby's jacket and clutched an old-fashioned string shopping bag bulging with onions. Graham smiled at her. He liked old people, most of *them* had manners. 'Hello then love, been in the wars?' he asked, gently unbraking the chair and mentally promising her a smooth ride to X-ray.

'I like the outfit, that colour's exactly your eyes,' Joe commented admiringly as he and Nina arranged themselves at their table.

'Thanks,' Nina replied simply, smiling at him. She accepted a menu from the waiter and looked around. She felt strangely as if her real self was over by the window, watching the scene. She observed herself being self-controlled, not clumsily lobbing back the compliment with an 'Oh this old thing?' type of remark, or getting defensive and lying that it was in a sale, less than half-price. Those were things she might have said during the married time. She knew better now. And of course *now* it was none of his business. Other things were none of his business too, like the answer to the question she always imagined hanging unspoken from him to her: 'Have you met anyone?' If he asked she'd have to give him the quiet triumph of hearing her say no. She'd say she wasn't looking and he wouldn't believe her. He'd never believe someone wasn't looking for sex. That he should perhaps have not been, during their marriage, had been more than a small problem.

'Drink? Spritzer as usual?' Joe asked.

'Thanks, yes I'd love one, but *just* one. I brought the car.'

'You always do. I can't think why. You've still got the

minicab account if you want it. I sometimes wonder if you bring it to make sure you keep utterly sober,' he teased. 'That Polo is your minder.'

'You know I hate drinking at lunchtime. If I do, it means the day's over, for me. I might as well just go straight to bed.'

He grinned, looking wolfish. 'Hmm, now that I *do* remember.' Then he quickly rearranged his face to more suitable post-separation seriousness and ordered drinks. Nina felt awkward, and then cross. How could her ex-husband even begin to imagine she'd find suggestive remarks amusing? Perhaps he had some warped idea that she'd be *grateful*; that a discarded wife could do with the charity of the odd thrown-out sexy comment. Or perhaps he meant nothing at all, she reminded herself. Joe had never been a great one for deep thought before he spoke – it was part of the general flippancy that went with the advertising business. And from him, a composer of jingles that stayed annoyingly in the head, words weren't even required for work. He'd always been the first to claim it just didn't matter what rubbish he talked as long as the tune fitted.

'This is such a pretty place,' she said, resorting to commonplace observation, looking around and admiring the strong Mediterranean colours, solid bold blues, acid-free yellow. 'It's got the kind of freshness that makes you feel you can hardly wait for summer to come.'

'It was always your favourite time, wasn't it?' Joe said, leaning back in his chair and grinning at her over the top of the menu.

'It still is,' she replied rather crisply. 'I haven't suddenly taken to wallowing in gloomy winter just because you're not around, you know.'

Joe held up his hands in mock surrender. 'OK, OK! Sorry, I didn't mean anything sinister. Anyway I'm glad you like it here, I thought you would. What do you fancy to eat?'

Nina studied the menu and chose quickly, allowing herself time to think about the *when* and *who with* aspects of Joe having visited the restaurant before. Horrendously, the part of her that was still somehow disconnected heard her say, and tried uselessly to stop her saying, 'Have you been here with Catherine?' Joe was concentrating hard on the menu.

'Huh? Oh yeah. And some people from Channel 4. It was Catherine's idea actually, bringing you here. She just mentioned on the way home that you'd probably like it.' He sounded casual enough but she noticed he didn't actually risk looking up and meeting her gaze.

Nina felt her skin chilling. How wonderfully *clever* of Catherine, who'd only met her briefly and twice to know just what she, Nina, would like. She also felt the envy elves gather inside her and present a little scene to her unwilling brain. It was of Joe, arm round pin-thin Catherine (colt-legs, plainly elegant clothes but peculiarly prissy jewellery), a wet night, yelling goodbye to friends under the blue and white awning, bundling each other into a taxi and dashing home eagerly to . . . to fuck.

'I think I'll start with the salmon crêpe,' she said brightly. 'What about you?' There was a tomato tart on the list; she crossed her fingers under the table and silently bet herself that he'd choose that. He *always* chose something with tomatoes, if only so he could complain about the indigestible qualities of the skin. She'd accused him of 'enjoying' the delicate health of a swooning Victorian, the day he'd sat shivering by a radiator in his ski jacket, claiming his fifth bout of flu that winter and berating her for lack of sympathy.

'Well if they've peeled them . . .' he muttered, patting his stomach. Nina giggled delightedly and he looked up. 'Oh I know, ever predictable,' he agreed. 'The tomato and olive tart. Then the lamb. Now, tell me about the girls. What are they up to?'

'Well, seeing as you only had them last weekend, you can probably tell me more about them than I can tell you,' Nina said. 'Not much has happened, really. Lucy modelled a dreadful polyester selection in a fashion show in the Morley Centre on Monday afternoon. Apart from that, not a lot. Emily's working quite hard. At least she's in her room a lot, which I'm supposed to assume is the same thing.'

Joe frowned. 'Did Luce take time out of school? You know I think she shouldn't. She's coming up for eleven, changing schools soon, it's not an easy time for her.'

Nina sighed. They'd been having this one out for the last couple of years. Their differing opinions over Lucy's highly successful career as a child-model had been one of the first serious fissures in their marriage. *He* said she was just a pushy stage mother, forcing her daughter to fulfil her own lost ambitions, whereas *she* claimed it gave Lucy confidence and a useful nest-egg for later. 'She only missed the last hour or so, and it was only games.' Nina bit her lip, which made him grin knowingly, identifying her guilt. 'I told them she'd got a tap exam,' she confessed.

'Good God, and they thought that was OK, where mincing down a catwalk with a bunch of underage crumpet wouldn't be?' He shook his head.

'Well yes they did, actually,' Nina admitted. 'It's that trigger-word "exam", isn't it? Even with dancing the school likes to think the kids are notching up points for the old CV. They'd probably give her an afternoon off even if she was going off to do a test in shoe-lacing, so long as there was a certificate to show.' She wanted to tell him that the afternoon had actually been a disaster, that Lucy had fallen off the catwalk and put her foot through a silk lace wedding veil. She *could* tell it in a way that would have had him choking with laughter – but only if it was someone else's daughter, and only then if they were safely well over the legal marrying age. But she knew he'd only be furious that his daughter had been parading about in public dressed as a child bride. She'd felt horribly uneasy about it herself; it was somehow far sleazier than swimwear and underwear, which she'd agreed with Joe Lucy was not allowed to model. 'Just a cute novelty finale for the kiddies' fashion show,' the organizer had gushed. She'd check the schedule more carefully next time, if there was one – child modelling was a fickle business. However beautiful and confident Lucy was, there was always the choice of another who could be relied on *not* to fall off the stage.

Joe laughed, 'Pity there aren't A-levels in plane-spotting. Your brother would qualify for Cambridge. How is he, by the way? Still with your mum?'

Nina shrugged and smiled. 'I don't know why you even ask. He'll be there for ever, you know as well as I do. So long as she's willing to do his cooking and cleaning and washing and ironing, neither of them sees any reason to change things.'

'But suppose he met someone . . .'

'He won't,' Nina interrupted, laughing. 'He's comfortable. He and Mother are two of a kind. Just like small children they want every day to be the same, no surprises, no challenges. They haven't even got round to semi-skimmed milk yet. They've still got a phone with a dial.'

'Not a bit like you,' Joe said.

'Oh I don't know,' she told him. 'Now I'm on my own I'm beginning to feel there's a satisfying security in knowing what's coming. And what's not.' She glanced up at him, wishing as she said it that she *wasn't* going to say I think I've had as many surprises as I can cope with for a while.

'How's old Henry? Still cadging our lawnmower?' Joe asked. 'He always fancied you. I expect that's why he never liked me.'

'*Our* lawnmower?'

'OK, yours.'

'Actually Joe, Henry didn't like you because you were a lousy cheating womanizer and you made me cry. He doesn't like to see his neighbours weeping over the weeding.'

'Just like I said, he fancied you.' He grinned comfortably.

'Not so much of the past tense.' Nina glowered at him.

Joe, thankfully, was distracted by the arrival of food. 'Too much to hope that this puff pastry is made with butter,' he was murmuring as he inspected the tomatoes for lurking skin.

'Well mine looks wonderful. I don't care what it's made of, I'm just glad I didn't have to do it,' Nina said, suddenly feeling frantically hungry. 'How've you been anyway? Still love's young dream with Catherine?'

Joe frowned and put his fork down.

'Tomato skin?' she queried.

'Babies,' he said, looking thoughtful. 'I promised myself I wouldn't mention this. I promised Catherine. She wants it just between us.'

Nina felt tense. 'Better *not* mention it then,' she advised, her hunger evaporating and being replaced by reluctant but craven curiosity. There was still the main course to go, so they'd better stick to talking about their own children if she was to do justice to the menu. But she was only human: if he now refused to elaborate and changed the subject to holiday plans she'd never forgive him.

'Sorry,' he said, picking up his fork again. 'No it's nothing, really. It's just Catherine . . .'

'Look, Joe, I'm sorry, but you really can't expect me to want to come out and discuss your new home life. There are people you can pay for that. Or there's blokes in the pub.' *Now* he'd tell her.

'No. No you're right.' He sipped his wine, then finished the glass with one determined glug and gestured to the waiter. 'She makes me nervous, that's all. She mentions babies sometimes. Quite often, actually. I mean, God, we've only been together a few months.'

That was something, Nina conceded privately; at least Catherine wasn't the cause of their marriage ending. If Other Women had been part of the reason, at least it hadn't been one particular Other Woman. In fact the saintly Catherine, super-accountant, super-body, super bloody everything, wouldn't slip from her pedestal of perfection to be an ordinary adulterous marriage-wrecker. Nothing would ever be *her* fault. There was nothing of the mistress about Catherine, from what Nina could gather, unless it was mistress of her own fate. And now possibly of Joe's.

'So what's she been doing – dragging you into Mothercare when you'd rather go to Conran?' she gave in and asked. He was clearly going to tell her what was going on, she just wished he'd hurry up. He shrugged, as if it was enough to have dropped the hints

25

and he could now leave her wondering. Slowly and irritatingly he ate the last of his pastry.

'You shouldn't be too surprised, you know; she's probably thinking she's getting to that age, that body-clock age. Though, God knows, she isn't anywhere near it. She's probably just hearing a louder tick than she used to.' Nina smiled and added with the pleasing glow of callousness, 'Get her a kitten.'

Joe fidgeted with the tablecloth. 'I've done babies.' He leaned forward, looking at her intently and saying in barely more than a whisper, 'I've done babies, that's the thing I did with *you*. Babies were *us*.'

Chapter Three

'He made it sound like a shop,' Nina was telling Sally. '"*Babies were us.*" As soon as he said it I pictured the "r" the wrong way round and lots of multicoloured jolly lettering.'

Sally giggled, her ample thighs wobbling dangerously on the delicate little gold-painted chair. She couldn't be comfortable, she overhung by a good fleshy bit. Her feet, in elegant black suede slippers which rivalled the chair for fragility, were planted solidly apart for balance. Nina wondered if she should tactfully suggest she sat somewhere else. The purple velvet chaise-lounge, still on sale or return after eight months, would be ideal. The pair of pretty chairs were part of their gallery's stock, and like many of the items were quite definitely more about ornament than function.

Sally commented, 'It's the "*were*" that gets me. It sounds like a shop that's closing down. You can just imagine old greying Babygros, curled-up bibs and grotty potties and third-hand high chairs.'

'With food stains. And worse,' Nina laughed, and then was struck by a sobering idea. 'Perhaps that's how Joe sees me, since Catherine came along, someone with the final sale signs up: "Last few days, everything must go", all moth-eaten carpet and dingy paintwork. Everything about her is so taut and shining, when he looks at me I must remind him of an unmade bed.'

27

Sally gave a disbelieving snort. 'Huh, if anything, since he moved out, I'd say you'd gone in for pretty thorough refurbishment. I mean look at your hair – having it cut all short and feathery took five years off, at *least* – not to mention you lost a few pounds.'

'I could pretend that was trauma and misery,' Nina confessed. 'But it's just that there's only me running round the house doing the laundry, taking the rubbish out, striding round the Common with the dog. I should probably make the girls do more, but I quite like being able to fit into my snuggest Levis again.'

Sally and Nina's gallery, Art and Soul (Joe's idea), was quiet. It always was on Friday mornings. It wasn't a good time for browsing lazily around, choosing between paintings that consisted of more square inches of frame than of art, silver jewellery that resembled paperclips twisted in frustration and contorted steel cutlery with hand-whittled sustainable-teak handles. Everyone who was shopping in the area was across the road in the delicatessen or the organic butcher's or in Scissorhands next door having their hair perked up for the weekend. A few bored young nannies and au pairs sat on benches on the green near the pond huddled into their collective resentment that 'SW London' could extend so very far from the vibrant centre of the capital. They smoked sullenly and watched their charges throwing bread to ducks that were growing plump on *focaccio* and sun-dried tomato ciabatta.

Through the gallery window, from between two post-modern interpretations of terrazzo statuary, Nina could see a queue at the florist opposite, and the wine bar on the corner was filling up early with those who would have to pretend not to be dozing at their desks after lunch. Until the afternoon, when there'd be the usual rush of people looking for just the right little one-off, so cleverly original present to take for the weekend/dinner hosts, there was no need for the two of them to be sitting there waiting for customers and getting through endless coffee.

Friday morning was Sally's turn but Nina had been almost choking with the need to talk to someone about the lunch with Joe.

'I mean why did he want to tell *me* about it? Why does he think *I* want to know if Catherine's getting broody?' she asked.

'You've already said that twice,' Sally pointed out, getting up and rearranging a display of silver-painted octagonal cups. I'm not sure whether you want me to give you several possible interpretations or whether you'd rather keep it rhetorical and think about it on your own.'

Nina looked at her doubtfully. 'I don't *want* to think about it at all. That was the point of the parting. When we lived together, Joe made me think about him all the bloody time, what he was up to, where he *really* was, who with, all that. He was worse than a naughty toddler for needing attention. I keep telling myself I've got my own life to get on with now. I'd been doing fine till yesterday. Joe *was,* not *is.*'

'Too soon for that,' Sally, veteran of two divorces, told her. 'You'll need at least a year. Or another man, of course, though I bet you're the sort who thinks they don't need one. It's women like me who rush out for a new puppy the minute the old dog dies. That's probably why, metaphorically speaking, I always end up with a stray so utterly cute I just don't notice it simply isn't capable of being house-trained till it's too late.'

'Well even if I was on the look-out, there's hardly a vast choice of available men around here. Anything on the loose would get snapped up faster than a half-price

29

Armani number at Harvey Nichols,' Nina said, peering through the window again. 'Look there's one – just coming out of the deli, not bad actually, but he's got that "I'm just going to run home and marinade the free-range chicken before picking up the kids from the Montessori" look. For every "Not Bad" out there, there's some gorgeous, brainy, creative, *young Mrs* Not Bad, you can bet a heap of folding money on it.'

'Well you know what I think: you should do what I do and simply shop for men in the *Sunday Times* Encounters column. That way, you just go out with them as and when you feel the need for an ego-boosting date. No hassles, promises, breakfasts or blame.'

Nina laughed, 'Yes, but more often than not you come home complaining that they were a total waste of time and make-up.'

Sally wagged a finger at her. 'Learn by my mistakes. Never go for one that describes himself as "bored" – that means married. Or one that specifies a Good Sense of Humour. You should be able to take that for granted. They can use the line space to list more important attractions, like the Ferrari or the VIP.'

'When you say VIP . . .' Nina sensed a rather ruder interpretation than the usual one.

'Very Impressive Penis, of course,' Sally said. 'Anyway, what about your dependable old Henry-up-the-road,' she suggested. 'You wheel him out for supper sometimes and he's quite presentable. Haven't you ever—'

'*No*. Absolutely never. Henry is a brilliant neighbour and friend and has been for years and that's all. We don't fancy each other in the slightest,' Nina stated, adding to make sure Sally got the idea, 'Not even the teeniest slightest bit.'

'OK, OK, though some, less worthy folk than I,

would suggest that perhaps you doth protest too much.' Sally smiled slyly at her.

'No, really. I'm afraid I always think Henry's most attractive asset is his set of drain rods. Forget finding me a replacement man,' Nina insisted, 'I'd rather take up tap dancing or archery.'

'So do,' Sally suggested, looking at her sideways. 'You haven't actually *done* anything very different since you two separated, have you? I mean you just plod on. Well we all do, I suppose,' she conceded, worrying that she was being hurtful.

Nina said nothing, just went on looking out of the window. 'Look at those nannies out on the green. *They* have all the world's chances to change what they're doing, where they are. They've got qualifications, youth, energy and still they sit there smoking and sulking by the pond, watching someone else's kid getting muddy. They don't have to sit there in the damp air wishing this was Knightsbridge or Beverly Hills; they could *be* there. I've got Lucy and Emily and the house, hamster, cat and dog, an ageing mother plus the creeping wistaria and this gallery to deal with. You can only change small bits at a time.'

'Emily Malone!' The shout pierced straight through the collective clamour of fifty sixth-formers chatting their idle way down the stairs towards the school lunch hall. Emily looked round quickly, not for the voice, but for an escape route. She hadn't done the French essay, hadn't even finished reading *La Peste*, didn't at all care about rats, plagues, allegory or Algeria. If pushed she would admit that the only French words of interest to her were *Marie Claire, pain au chocolat* and Renault.

'Shit. Bollocks,' she murmured to Chloe next to her.

'Emily!' came the voice again, 'Tomorrow at the latest!'

'Lucky you. She's given up. She wouldn't do that for me,' Chloe said, turning to see where the voice was going.

Emily didn't look, didn't want to risk catching sight of Mrs Hutchins and her so-sympathetic spaniel eyes. Emily had been offered counselling by the school welfare officer, as soon as her parents' separation had become known. Now *that* had been a day of Embarrassments to be Remembered, when both parents, all smart prim suits like nervous Speech Day guests, had turned up together to do what they called the right thing. 'If you get stressed, or whatever, they need to be aware of the pressure you're under,' her dad had explained while she cringed and argued. They were such bloody *Guardian*-reader parents – all emotion-sharing and fervent reassurance. Couldn't just sodding well do the *other* right thing and stay together though, no chance. Whatever they said about putting her and Luce first, there was no stopping Dad from going to find his own path through the woods, as he put it. No stopping Mum from helping him pack.

Emily had refused the counselling – there was nothing to talk about. Nothing she'd let the school know about anyway. What could she tell them? The awful truth? A couple of Dad's advertising jingles (ice-cream and a cheap car) turned into mega-hits, he decided he was Andrew sodding Lloyd Webber and went all irresponsible and big-time, and Mum was being such a stroppy feminist she did everyone's laundry except his, and kept telling him his kind of success was only a fluke, like the lottery. It would be all round the staff room. Instead she kept an enigmatic silence, gaining a hefty amount of sympathetic leeway where homework was concerned, and a convenient assumption that the only reason for flagging concentration must be unhealthily repressed emotional angst. Emily was quite happy to take advantage.

'S'OK, she's gone. I thought we were in for one of her "I do *understand*, I *was* young once" rantings,' Chloe mocked.

Emily laughed. 'Do you think she was one, though? *Really?* Do you think if I asked her if she'd tripped or done speed or shagged someone whose name she didn't even know that she'd actually say "*Oh yes, yes,* happy days"?'

Chloe thought for a moment, pausing outside the hall to give the menu a quick glance. She didn't really need to, it was Friday, so lunch was therefore something fish-shaped with chips. 'She might. She might like the chance to "share". Perhaps she did the Paris riots back in 1968 and met some Gauloisey piece of French rough.'

Emily shrugged. 'I haven't shagged anyone whose name I don't know either so it would be just a pose,' she laughed. 'How disgustingly, typically *teenage* of me.'

'Well you are from a broken home, you're sure to be kicking at the barriers a bit. Doesn't your poor despairing mother find you moody and uncontrollable and your father not know what to say to you? Don't you put your little sister through secret mental torture?'

Emily joined the end of the queue and stared past a crowd of jostling boys at the food. It all looked orange. Bread-crumbed fish, lurid chips, glistening beans. Her father had told her, that weekend when he'd asked her to help choose paint for her and Lucy's room in his wondrous loft/flat, he'd told her about when he was fifteen and painted his bedroom ceiling orange. He'd told her about the paint blobbing onto the carpet, his bed, his head, and how his mother had said, "Oh that's lovely, darling," because she'd thought everything he did was God-perfect. No wonder he'd gone off and slaked his ego on every little slapper who laughed at his jokes. Mum should have known he'd do that, Gran had warned her often enough that men need careful cherishing, like delicate plants. It even said all that in *Man-Date*, Emily's new guide to getting and keeping the man of any woman's dreams.

'No,' she eventually replied to Chloe, who had lost interest and was using both her inky hands to sort her way through the contents of the hotplate for a decent fish. 'No. I'm a perfect child. I'd say a model child, but that's my beautiful little sister's role.' Emily picked up a tray and then laughed, 'Lucy doesn't get out of bed for less than two Snickers bars a day.'

'There are girls in our year,' Chloe murmured, looking surreptitiously around, 'who will get *into* bed for less than that.'

'I would too,' Emily said, absentmindedly scooping chips on to her plate. 'I met a man.'

'Man? Not boy? And what about the faithful Nick? You'll break his scummy heart. If he's got one,' Chloe said as they made their way to a table strewn with abandoned salty crisp packets, spilt yoghurt and cold, dead chips. Across the dining room, Nick, the school's most desired male, was sprawled across a table with friends, talking about football and pretending not to care that Emily wasn't about to come over and sit with him. Around the room, girls flicked their long clean hair alluringly, hoping he'd notice *them*.

'Nick's irrelevant, don't mention him. He's just a *boy*, just someone I learned to do sex with. But last weekend,' Emily confided, 'when Luce and I went to see Dad . . .'

She hesitated, both scared to tell and at the same time keeping Chloe hanging onto her words. '*Well?*' Chloe reached across and shook her plate.

'Sorry. It's just in here, with all these *children* and the squally schoolkid racket.' Emily sighed, chewed a chip and continued, 'OK. Well, this Catherine woman he lives with now, her brother was there to see her. And he's younger than her. Only about twenty-three or so.'

'But you're seventeen,' Chloe pointed out, looking disappointed. 'It's not much of an age difference. Where's the big deal? I mean, come back and tell me when you've pulled a bald sixty-year-old with grand-children and a pension and prostate trouble.'

Emily shrugged and flicked her hair back. Her hair was long and thick and red-blond. He'd said it was the colour of sunset, but he'd said it as if he was laughing at her, like a joke so she wouldn't think he was sadly drippy. He'd also said it in front of her father and Catherine, picking up a hank of hair like it was a sleeve of something in a shop to be felt before it was tried on. His fingernail had trailed across the back of her neck, very slowly. The other two hadn't seen that.

Nick didn't trail his fingers anywhere. His hands made a mad straight-there dash up her skirt, no loiter-ing, no hanging about and tantalizing. It had seemed all right at the time, exciting enough when she was in the same amount of hurry and didn't really know any better. She looked at the girls who were gazing at him so adoringly: suppose she went up to one of these romantic little innocents and told her that his dick tasted of old sock?

'Seventeen but a pathetic schoolgirl,' she said and then looked down in disgust at her moss green pleated skirt. 'And this place must be the only school left in the world where the sixth form still have a uniform. It's like living in a piece of fiction from grandmother days. Even the boys here are pathetic, sad things.'

Chloe nodded sympathetically and munched a handful of chips, waiting for Emily to go on: having kept it bottled up all week there was going to be no stopping her now. Emily pulled a bone from her fish and waved it at Chloe. 'Look, it must have been a real fish, unless they slide a few bones into this stuff just to make us think they are. Anyway, about Simon, I mean I'm only just thinking about my gap year, *if* I pass my As, and he's had his *and* university. Six years when you're both working is nothing, but *these particular* six years, loads happens. Plus, and it's a big plus, he's my dad's girlfriend's brother. I have a suspicion, but don't quote me, that with Mum that could be an insey-winsey problem.'

Chloe giggled. 'If you all married each other, you'd be your stepmother's sister-in-law. If you all had children, your dad would be his grandson's er . . . uncle?'

'I can't say anything to Mum. Not that there's anything *to* say.'

'No you can't,' Chloe agreed. 'But that's mostly because secrets are sexy. Is *he*?'

Emily put down the bone she was holding and pushed her plate away, all hunger, at least for food, gone. 'Yes. Oh God Chloe, *yes*.'

Nina sat in the Polo outside Lucy's school and watched the stream of children emerging. Mostly they were running, hurtling towards the freedom of the weekend like puppies let off their leads in a park, their mothers trailing behind, weighed down with their children's bags and coats and buggy-loads of baby siblings and shouting to mind the road. It all seemed such a time of burden, that phase when the children were so little, always constantly hung round with paraphernalia and worry. Even in the park there was the running in front of swings, bad dogs, evil men who just wanted your back to be turned for a second. Sally's boys were grown up now and she still worried that they might get run over by a bus or electrocuted in a launderette – so obviously it never ended.

'Don't be late out, please don't be late,' Nina murmured to herself, feeling anxious. They had to drive to Kensington, no fun on a busy Friday afternoon, for what Lucy's agent Angela, at Little Cherubs, had described as the 'go-see of the season'. This, when she'd got Angela to dispense with the persuasive hype and come across with genuine information, turned out to be an audition for a chain-store's new clothes catalogue. 'They're talking Caribbean, darling,' Angela had persuaded breathily. 'And terrific *money,* of course. Don't forget Lucy's book.'

Nina flicked through the 'book', a photographic CV of the best of Lucy's modelling work. Some of the earlier ones should be removed now – a few were a couple of years old and Lucy was now changing fast, losing her podgy baby-tummy and gaining cheekbones and pre-pubescent angles that would later become curves. She was a tall girl, and had probably inherited her mother's tendency to early maturity. Nina herself still recalled the humiliation of being the first one in her class (age eleven) to start her periods. Her mother had told her it was a perfectly natural thing, that she should be proud to have reached womanhood and not to be ashamed of it. 'It's not a curse, you ignorant girls, but a blessing and don't ever forget it,' Monica had boomed at them when Nina and her friend Paula had been sniggering over Nina's off-swimming letter.

'Can I go to Sasha's?' Lucy opened the car door, flung her bag on the floor but didn't get in. She looked expectantly at her mother, large cat-like blue eyes eager for an instant 'yes'. Sasha, stumpy and stolid, hovered in the background, kicking at stones on the pavement.

'Oh Lucy, I'm sorry but not today. You know you've got an audition at 4.30.' She smiled past her daughter to the stone-kicker: 'Sorry Sasha, another time?'

Lucy slumped into the car, her slanted eyes narrowed and her mouth pouting sullenly. 'I forgot. I *never* forget. Why did I forget? Have you got my stuff?'

As Nina pulled away from the pavement, she could see Sasha waving but Lucy ignored her, she'd moved on mentally straight from school to work. She was already turning round and searching through the bag on the back seat for a change of clothes and the essential box of food. Nina joined a trail of slow-moving traffic approaching Putney Bridge.

'What would you like to do this weekend? Perhaps Sasha could come over tomorrow and I'll take you out somewhere,' Nina offered.

Lucy, her mouth full of her favourite Dairylea cheese and salami sandwich, carried on munching but waved her hand to indicate something was about to be said. Eventually she swallowed, laid the half-eaten sandwich down in her lap and turned to her mother. 'Mum. There's something I want to say. You mustn't be cross, promise?'

'Well it depends. Have they just invented Saturday morning detention at school and you're about to tell me you've got one?'

Lucy laughed. 'Huh, no I'm too much of a *goody* for that. No it's weekends. Since Dad, you know, went.'

Nina pulled up at the traffic lights behind a Body

Shop truck, and the hope that it was using lead-free petrol crossed her mind.

'What about weekends? Don't you like going to stay with Daddy?' she asked anxiously. Perhaps Lucy detested Catherine. The shaming truth was that she rather hoped she'd say exactly that.

'Weekends, they've got like . . .' Lucy sighed with the frustration of finding the right expression '. . . like they're *weekends*, something different, something that's got to be really special, *every single time.*'

Nina thought for a moment, choosing words carefully. She heard Lucy crunch hard into an apple. 'Well that's because they have to be shared out. I expect Daddy just wants to give you a really good time so you'll want to keep coming to stay with him. It's he and I who are getting divorced, you see, not *you* and him.'

'Mum. It's not just Dad. It's you *as well*. You're always wanting to make them sort of special too. I mean when Dad was there we never got dragged out to the zoo or the Kingfisher pool or to the theatre. Well we did, but not all the time anyway. Now you're both doing it. I want to be just ordinary, do nothing.'

The traffic was on the move again and Nina concentrated on manoeuvring beneath the Hammersmith flyover. For a Friday evening, as many people seemed to be hurtling into London as out of it.

'Well tell me what you'd really like to do then. What's your idea of a perfect Saturday?'

Lucy didn't hesitate: 'Getting up at 10.30 and lying on the sofa in my dressing gown and my Totes and eating Coco-Pops right there, not at the table, and watching cartoons on telly for as long as I want.'

'Is that it?' Nina laughed, though it didn't sound too bad. It was the child's version of lazy Sunday mornings in bed with a choice of both intellectual and inane newspapers and coffee and croissants. She remembered mornings like that with Joe. Before the children they'd involved making love among the itchy crumbs, sharing a shower and then going to the pub. Now he probably did all that with Catherine, who, just as she had, thought they were making the most of the prebaby stage.

'Yes.' Lucy turned an anxious face to her. 'And can you tell Dad, because Catherine thinks television is all rubbish unless it's a documentary about old dead history people and she thinks we should only eat muesli with no sugar, and *never ever* on the sofa.'

Nina smiled. 'I don't expect she'll change her mind about that until she has children of her own.'

'She doesn't need any though, does she,' Lucy decreed firmly, 'because she's got Dad to look after.'

Nina sighed heavily. 'Oh Lucy, how can you of all people have picked up the idea that men are there to be looked after by women? He's a *grown-up*, not a baby or a pet.'

Lucy went into peals of gleeful laughter. 'I *knew* you'd say that!' she shrieked. 'It's so *easy* to get you to fall for it!'

Nina listened to Lucy's laugh. Even with the indulgence of a mother she had to admit it wasn't a pretty sound. From somewhere among her and Joe's ancestral way-back, their younger child had inherited an irritating high-pitched bray that ended on a cackle. If there was, as now, just something small to be delighted about there might just be the cackle on its own. Once it had been a sort of party piece, this donkeying, egged on by any amazed audience to almost uncontrollable shrill hysteria which only ended with Lucy streaming-eyed and choking and threatening to throw up. Nina

40

had hoped she'd grow out of it. There was still time, but it was hard to fight habit.

The audition was at a dingy rehearsal studio close to the Albert Hall. Nina thanked the patron saint of car salesmen for allowing them to persuade her that all she needed was the little Polo to replace the Passat she'd shared with Joe. In a couple of years when Emily went off to university, she'd probably be open to the suggestion that all she needed was a motorbike. It was quite an exhilarating thought, speed and power, leather, freedom. There she'd be, magnificently mid-menopausal, flying on her Harley Davidson and there Joe would be, changing his tiny son's (son's?) nappies and wheeling a slow buggy round the park, worrying about swings, dogs and bad men . . .

'Ready?' she asked Lucy. Lucy's school uniform lay in an untidy heap, thrown onto the back seat from the front. She'd changed, expertly managing not to expose her young body to bus passengers and van drivers, into jeans and a sweatshirt.

'I'll just brush my hair,' Lucy said, delving into the vast canvas bag that always went with them on these outings. 'Do I look OK? Are you sure this is what Angela said they wanted?' Her triangular little face, peering through the long hanks of pale hair that she was vigorously brushing, looked anxious. Nina felt sudden sympathy for her. Perhaps Joe was right, perhaps there was more of an element of pushing Luce into this than Nina was prepared to admit.

'"Clean casual,"' Nina reassured her. 'That's exactly what Angela said. *But* – you don't have to do this, you know, we could just go home. We could have a pizza, go to a film if you want.'

Lucy leapt out of the car, throwing the hairbrush onto the seat and slamming the door. 'No! No I want to do this!' she yelled through Nina's window. 'I *like* it. I like everyone looking at gorgeous lovely *me*!' Nina climbed out of the car and fed the meter while Lucy fidgeted and scuffed at the pavement. 'We can have a pizza later, if you like,' Lucy said, sounding, Nina thought, as if she was the grown-up calming a truculent child. Everything felt upside down.

Monica Dyson's diary hung from a shabby old orange silk bell-rope next to the phone. She picked it up and flicked through the pages, squinting and holding the book at arm's length. Just as she did every time, she then sighed deeply and put on the reading glasses that hung round her neck. It always felt so like giving in to despicable weakness. She peered over the top of them at the book and then turned to Graham who was halfway down the stairs, up and ready for the night shift, smelling of shaving foam and cheap deodorant.

Monica sniffed and wrinkled her nose. 'You'll make them nauseous,' she complained. 'Those poor patients of yours - the pong of hospitals is bad enough without you adding to their woes.'

Graham sat on the bottom step to put his shoes on, smiling gently and ignoring the complaints. He heard them every day: that one, or the one about the colour of his socks ('Purple? With brown shoes?') or the way he'd parted his hair ('Are you sure about the left? I always thought the left was for men who *bat for the other side*').

'They don't mind what I smell like, as long as I smell clean,' Graham told her patiently. 'And anyway it's for me. Takes my mind off all the Dettol and pee.'

'Ugh! Just don't tell me!' Monica shuddered, an all-over undulation that started from her gritted teeth and quivered down through her shoulders, body and rather weak knees. She sat down on the flower-embroidered stool at the walnut Davenport from which she did all her telephoning and letter-writing.

'I was just checking the diary,' she told Graham. 'It's this Sunday I said we'd have lunch at Nina's. Don't forget.'

Graham stood up and went to the hall mirror to adjust his tie. He did it slowly, as he did most things, his fingers working laboriously as if he had to instruct them individually what to do. His face was becoming pink, Monica could see in the mirror, and she waited in quiet triumph while he battled for the right words.

'I can't come, not this Sunday. There's a couple of F-117s flying in to Waddington. We're all going.'

They both knew, from years of experience, that there was a choice of reactions from which Monica, this time, selected wounded disappointment. She could have had let-down anger, or stalwart resignation. Graham's announcement was a nuisance but didn't rate a deep sulk.

'Oh but darling you *promised*!' she wailed, waving her arms and letting them settle into an outstretched entreaty. 'Nina will be so disappointed, and you haven't seen the girls for simply *ages*.'

Graham turned to face her, the tie no more straight than when he'd started. 'It's all right, I've already told Nina. She doesn't mind at all. She says she'll send a taxi to collect you so there's no problem about you getting there.' He opened the front door. 'I must go, I'll be late. Will you be all right?'

Monica was looking petulant, slumped at her little desk. 'Why can't she drive over and get me herself? Too much trouble I suppose.'

'Because she'll be doing the cooking, that's why,'

Graham told her. His quiet but affectionate 'goodbye' was completely lost in the slamming of the front door, leaving Monica sure that he'd simply walked out on her. She felt thoroughly aggrieved, and was determined to enjoy it.

Chapter 4

'Emily! Lunch in half an hour! Grandma's coming up the path *right now*!'

Nina's voice cut through even Alisha's Attic in the headphones and Emily knew that this time, the fourth time of asking (demanding), she really did have to get up. She opened her eyes and squinted into the semi-darkness of her room. There were shadows of abandoned clothes hanging everywhere: over the back of the futon, on and under the futon, across the desk, all over the pink deckchair, and a huge collection – every coat and jacket she'd bought and borrowed over the past five years – shoved onto the hook on the back of the door. At night in the real deep dark, just before she went to sleep, she sometimes imagined that the bulging bundle hanging on the door was a real person, a massive, hunched-over evildoing sandman come to sprinkle nightmare dust in her eyes. Come to think of it, she decided now as she pulled the headphones off, the idea of *any* dust, good dream-making or bad, being sprinkled in your eyes was a horrible one, like a cold gritty day on the beach. I'd rather have no dreams at all, she thought, stretching and yawning.

Lucy opened Emily's door, but wisely, since she had forgotten the rule about knocking first, didn't come any further.

'It smells disgusting in here,' Lucy complained, holding her nose. 'It's even worse than Humphrey's cage. I've come to remind you it's your turn to clean him out. And I can't find his exercise ball.'

Emily slid out of her bed, picked up a black crumpled jumper, sniffed at it and hurled it towards her overflowing laundry basket. 'Me and Chloe couldn't find an ashtray so we used it, well half of it anyway. It's probably still in the garden. Look, the other half's right here.'

From among the dusty muddle of discarded home-work, candlewax, old tissues and cluttered make-up on her desk under the window she picked up a half-sphere of transparent plastic, part of the ball in which their hamster liked to roll around the sitting room, looking exactly like, Emily remembered her dad say-ing, a total loser from *Gladiators*. She felt a twinge of guilt about that; he'd also said, one of the last things before he moved out, something really obvious about making sure the cat didn't get in while Humphrey was running around. He'd said it as if he was trying to think of things to say that would make them remember him, so they'd go round the house saying 'Dad says . . .' and keeping him with them. It had made her really angry that this way he was doing leaving and staying at the same time. The very next time she'd been in the house on her own, she'd hauled the cat out of its sleep on the top stair to show it the rolling hamster, and had watched, wondering if she really had the cold soul of a torturer, while the frantic cat batted the helpless little rodent round the room.

'It was Dad's fault,' she muttered now, like a life-saving mantra as she shuffled through the knickers in her drawer, looking for some that didn't really matter, seeing as it was only a boring Sunday, with just Gran (or *Grandmama* as she preferred being called) coming for lunch.

'What's Dad's fault?' Lucy still hovered by the door. She was very interested in breasts at the moment and hoped to catch sight of Emily's, so she would know, if these things ran in the family, what she could expect hers to look like quite soon.

'Oh nothing, just sod off,' Emily hissed at her, throwing her copy of *Man-Date* at her.

'Mind my face!' Lucy yelled, chucking a shoe back, 'I've got a re-call for *Barbados* next week!'

Emily stalked across and slammed the door, though Lucy, fearing more violence, was already halfway down the stairs. 'You and your fucking *beauty*!' Emily shrieked after her.

'Goodness, that girl's got your temper!' Monica said to Nina in the kitchen. She pattered about, dipping her finger in the mint sauce, looking for napkins in the wrong drawer and downing most of her sherry in three fast slugs. Nina concentrated on stirring the gravy, wondering what would be the least petulant and childish reply to that little comment of her mother's. Only Monica had really been allowed full use of good old-fashioned anger in the house when Nina had been a child. Lack of consideration of any sort would set her off, directing equal rage towards a neighbour with a waywardly overhanging tree and towards her husband for going off to Bognor with a barmaid. Any display of rebellious fury by Nina or Graham would be skilfully quashed by recourse to a threatened migraine. 'You're making me *ill*,' Monica would plead as teenage Nina stormed 'It's not *fair*!' when Graham, two years younger, was allowed to stay nights with friends and Nina had to be home by ten. Monica would drape a purple crocheted shawl round her broad shoulders and put one delicately probing cyclamen pink fingernail to the pulse on her temple. '*Throbbing*, my skull is *throbbing*!' she would wail, throwing herself on the lavender chenille sofa and pleading for the curtains to be closed and camomile tea to be brought. Graham learned very young that anger was a profitless emotion and became doggedly passive, learning how to get his own way by appealing to his mother's awe of his male supremacy, watching, placid, treasured and contented as Nina battled her way through adolescence.

'Hi Grandmama.' Emily, smelling of an optimistic overdose of deodorant, drifted into the kitchen with her hairbrush.

'Not in here, Em, go and brush it in the downstairs cloakroom,' Nina told her.

'Hello darling,' Monica air-kissed Emily, and sniffed. 'Interesting perfume,' she said. 'Peach blossom and *L'Air du Silk Cut* if I'm not mistaken. Poison, darling, absolute poison.'

Emily smirked cheekily, 'What, the peach blossom, Gran? You're right – it's disgusting. Just didn't have time to shower though. I'll be back, just got to brush hair.' And she was gone.

'She's just like you were,' Monica said admiringly. 'Nothing but trouble.'

Nina laughed. 'You make it sound as if I was the perfect daughter. I must say it would have helped if you'd given me that impression at the time.'

'Oh but I was your mother. Mothers are for laying down the tracks and making sure you children run properly on them. Grandmamas are for indulging and adoring from a safe distance. She'll turn out fine, one day, you'll see.'

Nina poured the gravy into a jug. 'I don't even begin to doubt it actually. She's not a problem, you know.'

Monica laughed heartily, almost choking on the last of her sherry, 'Oh darling of course she's a problem!

She's a girl – they're always at loggerheads with some-body, especially their mothers. Boys now, they were born to *please* their mothers. They do it all their lives, it's that special bond. You wouldn't know of course, only having girls.'

Nina slowly counted to ten. 'Let's eat, shall we?' she sighed. 'Everything's ready. Can you call Lucy while I put the vegetables on the table? She's outside, up in the treehouse playing with the hamster.'

Monica went to the kitchen door and looked back at Nina. 'You'll have to carve, won't you,' she said, eye-ing the steaming, rosemary-spiked leg of lamb doubtfully. 'Such a pity Graham couldn't come. Carving does need a man.' She was out in the garden before Nina could reply.

Nina sighed and picked up the carving knife. 'Any fool can carve meat,' she muttered, piercing the skin viciously with a fork. Hot juices spurted up and caught her on the chin, making her suddenly want to cry. 'Any fool with enough practice.'

'Cheese and prosciutto croissant or smoked salmon bagel?'

Joe had both the huge stainless steel fridge and the emerald Perspex breadbin open and was peering into them alternately. Sunlight streamed in through the window, making all the apartment's pale wood sur-faces look bleached like parched driftwood.

Catherine lay nestled in the cushions on the cream sofa surrounded by newspaper. Joe looked at her, watching her sleek yellow head turn prettily sideways to an attitude of cute thought. If she puts her finger to her chin, like 1950s fashion models, I'll know she's deliberately posing, he thought. It occurred to him that this might be a near-critical thought about her, the first in their three cohabiting months. It might be something to do with the hints about babies: now he was just waiting for her to drop in something about being hungry enough for two, or to catch her shoving a cushion up her dress to check out what pregnancy would look like in the mirrored door of the wardrobe. He was quite relieved when she simply turned to him, pose-free and said, 'Both, if there's enough. I feel wickedly greedy.' She grinned and bit her lip, resting her chin on the back of the sofa and watching him. *Now* she's posing, Joe decided, turning away and reaching into the fridge for the cream cheese. 'It's all that exercise,' Catherine said, narrowing her eyes at him suggestively.

She has a smaller, neater mouth than Nina, Joe was thinking as he put her croissant into the microwave. Being fellated by Nina had been an act of delicious terror. Her big, roaming lips had reminded him of overgrown exotic sea-anemones, threatening to devour him, penis, balls, body, brain and all. Catherine was more of a nibbler, making him think, even at the most unsuitable moments, of Lucy's pet hamster. I wonder what they're all doing now, he thought as he crossed the many metres of blond polished ash floor to serve his love with delicacies. With just a little masochistic nostalgia he recalled the wafting odours of roasting meat and crisp, floury potatoes. The smoked salmon, as he bit into it, felt limp, cold and hostile. His stomach rumbled, an old man's noise; he hoped Catherine hadn't heard.

'Next Sunday when the girls come, I'll cook us all a proper roast dinner,' he promised her. She looked up at him in wide-eyed surprise. 'Heavens, whatever for? It'll take half the day.' *The sexy half, before the girls get here* hovered behind her frown. Joe took no notice – his plans had moved on to the vegetables. 'Mm,' he

50

murmured. 'With carrots poached in butter and tar-ragon . . .'

'You girls will do the dishes for your mother, won't you darlings?' Monica smiled from Lucy to Emily.

'Mum and Dad always say we don't do things "for" her, like we're helping, because that makes out that all housework is just her job really and no-one else's and that's wrong,' Lucy corrected Monica, managing to sound as if she was reciting Holy Writ without quite understanding it.

'Quite right,' Monica agreed readily. 'There are now three grown-up women living in this house and chores should be shared equally. So that means you'll *definitely* be doing the washing up, won't you?' She piled plates together and passed them across to Emily who scowled, but took them across the kitchen to the dish-washer.

'Give us a break, we've only just finished. Why don't you and Mum finish the wine and Luce and I'll clear up in a minute?'

'OK, but just stack that lot first, please Em, then you can go off for a while if you want,' Nina told her. She felt depressed. Lunch seemed to have taken an un-sociably short time, as if none of them had really felt like making much of a conversational effort and it had simply been a matter of functional feeding. Reluctant as she was even to think it, she was pretty sure it had something to do with the lack of men. As a family of women dining together they suddenly seemed an apologetic, sad lot. She and her mother were *leftovers*, and probably about as unappealing as the lamb would be by tomorrow. Perhaps she should have invited Henry, just to balance things a bit; he was always happy to accept a free meal. But then he'd have so charmed Monica she'd be forever after dropping comments about *that nice man down the road, how silly for you both to live alone* . . . She poured more red wine into her glass and took a deep swig.

'*Château La Lagune*,' Monica read from the label, waving her glasses vaguely between her nose and the bottle. 'Rather nice. I don't think Graham would have liked it though. Did Joe buy it?'

'No, I did,' Nina snapped. 'I know what I like.'

'All right, no need to get touchy, darling. I just wondered if it was left in the cellar from before . . . well, you know.'

'Before Joe left. Yes I know.' Nina could feel herself getting crosser and searched her mind for a decent reason. 'Sorry. It's just that Sunday feeling,' she said, shaking her head as if it was surrounded by summer midges, hoping to clear a space in her mind for some cheerfulness.

'Would you like some cheese? I've got Brie and Yarg and something from Italy I think.' She walked across to the fridge and pulled cheeses from the top shelf. If Joe had been there he'd have remembered to get them out well before lunch. He'd have laid them carefully on a leaf green plate with ice-cold grapes and a fat bunch of purple sage from the garden. She shook her head again – he had no business trespassing in her mind at all. He'd been neatly tidied away long before now.

As she went back to the table she looked around the room. It seemed very cluttered, suddenly, being, in estate agents' terms, 'a large family room' and therefore a collecting place for books, homework, television, assorted pet baskets and chatting, in addition to cooking and eating. The houses on this side of the road were built on a front to back slope and the kitchen took up all of the large basement, leading out by way of a small conservatory to the walled back garden where the shrubs she and Joe had chosen so carefully ten years before now threatened to strangle each other and block out most of the sun.

That all needs clearing out as well, Nina thought, turning away and inspecting the cool blue walls of the kitchen that had collected smudges and plaster chips where Lucy's school artwork had been blu-tacked up and then carelessly pulled down again, and mystery smears that might have been from the exuberant killing of wasps. There were, too, the sad pale patches where Joe had taken framed photos of the girls to put in his new flat. The floor-to-ceiling bookshelves were crammed with paperbacks that Nina had read so long ago that many could reasonably be passed on to the school fair, and the window shutters had grey finger-marks because nobody ever bothered to use the awkward little (tarnished) brass rings to close them. Even the cushions strewn on the sofa annoyed Nina, being of the fussily 1980s chintz-and-frill variety. Suddenly she longed for plain cream linen and the smell of fresh paint. And the sharp Mediterranean colours of the restaurant she'd been to for that strangely unsettling lunch with Joe.

'Yes it could do with a lick of paint,' Monica said, surprising Nina with her accurate thought-reading. 'You'll have to get someone in.'

'Well I might do it myself actually,' Nina decided, though even as she said it, she felt her right shoulder tweak with anticipatory pain at the very idea of painting what must easily be 600 square feet of ceiling. Perhaps Henry . . .

Nina went to the window that faced the road at the front and inspected the curtains. They needed cleaning, or better still throwing out. Up in a bedroom window across the road at number 26, someone else could be seen measuring a window. 'We're getting new people across the road,' she said. 'They're in there now, measuring up.'

'Really? That'll be nice for you.' Monica came and stood beside Nina and peered across the road. 'Look at us, aren't we shamelessly nosy,' she said. 'Why don't you run across and invite them in for coffee?'

'I will soon, but not today. Let's just leave them to it, I expect they've got loads to do.' She dropped the curtain edge and turned away. She imagined a young, optimistic couple strolling round their new house together, laughing over paint-chart disagreements, picturing their furniture, where it should go, what they would need. The emptiness she'd been feeling all day gnawed harder at her.

'Mum, Mum do you mind if I go out for a while? After we've cleared up?'

Nina looked suspiciously at Emily, who had tied her hair back in honour of asking the favour. 'No I don't mind, as long as there isn't homework you should be doing. Where are you going? Chloe's? Nick's?'

Emily went to the sink and started rinsing cutlery. 'Er, no actually, I just thought I might just drop in and see what Dad's doing. He said we could, any time.' Her face was hidden as she bent to drop knives into the dishwasher.

Nina was on the point of saying, But its not his turn . . . but stopped herself. She and Joe had agreed it wouldn't be a matter of 'turns' and complicated arrangements. Emily was nearly eighteen, long since capable of getting on a bus to Chelsea and visiting her father by herself.

'OK, good idea. You could discuss your gap year

with him, see what he thinks,' she said. 'Have you phoned him?'

'No. I just thought I'd surprise him. He might not even be there, but I don't mind chancing it.'

Nina smiled. 'It'll surprise Catherine too.' The thought quite cheered her up.

Up in her room Emily undressed completely and padded across the landing to the bathroom she shared with Lucy. Under the shower she soaped away the stale lingering smells of last night's cigarettes and the grubby pub that she, Chloe and Nick with friends from various local schools and colleges frequented at weekends. The night before there had been a bizarre tweak of pleasure in *not* going on to his house and having sex with Nick: nothing, not even a goodnight kiss. He was nice to snog, but if you got as far as kissing him it was as if all the right buttons were suddenly pressed and he was on autopilot till the after-sex cigarette. If you stopped him halfway, you did damage: his mother had told him this, told him it wasn't safe to stop once he'd got going because he'd end up with prostate cancer or something. According to Nick, that would mean it was all Emily's fault if she refused to finish what she'd started. That meant, Emily reasoned, that it followed it was all his mother's fault that she, in the interests of his health, had therefore refused to start anything at all. So tough luck.

Back in her room, she chose underwear far more carefully than she had before lunch. 'Well you never know, Simon might be there, and then he *might* just want . . .' she murmured to the cat sleeping on her unmade bed as she picked out the scarlet satin bra and knickers that she'd bought with a Knickerbox gift token the previous Christmas. The bra was now rather tight, she noticed, which meant she'd grown in the past three months. The mirror told her it gave her quite a cleavage, which, being used to a fairly flat teenage figure, slightly unnerved her. 'God I look like a *woman*,' she told the cat. 'Proper tits.' She felt quite shocked, as if she was looking at someone else, someone she didn't know very well.

'Can I come too?' Lucy knocked and came into the room at the same time. 'That looks nice. Like a bikini,' she said, admiring Emily's underwear. '*Is* it a bikini? Are you going to the pool?'

'No, I'm going man-catching,' Emily told her, turning to the wardrobe and flicking hangers past, looking for something to wear that would hint at the treasures beneath without looking too obvious.

'How do you do that exactly?' Lucy asked solemnly.

'I can't really tell you,' Emily said, holding up a very short black velvet dress and checking for old, unattractive stains. 'It just comes naturally when you get to the right age.'

'I thought you were going to Dad's. That's what you told Mum,' Lucy continued. 'She said we should always tell *someone*, even if it's not her, the truth about where we're going just in case of accidents. So you'd better tell me, hadn't you?' she smiled persuasively at Emily, who grinned back at her. No wonder she gets all this modelling work, Emily thought, she really has got the most peculiarly pointy little cat-face. Not so much pretty-pretty as unusual. And her mouth's too big, in every sense. No way would she ever tell Lucy a secret.

'Actually I *am* going to Dad's. And this time no you can't come in case I go on to see Nick later. Sorry, maybe next time,' she said, patting Lucy on the head in a gesture she hoped the child would take as the nearest she'd get to open affection, and not simply feel she was being put down.

'I'll have to go for a walk on the Common with Gran, then,' Lucy complained glumly. 'She *always* wants to walk on the Common. She says it's good for the digestion. And she always goes really fast so that she can get back home in time to cook something for Uncle Graham.'

'Well it's good for the dog. Genghis will love it, and then it won't be your turn to walk him tomorrow will it?' Emily grinned at her, opened the door and ushered Lucy out ahead of her. She shut the door firmly, so Lucy would know she wasn't expected to make a return curiosity visit in her sister's absence. Together they went down the stairs, back to the kitchen.

'Joe shouldn't have left the dog for you to look after. You'd think he could have taken it with him,' Monica was saying as she watched Nina attaching a stout lead to the collar of the ancient and supremely idle Afghan hound.

Emily laughed, 'No *way*. These dogs are just so uncool now, Dad wouldn't be seen dead with him.'

'Come on Emily, that's not true. He could hardly live in the flat with Joe. It wouldn't be fair.' Nina patted Genghis's soft shaggy head. 'Not fair on *whom*?' Emily asked as she gave Monica a goodbye hug.

Graham sat in his Fiesta in the Waddington Aviation Viewing Enclosure, notepad and book of *USA Military Aircraft Serials* in hand. A satisfying day. A rare day off from the demands of both home and hospital and no fewer than *three* F–117 Nighthawks had arrived, slinking over the horizon and down on to the runway just in front of him. Their weird black shapes reminded him of sinister origami. No wonder the media liked to call them Stealths. They even looked fragile, but deceptive like the small plain spiders that have the deadliest venom. The Brits had nothing like the F–117, not military, though he was sentimentally both fond and proud of Concorde. And if they *had* got something that special, it definitely wouldn't be out and flying on a Sunday. Weekends and three weeks in August: any amateur aircraft enthusiast could tell a hostile nation that that was the time to invade.

Right now his stomach told him it was more than lunchtime so he waved briefly to the small band of equally committed hobbyists comparing their electronic scanners by the airfield fence and drove towards the village. As well as hungry he felt quite old. The others waiting in the WAVE with him were, at the most, only just out of their teens. Partly this was cheering: that youngsters hadn't all gone over to mugging and computer games in place of plane-spotting and bird-watching. But it reminded him uncomfortably that people generally, most people, expected to grow out of it. He hadn't. He didn't want to. His military aircraft log must be about the most comprehensive in the country, way back to 1971. If it had flown in, from whichever world air force, he'd been to see it, photographed it, written it down.

He looked at the car's clock. Only 2.15. After the burger (which Mother mustn't know about because of BSE), if he drove fast, he could get home and get in a couple of hours of number-logging on the computer before his mother got home and started her 'Oh you're not shutting yourself away again with *that* stuff are you?' nagging again. If he went out she'd moan about being neglected. He couldn't win.

'So tell me about Barbados. When are you going?'
Monica strode along across the breezy Common

beside Lucy, trying not to gasp at the pace. The dog, too hopelessly unreliable to be let off its lead in an open space, hauled Lucy along in an attempt to get her to run with him.

'I might *not* be going. They liked me, but they liked about ten others as well and we've all got to go back next Thursday for a re-call. I think we'll have to try some of the clothes on. That's what usually happens. And if they don't look good on us we don't get it.'

'Barbados though, that'll be lovely won't it, darling? I'm sure you were easily the prettiest, you're bound to get it.'

'Don't build her hopes up, she might *not*, you know.' Nina murmured a warning to her mother. Monica frowned at her.

'Oh don't be so defeatist, let the girl fly while she can. *You* did, in your day. Of course she'll get it. She usually does, doesn't she? And of course you'll get to go as well, chaperoning, but if you don't want to, I'll go.'

'Last time I got a hot country job, we only went to Ealing to a big shed. They'd made scenery and got loads of palm trees.' Lucy laughed. 'It was really cold and we had to dance about and pretend it was a party on a beach. That was an advert for Tropi-choc sweets. They were disgusting.'

'Joe isn't very keen. He says it interrupts her school work,' Nina admitted.

'But it was him who got her involved in all this in the first place, wasn't it, taking her to a casting for some awful ad for, what was it, yoghurt?'

'Yes, but he thought it would just be that one-off, just for fun. We used to argue about it quite a lot.'

Monica sniffed. 'Well, you know what I think. You could have found a way of sorting it out without resorting to *words*. You let that man slip through your fingers, simply because you've never managed the art of quiet subtlety. There's many a way to skin cats, you know. Perhaps if you'd given him a son . . .' She made it sound like a gift, or a bribe, Nina thought, as if for the sake of a son he'd have stopped showing off his manhood with a succession of dozy young girls and stayed home being dutiful. Sally, though, had 'given' each of her two husbands a son and they'd still gone off and left her, but then *she* was of the opinion that if you had a boy-child, they were so utterly treasured by their doting mothers that the husbands got jealous anyway . . . Either way, the female of the species, daughter, wife or mother, clearly couldn't win.

'Come on Genghis, let's go, shall we?' Nina took the lead from Lucy and started running. The Common was Sunday-afternoon busy. Lunches were being walked off, lone fathers were having parental access, quality time with sweets and promises. Children ran and squabbled and kicked footballs. Men and women, arms linked in domestic solidarity, strolled together and sorted their weekend differences. Dogs more biddable than Genghis were running loose, sniffing for rabbits and for each other.

'"Slipped through my fingers" did he? I'd say he prised them apart and forced his way through,' she whispered to herself as she ran. The dog loped gently just ahead of her, his big golden ears flopping. If she let the lead go he'd run till he dropped, unseeing and purposeless, for miles and miles and miles.

'The doorbell's ringing,' Catherine murmured into the pillow. Joe didn't move. He lay sprawled and exhausted beneath the duvet, trying not to fall asleep because, wise grown-up as he was, he knew he'd be in for a restless night later if he gave in now in the late afternoon.

'Joe. It's ringing.'

'Just ignore it,' he said, staring at the ceiling, conscious that he hardly had the energy left to blink.

'I can't. It might be Simon. I'll just have a quick peek.' Catherine sighed and hauled her naked self out of the bed, pulling on a pink satin robe and tying the belt tightly. Joe was conscious of a small display of impatience in the act of the tying. The sharp tug of the fabric, the brisk knot. The leisurely tenderness of the past half-hour had evaporated. Catherine carefully positioned herself at the window where she thought she could look down at the street and not be seen.

A girl stood there, a girl with long hair the colour of butternut squash, blowing on her cold hands and looking up and around for signs of life in the building. His daughter. Catherine stepped back quickly from the window, telling herself she hadn't been seen, not from that angle. It was her turn to have Joe this weekend, not theirs.

'Nobody there, they've gone away,' she told Joe as she slipped off the robe and climbed back into bed, smiling.

Chapter Five

'Jeez, Mum what are you doing, you scared me! It's not even seven o'clock yet!'

Emily stood in the kitchen doorway, hair sleep-tousled and feet bare. She was wearing an old Metropolis Studios T-shirt that Nina assumed she'd purloined from Joe on her last visit to him. It stopped at mid-thigh; her long pale legs looked chilled and vulnerable.

Nina was sitting in her old blue towelling dressing gown on the floor in front of the bookshelves, sorting paperbacks and allocating them to various supermarket boxes.

'I'm clearing stuff out so we can paint this room. I woke up early and couldn't get back to sleep. Then when I was fidgeting about the cat came in and assumed it was morning so I thought I might as well get up and make a start. I won't have time later. Anyway,' she said, looking up at Emily, 'I could ask you the same. I bet you can't remember when you last saw this hour of the day. You're usually not out of bed till about thirty seconds before you need to leave for school.'

Emily rubbed the back of her left leg with her right toes. 'The birds woke me up,' she said. 'Um . . . shall I make some tea?'

She wandered across to the sink and filled the kettle. She's looking shifty, Nina thought. If she didn't look so obviously sleep-sodden, I'd wonder if she'd only just come home. She watched Emily reach up to get cups out of the cupboard and wondered what she got up to with Nick. She assumed it was *something*. The boy, struttingly confident of his own desirability, could clearly have his pick of the entire sixth form and probably most of the two years below that as well. With his lean, tall body and sun-streaked hair, he reminded Nina of an advert for surfwear. It was naive to imagine he'd put in time with a girl who wouldn't venture beyond a chaste good-night kiss, however astounding her personality.

'Are you still seeing a lot of Nick?' she asked, cursing herself for such an obviously mother-like question. Emily turned and smirked at her pityingly. As well she might, Nina conceded. '*Seeing?* What kind of a question is that?' Emily mocked. 'Do you mean am I having sex with him? Because if you do the answer is "Not right at this moment because I'm busy making tea for my mummy", OK?' She flicked her hair and did a pert turn back to the kettle and filled the mugs with water.

'Serves me right I suppose,' Nina said, laughing. She was none the wiser, just as she was meant to be. It was probably more comfortable for both of them that way.

Genghis, stretched out on the sofa, woofed gently in his sleep and lifted his head a few inches. 'Newspaper's here,' Nina said, looking at the end window and catching sight of the Nike-trainered feet of the girl with her delivery bag plodding up the path. 'He's quite good, old Genghis,' she said, reaching out and stroking his ear. 'He sensed she was coming before she'd even opened the gate.'

'Huh. He doesn't exactly do much about it though,'

Emily commented, handing Nina her mug of tea. 'Even if the mad axeman came creeping up, he'd just go "Oh woof-hello" and drift off back to dreamland again. About as much use as Lucy's hamster. We should get a great big evil Rotty, then we three girlies could feel safe in our beds.'

'*Do* you actually feel less safe without a man around the house?' Nina asked. It hadn't occurred to her before that it made a difference, since Joe had gone. Man as guard-dog had never really been an issue – it had been more a case of trying to keep Joe in than intruders out. 'We could get a lodger, I suppose, put him in the old music room.'

'*No*, no lodgers, *please*. I'm fine, truly. I feel just the same in the house as I always did. Anyway, it's not as if Dad was even here all the time, is it? He was often away, or in really late or whatever.' Emily picked up her tea and headed back towards the door. 'Actually I've got to make a quick phone call, so I'll leave you to the books. OK?'

'Good grief who on earth do you need to call at this hour? They won't thank you, whoever it is.'

Emily was halfway up the stairs now and her voice was trailing away, out of earshot. 'S'OK, it's just some-one about a Wordsworth essay. They'll be just getting ready for work . . .' If more information was being volunteered, Nina could no longer hear it. She didn't waste time wondering over why Emily didn't stay and use the kitchen phone. She was perfectly well used to the teenage need for phone privacy, even if it was only for checking the time with the speaking clock.

Concentrating again on the piles of books, Nina looked around the room and fought off the feeling of defeat which threatened to overtake her now she had started on this job. After the books there would be the pictures to take down, all the plates, dishes, vases and collected bills, catalogues and bits of paper on the dresser to be sorted and put away, the kitchen equipment to have cupboard space found for it, curtains and their rails to be dismantled. Then there was the actual painting. There seemed to be acres and acres of wall. It suddenly seemed a pity that her brother had never been the kind of man who'd taken to DIY, but then it was deplorably sexist of her to expect him to. Instead Graham did have an enviable address book full of tradesmen, which he consulted the moment Monica so much as glanced at guttering or gatepost and pronounced them sub-standard.

'No. I *can do* this,' Nina assured herself, turning back to the books and refusing to look towards any further effort till that one job was done, and done properly. That evening she would ring the local Scout group. They were sure to be having a fund-raising sale soon. She felt as if she was nesting, though for her own comfort, not for the raising of new babies. Presumably Joe would have to think about the baby sort of nesting soon, if Catherine got her way. Lucy and Emily would then have a half-brother or sister. They'd be connected with it, would have moved on into the future with Joe but she wouldn't. There was something in that which made her horribly miserable, left out, like being the only child in an infants' school class not invited to a party. She hurled a copy of *Brave New World* into the box of books for the jumble and then just as quickly took it out again. Lucy might want to read it one day – or even her little brother or sister.

The slam of a car door at the front of the house made her look up and out of the window. The day seemed to be starting early for the entire street. Across the road she could see the legs of two men climbing out of an

Audi and walking up the path of the empty number 26. Aha, the new arrivals, she thought, going to the window to indulge natural curiosity. She watched them on the doorstep, the taller, blonder of the two fumbling for the right keys. They both wore jeans; one of them also wore a long denim jacket and the other was in soft butter-coloured leather. Within seconds, she'd decided they were a gay couple, about to fill their house with interesting treasures, with souvenirs of unusually exquisite taste from foreign travel and that they'd hang soft silky kelims on the walls. They'd grow their own herbs. As an afterthought she gave them a small and ugly dog which they would make fat from treating it to Smarties. As she turned back to the book-sorting, smiling at her own ludicrous assumptions, she decided to take them a box of Maison Blanc's most delectable cakes as a moving-in token, and she already planned to be thoroughly disappointed if they didn't eat them with a stunning set of art nouveau cake forks.

'Hello Catherine? It's me, Emily. Emily Malone.'

Emily's feet felt cold, even on the sitting room carpet. She curled herself on to the sofa and wedged her knees up under the big T-shirt, and then quickly unfolded her legs again, smoothing the fabric down and crossing her legs neatly in a way that felt more suitable for talking to the immaculate Catherine. She imagined her, even at just after seven in the morning, already made up for work and wearing a sheeny Joseph suit set off with one of the horribly twiddly little gold-chain necklaces that she seemed to like. If I had clothes like that, she thought now as she had before, I'd wear chunky stone jewellery, or stark wide silver bands.

'It's awfully early.' Catherine's voice sounded like

Mrs Hutchins whingeing about an overdue essay. She didn't actually go on to say 'What do you want?' in a really rude way, but Emily could sense that she'd like to. Perhaps Joe was in the room with her, she thought, trying really hard to keep the picture of a fully dressed-for-the-office Catherine in her head and not replace it with one of her in bed wearing nothing but something tiny, rude and lacy.

'I'm really sorry,' Emily apologized resentfully. 'It's just the only time I can be sure to catch you at home and it is a bit of an emergency. You know your brother, Simon?'

'Well of course I do,' Catherine snapped. 'What about him?'

Fierce and unexpected tears stung Emily's eyes at this impatient rebuke. I hate her, she thought, but continued, trying to smile to make herself sound like a sweet, nice girl: 'Well it's just that when I met him we got talking about A-levels and he mentioned that he'd done a lot about Wordsworth for his degree and that he still had the essays and notes . . .' Emily paused for breath, sure that she was gabbling in a stupidly desperate, juvenile way. Catherine remained silent. Emily imagined her inspecting her fingers, picking a teeny crumb of stray wholemeal toast that had dared to creep under one perfectly varnished nail. A big tear trickled down Emily's face. What was her dad doing living with the kind of woman who spent a whole hour doing the base, polish and topcoat ritual with nail varnish? What went through her head while she did it? Why isn't she pleased to hear from me, *why doesn't she even ask how I am*?

'It's just that he said I should call him if I had any problems about the Wordsworth stuff, and I haven't got his number. So please could you give it to me?'

67

It felt like begging, especially into the prim silence that was at Catherine's end of the phone. If Emily told Nina, Nina would probably say something kind like 'Oh perhaps she's shy, not everyone's comfortable talking to teenagers.' Too generous by three-quarters, that was the trouble with Mum. What would it take for her to know, just *know* that Catherine was a cow?

'Your father could have given you the number at a more reasonable time of the day. It's in his address book too, you know. Just wait a moment.' Catherine put the phone down and Emily could hear her footsteps trit-trotting across the miles of wooden floor in the flat. So she *was* up already then, *and* not in the bedroom *and* dressed in proper shoes, Emily realized, feeling a snug glow of satisfaction warming her.

'I've got his home number and the one at work. Which do you want?' Catherine demanded.

'Oh both please, if that's all right, then I can be sure to catch him. It is a bit of an emergency.' Emily, hating herself, heard herself grovelling. Never apologize, never explain, wasn't that the saying? But who could ever live like that? Only Catherine, probably. She scribbled the number down on the back of her hand and drew a quick heart round Simon's name. 'Thanks *so* much,' she purred. 'You've been really kind and I'm terribly sorry to have bothered you so early in the morning. Love to Dad.'

She put the phone down carefully and wiped her hand down the T-shirt. 'Bitch cow from hell,' she then said, racing up the stairs back to her room, passing Lucy on the stairs on her way down for breakfast.

Emily glanced at her watch and smiled. Somehow she'd managed to use up the time quite satisfactorily; it was now, as her mother put it, about thirty seconds before she should be leaving for school.

* * *

Henry looked so comfortable sprawling on the sofa, cradling his mug of coffee to his chest. Nina felt quite a pang, sharply missing the sheer rangy *bigness* of a man around the place. They took up such a lot of room, like Irish wolfhounds – you couldn't just not notice them. Even when quiet, just like naughty children being suspiciously silent, they tended to draw the eye. Joe had been a great one for slouching around. He'd done a lot of reclining upstairs on the music room sofa, eyes closed, pained that anyone should mistakenly think he was not actually working. Even now, some-times when she went up the stairs, she half expected to catch sight of a naked foot dangling over the sofa's edge. Then as she came level with the door and there was just the empty room, the sofa gone to the flat with Joe's recording equipment, there was a small shock as if she'd just realized she'd been burgled.

'So what do you think? Cream? Yellow? What about blue? Or is blue too cold?' Nina asked the lolling bulk that was Henry. She strode around the room, stacking magazines, collecting up stray bills and school notes, trying to imagine a clutter-free, refreshingly empty space, just solid blocks of fresh flat stain-free colour. She didn't want any twiddly, dated fancy paint fin-ishes, no splattered stippling or wobbly dragging, not even soft and tentative colour-washing, that much she knew, but deciding which *colour* was a problem. Joe had been so very good at that sort of thing. Even when they'd settled on just plain basic white for their bed-room, when they'd first bought the house, he'd pinned up a selection of at least twenty different white shades round the room, waiting for the right light to catch the right one. This was the first major change she was planning to make to their home since he'd moved out.

It seemed important to get it right, prove that her own taste was competent and confident. All the decisions were now hers and she would have to live with the results.

'You could just have white,' Henry suggested, lazily closing his eyes and sighing. 'Have you got a bun to go with this coffee, Nina my darling? Breakfast seems to be a long-distant memory.'

'You look as if sleep is a long-distant memory too,' she said laughing, 'What were you getting up to last night? You look terrible.'

'Drinking for Britain: I think I won a gold,' he said with a groan and a hand to his head. 'Down at the Fox – darts night. They were asking about Joe, no-one's seen him for months. I told them he was working away.'

'You could have told them the truth,' Nina said with a frown, handing him a packet of Hob-nobs, 'I mean it's not as if he'll be back. I don't think he's much of a pub-goer any more. I get the impression Catherine's more into dinky dinners at home that her mummy told her were the motorway to a man's heart.'

'Ooh, I hear bitchery!' Henry said, sitting up to pay attention. 'Go on, what else?'

'Only if you promise to paint the ceiling for me,' Nina teased. 'And then I can do the rest myself.'

As she walked past the sofa, Henry's hand shot out and took hold of Nina's wrist. 'You said you were over him,' he accused. She wriggled her hand out of his grip. 'Hey, that hurt,' she complained, rubbing at the pulled skin. This sudden, rather sinister gesture was quite alarming. It showed deep-rooted dormant power, capacity to hurt like the swift clawing of a normally fond cat, disturbed from sleep.

'I'm really sorry,' he drawled with no real concern,

slapping the back of his right hand with his left. 'Don't know my own strength. And of course I'll paint the ceiling, any old colour you like. Friends again?' he looked up at her, mock-humble and casually sure of forgiveness.

'OK. And we'll do it white. Clean, fresh-start white,' she said. Henry chuckled. 'White. Fine. But only *some* of it white. The ceiling and some wall. But I can see you want colour. You're *yearning* for colour. You're just holding back.'

Nina sat on the arm of the sofa and picked at loose threads that the cat had pulled from the fabric. She wondered, after the wrist-grabbing business, if they were really still talking about paint colour or if there'd been a subtle detour in the direction of her sex life. She decided that she was imagining things, this was only Henry. If she chose any other interpretation, then *he'd* be the alarmed one and she'd have to get professional decorators in, chosen at random from Yellow Pages.

'You're right,' she told him. 'For someone who spends their working life selecting and rejecting bits of art and craft and trusting my taste, I'm being pathetically indecisive about my own home.'

'Hmm. It's only lack of practice,' Henry decided. 'We'll start with white and you can add. Take it one step at a time, like alcoholics.'

'And babies,' Nina added, wondering where that little notion had sprung from.

Emily stood as close as she could to the girl using the school payphone, hoping to intimidate her into cutting short her call. She was practically breathing in her ear. You sure have to suffer for love, she thought, trying not to inhale the soupy smell of exuberant hockey-field perspiration. 'Get on with it!' Emily hissed at her, prodding her muscly hip. 'Some of us have a life to get on with, you know.'

'You're so fucking rude,' the girl told her, face blotched red with anger as she hung up the phone. 'That was an *emergency*, my mum's having a *baby*.'

'You're joking,' Emily said. 'Whoever would want another kid like you?'

The end-of-break bell rang and Emily swore as she punched in Simon's numbers, copied from the back of her hand. 'Oh shit,' she murmured as a recording told her to leave a message after the beep, he'd get back to her later. He sounded so strangely adult, almost like her father. This was probably a serious mistake. Nick's mobile had a silly message, 'Leave a name, dame,' that kind of thing. Everyone's did, silly attempts to be slick or cool and not managing to be either.

Simon's beep sounded before Emily had decided what to say. There hadn't been time to rehearse any-thing impressive in her head. She should have just hung up and started again but she had no more money. 'Er, it's er . . . Oh shit,' she waffled and slammed the phone down. 'Jesus, what a stupid prat he'll think I am, like some dopey little lovestruck kid fancying one of Boyzone,' she muttered. She'd have to try later, try his work number this time and pretend the other mess-age was nothing to do with her. She picked up her bag of books and swung them over her shoulder carelessly, banging her hand hard against the wall. 'Ow!' she yelled, licking the bruise and rubbing at it. Too late, she realized what she'd done: the phone numbers were no more than a blue blur smeared across the back of her hand. Oh well, she thought despondently, it must be fate.

* * *

'Emily's gap year. Do you think it would be a good idea to meet up and discuss it?'

Joe sounded very business-like, Nina thought, as if Emily's future was simply the next thing on life's agenda. He'd probably had this programmed into his electronic organizer since before her GCSEs and now it had made a punctual 'bleep' and reminded him. Nina felt defensive: she didn't like it when he called her at the gallery, for out of sheer consideration to customers she was forced to be politely acquiescent, whatever he said. The gallery was unusually full. Nina wished she'd remembered to put some music on. At least seven browsers drifting near her desk were able to hear every word she said and interpret for themselves what Joe's end of the conversation might be.

'With Emily as well, do you mean?' she asked. 'After all, it is her own time, isn't it. She's sure to have been thinking about it.'

'Well, I just thought the two of us to start with, and then see what she comes up with.'

'Actually I think it should be the other way round, but whatever. Funny you should be calling about this now,' she went on. 'I told Emily to have a word with you about it when she came round to see you last Sunday. If you'd been in, you could have chatted to her, see what ideas she's got, if any.'

'Sunday?' Joe sounded as puzzled as if he'd never heard of the day. He used to do that sort of thing a lot, Nina remembered with irritation, doing one-word questioning, head on one side, whenever she asked him something he didn't have an honest reply ready for. 'Holidays?' he'd puzzle, when she'd try to pin him down to discuss the wheres and the whens, as if waiting for her to define the term. Later, just after the first of his many extra-mural romances, she realized he used it simply to give himself time for the concoction of excuses.

'Yes *Sunday*,' she hissed into the phone. 'God's day off, great hunks of roasting meat, you know. Emily came round to see you after lunch, and you weren't there.'

'No. Right,' Joe said blankly. Nina gave up. Why should he tell her, anyway, where he'd been? Did she really want to hear that he'd had some socially thrilling day out with stimulating and amusing people so that she could have a good masochistic brood about walking her aged dog and mother round the wind-swept Common?

'OK, maybe we should get together. Why don't you come to the house?' she said. Don't, she prayed, let him him say 'House?'

'Better than that, what about a mid-month lunch? Just a sneaky little extra one,' he suggested. She could hear by the increased breathiness of his voice that he was now holding the phone very close to his mouth, being secret from those who might be tempted to over-hear. She'd seen him do that at home, when one of his silly smitten girlies, despairing (rightly) of ever hearing from him again, had plucked up the courage to call him and he'd had to do some swift verbal fending off. She remembered how vivid and excited he'd looked afterwards, positively sparkling with the danger of illicit naughtiness, hovering around her grinning and waiting like a puppy for her to notice. This time, he must be gleefully anticipating *not telling Catherine*. Sally, battle-wise from long experience, would say this was the typical behaviour of a man who liked the idea of infidelity far more than the reality.

Nina, now faced with two people lined up at the counter tapping their feet and waiting to pay, agreed quickly and hung up. She smiled at the customers. 'I'm so sorry. I do hate it when people in shops do that,' she apologized to the first one, a neat woman in stiff navy blue with a white crisp collar standing to attention round her neck. 'When they conduct their private lives over the shop phone and you feel you're interrupting.'

'Quite. Absolutely,' the woman said brusquely and with no smile, handing over a velvet beaded evening bag to be wrapped. The tall, youngish man standing behind her stuck his tongue out rudely at the back of the woman's head and winked past her to Nina who had to fight down a schoolgirl giggle.

'Forty-five pounds fifty please,' she said, trying to sound efficient and rummaging in the till to hide her face.

'Well *she* wasn't the forgiving type, was she?' the man said as the woman left the gallery, shutting the door behind her with a smart, cross tug. He looked familiar, but this was an area inhabited by many actors, so Nina was careful not to assume she'd actually met him.

'No, she wasn't. But then I expect she's one of those lucky people whose life slots into convenient compartments that never overlap.' He was buying a pink and white spotted teapot with a silver-edged lid. Nina found herself speculating as to whether it was for him, his wife, mother, girlfriend or boyfriend. It was probably just for himself, she decided as she folded it carefully into bubble-wrap. He had a kind of confident, arty look (old black jeans and a collarless teal blue shirt that looked vaguely Chinese) that would easily carry off serving tea from something boldly pink. The tea would not be in bags and would not be cheap and there would be coffee cake oozing gloopy chocolate cream with a hint of brandy . . .

'I've seen you in the Crescent. We've moved into number 26. Am I right to take it you live there too?' he went on. Without waiting for a reply he held out his hand: 'I'm Paul Brocklehurst.'

'Oh of course! So that's where I've seen you. A few mornings ago, early,' Nina said. She shook his hand over the counter, feeling foolish. She must have sounded as if she spent every waking moment peering across the road. When he went home, he'd probably be looking to see if she had net curtains twitching. She wondered who 'we' referred to, whether it was a wife, or the man she'd seen him going into number 26 with.

'I'm Nina Malone,' she told him. 'Number 23. Welcome to the Crescent. I'm sorry if I've been very remiss as a neighbour, I should have been round with a bottle or a cake or something.' Nina had a qualm as soon as the words were out. He could interpret it as fishing for another meeting. That was another irritating difference from the days of Joe: the simple change in implication that so-ordinary sentences could have. It could only matter to her: there was no way he could know she was a Lone Woman, unless there was some special alerting scent that went with the state, Eau de Solitude, or Abandonée, that only men could smell, a warning like the kind of whistle that only dogs can hear.

'That's soon remedied. Come over tomorrow night for a drink, I was going to put a note through your door. Er . . . with your husband?' Well if she *had* been fishing, it had more or less worked, she then thought with a tiny tweak of triumph. She was too old (she supposed) for him, (and possibly the wrong sex), but this was just a spot of flirt-practice.

The gallery doorbell clanged and she saw Sally

come in. Sally caught her eye, winked and mimed a disappearing act before creeping out again with exaggerated tact.

'I don't have a husband,' Nina admitted. 'Not any more. There's just me and the daughters now.' And a gruesome hell-house full of ricocheting hormones *that* sounded, she thought.

'Oh I'm sorry. I thought, well I saw you leaving the house the other day with that chap with the grey hair, and I just assumed . . .'

Nina thought for a mystified moment and then burst into laughter. 'Oh no, that's just *Henry*. He's from number 7. Very good at borrowing, but also very good at tap-fixing and video-tuning.'

'Any good at babysitting?' Oh well, thought Nina, he was bound to be married, really.

'Your babies?' Well he could have meant *hers*, she thought.

Another customer approached, clutching a pleasingly expensive vase. Nina bent to retrieve more bubble-wrap from under the counter. When she looked up, Paul had backed away without replying to her question, making space for the vase-buyer.

'Tomorrow night then? About 6.30ish for drinks?' he said, heading for the door.

'OK, thanks. See you then.'

At the door he collided with Sally making her way back in. Nina wrapped the vase, put cash into the till and then turned to Sally. 'Coffee?' she asked.

'Mmm, please. God, the traffic. So who was *that*? I could tell from right out on the street you were being blatantly chatted up.'

'Come on Sal, he's only about thirty.'

'Thirty *plus*. He's got a few lines.'

'Probably sunbathes.'

'Crows' feet. A teeny bit jowly too. Could be pushing forty, just.'

'Hey what is this?'

'Just finding you a new playmate. I can tell you need one.'

Nina sighed. 'Do you know, I'm beginning to think you're right. It's really annoying. When Joe and I finally split up, I felt nothing but relief. It was so blissful not to have to think about how to *keep* a man. So restful just to find I was perfectly OK without. Now I'm beginning to wonder. Do I really want to be on my own for ever more? Does staying celibate for the rest of my life just so I can feel restful really *compensate*?'

'Ugh! I should hope not!' Sally said with some vehemence. 'I don't approve of celibacy, I'm sure it leads to trouble in the downstairs area. I know, I'll take you out with me for one of those dinner party dating set-ups. They're good fun and much better for the beginner than the one-to-one, Waterloo Station/red carnation type of thing. Trust me, you'll enjoy it.' Sally was grinning happily as if all in Nina's life was now safely sorted, and she rummaged through her bag for a cigarette.

Nina stamped off into the little kitchen at the back of the gallery and switched on the coffee machine. 'OK maybe I'll give it a go. What's to lose, especially if Joe's moving right on to the baby-and-family stage? I don't want to be stuck for ever in the abandoned wife mould, like something turned to stone. It's all right for men. They all get snapped up by piranha women the moment they're back in the pond. Joe must have been on the loose for what? a month or less before Catherine sidled up with the handcuffs.'

'I thought you said Joe *always* behaved as if he was on the loose,' Sally interrupted.

'Not really, not now I'm looking back. He just played at it. He always came home.'

'Huh. Just like a little boy bringing his football kit home for Mummy to wash.'

'I suppose so. I suppose in the end I just decided the metaphorical washing machine was terminally broken. But then he found another mummy.'

Chapter Six

It was the lady with the pink baby-cardigan and the hurt leg. She was looking very peaceful now, laid out ready for collection, her white hair neatly brushed to show her at her dignified best for the viewing relatives. Graham wondered if she'd got any, if they'd been in to see her like this. They'd have been told, offered the chance. Some of them didn't want to know till they could visit days later in a chapel of rest when the undertaker had had a go, then they could say how wonderful the dead one was looking, you wouldn't think, would you? Seeing a body in hospital just moments after the event like this, well some of them, he'd heard them saying it was all too fresh, like it might still be just a silly mistake. They were afraid, scared the body might take one more heaving breath, or that some lingering reflex would make it sit up. They'd all heard stories like that, ones they never thought they'd believe but now weren't so sure, you could tell by the looks on their faces.

Graham pushed the big metal trolley further into the room, wondering what had happened to the bag of onions she'd had with her down in A & E. He couldn't smell them, but then when deaths happened, he was always careful not to breathe too hard. Some illnesses were more odorous than others. Some deaths made him sick.

'It was the shock, probably.' The nurse, clutching

the black bin-liner that contained the patient's possessions, stood beside Graham. 'She'd probably managed fine up till the fall. Some of them just give up.' She sounded sorry, and kind, which might be because she wasn't so young – probably a couple of years older than him. A silveriness that he couldn't quite pick out in her dark brown hair was catching the light as if grey hair was in there somewhere but doing its best to hide. Some of the younger nurses were really hard. He'd heard them *accusing* old people of 'just giving up' – saying it with contempt, as if they'd died on purpose, just to spite them. Then they'd hassle him to be quick getting the body out, they needed the bed.

Graham eyed the plastic bag. He hated it that dead people's stuff went into bags meant for rubbish. It diminished the owners, as if they and their things were now unworthy of a better-quality container. Didn't matter how rich or grand they thought they were: whatever smart luggage they'd brought in with them, on death they all got a bin-bag, standard issue. Perhaps the onions were in there. They'd make her pink cardigan smell. There might be a relative, a sister or a cousin, who'd want it. It had been so carefully knitted.

'I'll help you move her,' the nurse said. Her name tag said 'Jennifer'. As she leaned forward over the old lady, Graham watched her large breasts strain forwards in her overall. The buttons had trouble staying fastened. Graham moved the trolley in closer to the bed and closer to Jennifer. 'I'll take her feet, OK?' she said.

'OK,' Graham grunted. He had pictures in his head that he wasn't used to. Pictures of Jennifer's overall, pulled wide open and her big hips shoving against him. He looked away and concentrated on being more reverent. He was in the presence of death. The lady's soul might still be in the room, disapproving. *He* disapproved.

'Ready? One two three . . .' Together they lifted the dead woman onto the trolley. Graham covered her face with the sheet and closed the lid.

'When I was little,' Jennifer told him, 'I went to a hospital once to visit my grandad, and I saw one of these trolleys being wheeled in. I remember rushing round the ward telling the patients that their dinner was coming and pointing to it. I just thought it was a big tin box full of hot food, like the ones at school.' She patted the lid gently. 'Bye, Mrs Cox. I hope they give you a good send-off.'

'We could have a drink, after work,' Graham heard himself saying. He could feel a hot blush starting and sweat welded his shirt to his back. He looked at Jennifer, waiting over the canned corpse of Mrs Cox for her to answer. What he most wanted now was to be already far away in the service lift, halfway to the mortuary with his companion who would require no tricky conversation.

'OK, I'd like that,' Jennifer said simply. 'Do you mean tonight?'

'Er . . . yes.' He supposed he did. Tomorrow would be better, give him time to get used to the idea, but then she might be offended, think he was looking for a way out. Mother, with supper on the table at exactly 6.45, came into his head. 'Eight o'clock? The Green Dragon in Church Street?' he suggested, then added, as he felt he should, 'Or would you like me to collect you from home?'

She laughed. Graham looked down anxiously at Mrs Cox's trolley. They were talking across her, rudely it seemed, talking about life things. That couldn't really be bad, surely?

'I could collect *you* from home if you like,' Jennifer teased. Graham, for a moment, was horrified. Mother mustn't know about this. Mother would have none of it, would know just how to get rid of Jennifer, just as she had with all the others, and keep him for herself. She'd say she had his best interests at heart and convince him she was right, but right now this was something he didn't want to risk.

It was appalling really, just how little Nina knew about her neighbours. The Crescent was one of those shrub-barricaded roads where everyone was forever on their way out. There wasn't a play, exhibition or art film in London that any one household wouldn't be able to analyse and argue over. But if there'd been a grisly murder right next door, no-one would have heard a thing or known the victim even well enough to do holiday cat-feeding. TV news crews would find only a collection of diverse and bewildered folk who'd have to admit, in a prim, net-curtain way, 'We tend to keep to ourselves.'

'We've lived in the Crescent for over ten years, and I couldn't tell you the names of even half the inhabitants. I only really know Chrissie and Jack up at the top end and posh Penelope with the Weimaraner. And even that's only to chat to on the Common when we're out walking dogs. Isn't that dreadful and unsociable?' she was telling Emily as she applied mascara using the badly lit kitchen mirror.

'Hmm,' Emily murmured, from the depths of *Marie Claire* which was propped up at the table on a pile of neglected homework.

'After seeing them that once early in the morning, I didn't even notice number 26 moving in. And I don't think that actually *was* them, I think there's a wife. I must have been at work, unless they sneaked their stuff in during the night, like a reverse moonlight flit. Perhaps they don't *have* tons of junk like the rest of us,' she said, looking round the room, where, in spite of what she considered ruthless sorting and disposal, newspapers, homework and assorted shoes and bags seemed to be reassembling. It too seemed to creep in in the night, sneaking out of its pre-painting storage. 'Imagine being truly minimalist, like those architects in magazines who don't seem to have anything but one perfect chair and a glass bowl of a hundred white tulips,' she said wistfully. Emily, who owned much of the room's debris, didn't deign to comment.

'I suppose it's different for you,' Nina said, foraging in her bag for lipstick. 'Children grow up in a place and expect to move on, away from it. It's your duty *not* to get over-involved with the inhabitants, otherwise it might be difficult to leave. And of course it's not like it was when I was little, all the children sent outside to play together. I don't think I know of anyone's kids who are allowed on the Common without a parent. You just know that behind every tree lurks a crazed rapist.'

'Hmm,' Emily replied again. Nina, as she applied blusher, remembered her own childhood, making camps with friends in the woods, fishing for stickle-backs in a river that no-one even bothered to check the weedy depth of. Once, when she and a friend, at about Lucy's age, had been digging in the earth for shards of highly prized old broken pottery, a man had knelt beside them and asked if he could show them his own 'treasure' and had unzipped his trousers – bottle green corduroy, she could see the warm fuzzy fabric now, and could almost smell the dusty dried earth she and the friend were so solemnly scraping into with their seaside spades. She remembered how politely, with what must have been almost comic decorum, they'd told him, 'No thank you, we're busy.' By some sixth-sense agreement he had never been mentioned again, to each other or to anyone else. Talking about it, telling, would have meant the incident was significant and sinister and playing out in the woodsy freedom would never have been the same again. Girls who told parents about that kind of thing got kept in, confined to their own dull gardens, which felt just like a punishment, till only gangs of boys would be left to roam wild and free. Parents then didn't think things like the treasure-man happened to boys. Lucy didn't have that freedom, driven to school, kept safe, made wary. She still hadn't been out of Nina's sight over on the Common, wasn't ever allowed to use it as a short cut to the school unless she or Emily was with her.

'He mentioned something about babysitting, this Paul man. You could earn yourself some cash,' Nina suggested.

'How much?' Emily looked up, instantly interested. At Joe's expense she was having driving lessons, but buying and running a car along with her social life might well be at her own.

'Oh I don't know, you'd have to negotiate some kind of hourly rate. Ask your friends, someone at school will know.'

Emily flicked a few magazine pages, but Nina could see financial calculation on her face as she said, 'They might have real brats. I think the charge should be per child, as well as per hour. Suppose there's a teeny baby that cries all the time and needs bottles and nappies every couple of hours and stuff.'

'You're talking yourself out of it, I can tell,' Nina told her. 'Just think of it as a chance to do your revision in peace and get paid for it at the same time. What do I look like, will I do?'

Nina did a twirl. Emily inspected her, head to toe, slowly. 'You look fine. Your hair looks really good and I like that suede shirt thing.'

'It leaves ginger-coloured flecks on the black trousers, that's the only trouble.' Nina fussed at the hem of the shirt.

'Better let me have it then,' Emily suggested swiftly. 'Teenagers don't care about things like that.'

'How true.' Nina leaned down and kissed the top of her head. Her hair smelt delicious, like strawberries. She remembered suddenly the scent of newborn babies' heads, something primitive and beadily damp- ish, making her want to lick the downy scalp like a mother cat.

Lucy was born ten whole years ago, she thought; probably the next one I'll get that close to will be Emily's own: Unless of course Joe brought his new baby to their monthly lunches. Nina imagined it cling- ing in a denim sling, suspended like a baby ape. They'd have to go to an Italian restaurant where babies were cherished and given a breadstick to chew. Or per- haps there'd just be no more lunches.

'Emily darling, don't let Lucy watch too much telly. I'm only going over for a quick drink, I'll be back for a latish supper. You could get yourself and Lucy some- thing earlier if you like. There's plenty of pasta in the fridge.'

'S'pose,' Emily conceded, returning to her magazine. 'Have fun.'

Nina could hear party noises as she crossed the road. Paul's house was closer to the Common, with a small alleyway along the side of it that the residents had got accustomed to using as a dog-walking short cut while the house had been empty. They'd all have to go back to trailing round the long way now, up to the main road and along past the riding school. Henry, to her surprise, was sauntering towards her from his own house, hands as ever stuffed in the pockets of his old jeans and his matted blue sweater showing he made no concession to silly social niceties.

'Do you mind arriving with me or would you prefer to go in alone while I hide in the hedge for ten minutes so no-one mistakes us for a couple?' Henry asked politely.

'I think I can just about tolerate being seen with you, just this once,' Nina laughed, pushing open the gate of number 26, 'As long as it doesn't become a habit.'

'Not bloody likely,' Henry retorted, ringing the bell.

The door was opened by a child, a girl of about nine wearing army camouflage trousers, a paratroopers' red beret, and with her face striped with mud coloured make-up. So there *is* a wife, Nina thought, or at least a partner. Henry saluted: 'Neighbours reporting for drinks duty,' he said. 'Corporal Henry Perry and Field Marshal Nina Malone. Or have you gone back to Dyson?' he added. Nina shook her head, 'Well not yet.'

The child looked at Nina, put a finger to her temple and twiddled it in the universal 'completely crazy' gesture, glancing sideways at Henry.

'Do come in. I'm Megan. I see you've met Sophie.' Nina heard a gasp from Henry and took a look at her new neighbour, who had appeared behind the child. Megan Brocklehurst looked like a walking flower; a hibiscus came to mind, or a pale scabious. She was wearing several layers of white floating fabric (in early April) each piece of which had an asymmetric hem and so accurately gave the impression of layers of petals that it looked decidedly peculiar to see a hand holding a glass protruding from among the folds. Her stomach bulged gently with pregnancy, and she looked the absolute definition of 'blooming'. Her face, tiny among clouds of blond hair, was the kind of perfect heart-shaped one on which they would originally have based the drawings of Snow White.

'I expect you know everyone here much better than Paul and I do,' Megan said, ushering Nina and Henry into the sitting room and towards the drinks.

Nina looked around the room quickly. As in most of the Crescent's Victorian houses, this was a room that had been two smaller ones knocked through. There were large french windows overlooking the back garden, and in the high brick wall at the far end of the garden Nina could see a small door which would have led out to the Common in the days before the Council had been round issuing all the residents with official padlocks but no keys. No curtains were up yet, and the plain cream walls bore the sad grubby oblongs of other people's taken-down paintings. The floor was a rich syrup-coloured parquet which must have been hiding its lustre under the former occupants' figured green Wilton for a good fifteen years. It was quite crowded, so this was either far less impromptu a gathering than Nina had thought it would be, or the entire Crescent was as downright nosy as she was. She recognized most people from simply seeing them going in and out of cars, gates and doorways over the years. One or two were fellow early-morning dog walkers; Nina could see posh Penelope in her caramel cashmere and guessed from the lifeless expression of the man she was talking to that she was lecturing, as ever, on the rather fascist topic of the compulsory spaying of mongrels.

Megan handed Nina a glass of white wine and grimaced apologetically at the state of the room. 'Appalling to ask people in while the house is still so shabby, but I thought it might be a good way to find out who were the best painters and decorators in the area. I thought that between most of the Crescent's inhabitants, I should be able to assemble a useful list of artisans. Do you find you all end up using the same people?'

'To be honest I wouldn't know. Joe and I always did our own painting, though now I'm having Henry in to help. My brother's got quite a useful address book of plumbers and electricians though. I don't actually know what the others here do,' Nina said, laughing, 'I must confess I haven't really been much of a joining-in type of neighbour. Just the usual hellos and goodbyes and Merry Christmas,' she admitted.

'Oh well I hope that will change,' Megan said with a smile, 'because haven't you got a daughter of about Sophie's age?'

'I've got Lucy, she's ten.'

Megan grinned delightedly, showing a perfectly straight set of teeth as white as her dress. 'Oh that's terrific. Sophie's nine. It would be lovely if the girls could be friends. We've got Sam as well, but he's only five and, well boys just want to kick a ball around and don't care who they see. Sophie hasn't met anyone here yet, though I'm sure that'll change when she starts school on Monday.'

'Which one? Lucy's at St Clement's.'

'Oh good. That's where Sam and Sophie will be going. Sophie's already decided she likes it, because they let the girls wear trousers. As you can see, she's hardly the frilly frock type.'

Unlike her mother, Nina was tempted to say. Megan had tiny, delicate wrists and shining fluffy golden hair, like a brand new Barbie doll. Joe would, if he was still around, be offering his services as complete house renovator. He'd be reviving the old custom of borrowing cups of sugar, anything to spend time lolling on Megan's sofa gazing at her delicate features and making a total besotted fool of himself. Henry was hovering nearby, staring shamelessly at this vision of ultra-feminine loveliness. Beside her, Nina felt far too tall and clumsy. As she made neighbourly conversation with various guests, going over the grumbles by which they were linked (17's overhanging willow, the strange drainy smell outside 33, 19's perpetual builders), she imagined that her arms and legs were growing longer like Pinocchio's nose. She slid her feet out of her shoes and leaned against the wall, trying to feel smaller. It was the first time she'd ever felt uncomfortable about being tall.

'More wine?' Paul Brocklehurst appeared at Nina's side with a bottle. He was the same height as she was and she was looking straight into his eyes. She'd never been able to do that cute looking *up* thing that she'd always despised small women for doing. It was something irritating that she'd seen when women were appealing to a man's strength. Even Sally did it. Once at the gallery, Nina had watched in astonishment as Sally, capable and independent as she normally was, had shimmied up to a browsing customer, eyes wide and helpless, and coyly proffered a coffee jar with a stubborn lid to be opened. 'Thank you *so* much,' she'd then gushed, leaving the man convinced he'd achieved a historical engineering milestone.

'How could you *do* that?' Nina had asked her.

'The jar is now open, my nails and my temper are intact and it gives men simple pleasure to be asked. Easy,' Sally had explained. How pathetic of men to be so easily pleased, Nina had thought. She still thought it was something to do with eye level and putting

90

yourself in a diminutive position. She and Joe had been on the same level and she caught herself wondering if he, standing next to Catherine, would be tall enough to kiss the top of her head. That would be disgustingly cute.

'Are you planning to do a lot to the house?' Nina asked Paul, watching Henry, across the room, grab an opportunity to slide into place next to Megan. She wondered if he was asking if she needed help painting *her* ceiling. One upward appeal from those delphinium eyes and he'd probably roll on his back to be tickled.

'Not a huge amount. Structurally it's fine and the kitchen is bliss. The vendors slapped in a new IKEA one so it would look good just for selling and it happens to be one we'd have chosen, so that's all right. I suppose it's mostly just a matter of paint. Megan is good at colour. I'm an architect, more interested in form and function. And people. I'll be working from home, office upstairs,' he waved his glass upwards and drops of wine fell to the floor. He rubbed at them with his foot. 'So I feel the need to meet the neighbours, find out who's around for the odd coffee and chat when inspiration deserts me.'

'Henry's very reliable for that,' Nina told Paul. 'He's a painter, the art sort so he's always up for skiving if you don't mind oil paint smeared all over your worktops and a lingering smell of turps. Goodness knows what he actually lives on. Otherwise it's the usual suburban morning out, evening home, not a lot of casual dropping in. We do have the odd barbecue though, and there's Bonfire Night on the old bit of waste ground next to number 19, and it's quite good around Christmas.'

'You make yourselves sound like an antisocial

bunch. Last place we lived, everyone was forever in and out of each others' houses. Drinks, parties, Sunday lunches, all that.'

'Sounds idyllic,' Nina said, suddenly envious. 'Why on earth did you leave?' Paul's face clouded for a moment. 'Oh this and that,' he said breezily. 'Work, mostly. We architects, we have to move on to stay fresh.' There was something else behind his ordinary reply, Nina thought. If I wasn't directly on his eye level I wouldn't have noticed that.

Nina stayed longer than she'd intended and gravitated towards the kitchen. It seemed to be full of women and a high, squawking noise level, as if inevitably, having cruised the room, lone females should congregate together for comfort. She and posh Penelope sat at the table polishing off a bottle of oaky Chardonnay and grumbling about absent husbands.

'Oliver went to work in Dubai. "Only for three months, think of all the tax-free lucre," he said. And then he met a nurse. *On the plane out*, would you believe.' Penelope waved her glass at Nina. 'They're having twins.'

'Oliver and the nurse?' Nina asked.

'No, our hosts, Megan and Paul. Poor buggers. Got a cigarette?'

Penelope looked past Nina, round the room and towards the door. She looked vaguely hopeful, Nina thought, as if there might be an outside chance that a replacement for the adulterous Oliver might be just beyond the fridge. Nina realized she'd been doing the same, scanning the gathering with the tiniest corner of her mind wondering if there might be an adventure worth having among the men not yet met. All of them, apart from Henry, seemed to be there as anchors for their partners. The husbands stayed in one spot, discussing golf, BMWs and their cholesterol levels. The wives circulated, talking of education, au pairs, diets and tennis and then returned to partner-as-base. Some of them wandered into the kitchen, and sat for a while with the single women who could smoke without risk of being told off, before starting to look edgy, and sensing a need to go back and be sure of their men.

'Where are all the lone men? All the ones abandoned by *their* partners?' Penelope was murmuring drunkenly. 'Where do they *go*? You never see *them* drifting around at parties looking lost. I just know now that I'll never live with anyone else again.'

Nina looked at her face that in its lines and folds inadequately patched with make-up held all the signs of great disappointment and lost hope.

'I don't know. Home to Mum, bedsits with Kentucky Chicken, or maybe they go straight back out into the fray again, like getting back on a horse. Perhaps they're all out there looking for another Mrs Right, in case it's worth a shot.' She giggled, thinking of Joe and the speedy moving-in of Catherine. 'It usually is, and pretty quick.'

I'm not going to end up like Penelope, Nina vowed to herself, jolly and shrieking in party kitchens but with eyes like a bereft soul. I'm going to go on out and have a good time, like Sally. With Sally.

Graham took the balaclava that he used for night bird-watching and winter plane-spotting into the sitting room where Monica was waiting eagerly for *Crimewatch UK* to start. The balaclava was hand-knitted in finest alpaca, made to last by Mother when he was about twelve, had just taken up plane-spotting and was thought to be in need of protection from chills. Back then, it had been an embarrassing item, swaddling his head and making him feel conspicuous. Now everyone at the airfields had them, bought from army surplus stores and worn with nonchalant pride. His own was softer though, comforting even when he just felt it nestling in his pocket, soft like a sleeping rabbit. He didn't put it on now, just held it so Mother would see it and assume he was telling the truth.

'Popping out for a bit,' he said from the doorway. His shoes were by the front door, ready to be slid on fast before she thought of too many questions to ask.

'Going for a drink?' Monica asked, barely looking up.

'Well I might stop for just a pint, on the way back. There's a barn owl by the Common, just on the edge. I thought I'd go and have a look.' He took a deep breath, to stop himself rambling on. Keep it simple, don't over-explain. Then she won't get suspicious. *Crimewatch* was just starting and Monica lost interest in the comings and goings of her son. She didn't want to miss a second of the programme, being always convinced that she recognized most of the criminals and that she alone knew just how they should be punished.

Graham slipped out of the room and picked up his coat from the bottom of the stairs. She wouldn't come out now, he thought with a small gleeful grin, wouldn't see him going out in his navy blue jacket instead of the old Barbour he'd normally wear for owl-watching. He drove away from the house quickly, for once not putting on his seat belt till he was round the first corner, heading for the High Street. He just hoped he'd be able to stop grinning like an escaped madman before it was time to meet Jennifer. He also hoped, really really hoped, that she'd be there.

Chapter Seven

'The parents are going out to lunch today to talk about my gap year. They're going out together,' Emily told Chloe as they sat in the sixth-form cloakroom avoiding compulsory midweek assembly.

'Why?' Chloe asked, puzzled. 'What's it got to do with them? It's your time off.'

Emily frowned. Chloe had picked up on the wrong sentence from the two she'd just been given. How dense. What mattered was the 'together', but then why should Chloe be interested in that – she had two parents in the same house. Parents who went out together and stayed in together, taken for granted. 'Don't know,' she said. 'Maybe they want to give me shit-loads of money to do something wild. Perhaps I'm secretly a trust fund babe and they're working out how to tell me about it.'

Chloe inspected a spot in the mirror. 'Hard to tell if it's zits or if the mirror's just filthy. It's not near enough to the weekend for sod's law spots,' she murmured, then turned back to Emily. 'What *are* you going to do next year? I thought I might just work a bit then travel a bit, you know, what most people do I suppose. Unless I fail everything and have to do retakes.' That was something they all said, in case of exam disaster. It was like crossing your fingers, an essential calling up of good luck.

Emily sat down on the wooden bench beneath the

coat hooks. From the wire shelves beneath, fetid plimsolls and dilapidated trainers that no-one would ever deign to steal tumbled out onto the dusty floor. She kicked a shoe across the room where it clanged dully against a locker door. No-one used the lockers: the keys got lost and that meant a fine of one pound that nobody wanted to waste.

'I'm going to get a nice job in Marks and Spencer and a Renault Clio and get that Simon to ask me to marry him,' she said.

'Are you mad? Aren't you a bit ahead of the plot here? You haven't even got him to ask you out yet,' Chloe demanded, looking appalled. 'We're clever women, power execs in the making. We just don't concern ourselves with mere till rolls and checkout rotas. And *especially* not with diamond solitaire engagement rings.' She looked at Emily closely for signs of laughter. 'You are joking Em?' She shook Emily's impassive shoulder. 'You *are*, aren't you?'

'No, not exactly. But I didn't say I wanted to *get* married, just make him ask me. I've been reading this book called *Man-Date*, all about how to catch the man of your dreams. I want to see if doing all the things you're supposed to do actually works. It'll be practice for later, for when I really want one.' She yawned and stretched out full length on the narrow bench. 'I'm so tired, I don't want to do anything that means any more mental effort. I want to slog for cash in a department store and completely forget about it at the end of the day and blitz away *all* weekend *every* weekend without a single bloody essay to write. And I don't want to save a rain forest or the sodding panda either. If pandas weren't such picky eaters and appalling parents they wouldn't need our help. They *deserve* extinction.'

'No backpacking in Australia, no smokin' and surfin' in Goa?'

'No. Because even that's competitive. You hear them at parties, bragging on, like "Oh *we* got stuck without water, three days up a mountain in the outback, and Jamie got bitten by a redback." And then someone else says "Oh that's nothing, Molly got purple monkey fever in Zaire and a witch doctor swapped a miracle cure for her Walkman."'

The school bell rang and Chloe picked up her bag of books. 'And you'll be able to chip in with "There's been a hell of a run on black satin bras in 36D this week", won't you? They'll be riveted. Come on, miserable cow, it's French lit., your favourite.'

Monica was troubled. Graham had been looking shifty for several days. It was something to do with going out and with telling half, or even quarter-truths. That morning when she'd asked Graham about the owl on the Common, he'd said 'What owl?' and gone on stolidly eating his Shreddies. His balaclava was on the shelf in the cloakroom, folded neatly and put back in its usual place on top of the US Air Force Tomcats baseball cap that he'd bought at an airshow three summers ago and she'd told him he was far too old to wear. He wouldn't look at her. He kept his eyes on the cat which sat washing its back leg, with its toes spread like pianists' fingers. Even when she sat down opposite him at the kitchen table and made a lot of busy, companionable noise with the toast and marmalade, he just went on placidly munching.

'On the Common,' she'd persisted. 'The barn owl you went out to see the other night.'

He'd grinned then, silly and lopsided, as if he knew something smutty. He'd done that when he was five and gathered all his courage to say 'bum' to see what she'd do. He still wasn't looking at her, but was closely attentive to his cereal, as if he'd heard someone was going to drop a fly or a hair into it and he was determined to catch them out.

'That wasn't an owl,' he'd said.

'What kind of bird was it then?' she'd asked.

He'd looked at her then, beady-eyed and challenging, cocky with his own obtuseness. 'A big one. Not a turkey. For once,' he'd said.

When he'd gone off to work Monica fretted about what he'd meant. She paced the hallway, then went slowly up the stairs and paced the landing. The house was far too big for just the two of them, cluttered with old and looming furniture that was polished without enthusiasm or skill by a succession of bored young cleaners. They were girls in jeans too tight for proper bending who arrived late and left early and retuned the radio to something raucous whenever Monica was out. They never stayed long, she thought as she opened Graham's bedroom door. Perhaps it was dusting all his model aircraft that did it. The planes hung from the ceiling and covered every surface. The last cleaning girl, assuming from his room that Graham was still a teenager, had talked to Monica about how lucky she must have felt, having a 'late' baby. She had thought for an awful confusing moment that she meant a dead one.

Monica sat on the neatly made bed and picked up Graham's bedside reading. She wasn't going to find out what was going on in his head from flicking through *Wrecks and Relics*, or *The Military Aircraft of Europe*. He'd got a secret. She'd never get it out of him, not in the normal way of ask-and-tell. No-one could be as stubborn as Graham when it came to keeping silence. She wondered if it was a woman. There hadn't been many over the years, or at least not that she knew of. A daughter-in-law might have been nice, and goodness knows Monica had encouraged him, back when he'd been twenty or so and she'd decided it was time. Two in particular she'd made a real effort with and turned into very special friends, helping them choose his birthday presents, giving them hints on the food treats he liked, teaching them tapestry, booking theatre seats for them, but nothing had come of it. Really it was probably just as well – they wouldn't have given him the proper care that only a mother really could. These days it was all careers and cook-chill dinners. She'd bought Nina a pasta-maker but it was still in its box. She'd seen it, stuffed away in her dresser cupboard.

Monica sighed and left the room, leaving the door open at precisely the angle it had been at when she'd entered. It didn't do to pry, and it certainly didn't do to be found out. Later, talking to Nina, she would blame Graham's secrecy for the fall on the stairs. She was distracted, not concentrating. Nina would tell her it was because the stair carpet was loose and had been for years, and there'd be a hint about the frailty of age, but Monica would dismiss that, because Nina, who didn't even know enough to keep a husband, couldn't be right, not ever.

Monica was going slowly down the stairs now, wondering, not about Graham but about biscuits: Rich Tea or Bourbon creams with her coffee. She felt cold and folded her arms across her stomach, keeping her body heat in. Her last thought before she fell was that she should be holding onto the banister rail, but it felt, somehow, as if she was asserting her strength, youthful strength, sauntering confidently down the stairs scorning a safe handhold. She didn't, she told them later, actually hit the stairs, it was more that they came up and hit her. She was conscious of swift rushing air, the clogging smell of dusty carpet, a glimpse of scuffed cream paintwork and thick dull thudding that sounded so very far away. When the fast sensations stopped, she wasn't even down as far as the hall floor, but inelegantly upended, three stairs from the bottom with her skirt crumpled up around her hips.

I look ridiculous, was Monica's first thought, seeing her legs, one poked through the banister rail, the other bent beside her. Nothing felt broken, but nothing moved comfortably either, and her breathing and heart felt rushed and frighteningly unreliable. I'll be found looking a fool, she thought, trying to slide further down to level ground, making a move towards dignity before any real agony that was waiting beyond the shock could get a chance to set in. Inching painfully, crawling across the floor, she made her snail's-pace way towards the telephone, determined to welcome the ambulance driver entirely on her own terms.

'Remember all those Sunday brunches we used to have here?'

Joe unfolded his napkin and picked up the menu, gazing around at the familiar gleaming black and chrome Caprice décor. He looked up at a black and white photograph of Peter Blake on the wall, grinning as if at an old and loved friend. 'And they still have those lovely fish cakes. Remember those? I'm going to have them.'

'Of course I remember,' Nina said, smiling as she knew she was meant to. The meal hadn't even begun yet, so she opted for basic politeness in the interests of getting Emily's gap year discussed. She felt cross inside though, fuming that he could so cosily reminisce about their shared past as if those were the happiest days. If they were, why had he messed them up so carelessly? He'd behaved like a child with a Christmas puppy. Why had he so swiftly taken on a new love-of-his-life? And how soon would he have a new collection of things with *her* that he could do nostalgic reminiscing about?

'So. How've you been?' Joe asked as soon as they'd done their food-ordering, sipping at his mineral water. Was this Catherine's influence, Nina wondered, had she hinted about middle-aged waistlines? The Polo safely at home for once, she was the one drinking Chablis.

'I'm fine. Just as ever,' she told him. 'Lucy's got a new friend, Sophie from across the road.'

'Oh yes? I don't remember children across the road.' He looked puzzled, trying to recall.

'No, well you wouldn't, they're new. Moved in a couple of weeks ago.' Nina fidgeted in her seat. She was wearing tights that itched, which she put down to Lucy being the last one to operate the washing machine. Democratic in-house chore-sharing had its price; words obviously needed to be had about how much powder to use.

'I missed something then,' Joe was saying, looking mock-glum. Nina grinned. 'Well don't worry, I missed the moving-in too. Apparently only Henry got to gawp at their enormous medieval-style iron bed and the painted wooden zebra. Though actually I saw the zebra too, when they had their party.'

'Party? Things are looking up socially in the Crescent, then.'

'Don't patronize,' Nina snapped, then said, 'Let me tell you about Sophie. Lucy's besotted with her and she's only known her a week. She wears military combat gear and the only make-up she's interested in is camouflage stripes like the army wear in jungles. I take them out on the common with Genghis and they hide in the bushes so they can jump out and ambush dog-walkers.'

Joe laughed, 'I can't imagine Lucy doing that. She's so dinky and feminine. She's been into skin care since she was seven.'

'I know. It's a real clash of cultures. At night she spends hours taking the camo stuff off with gallons of my Clarins cleanser. It's costing me a fortune.'

This was the point, Nina thought, where he might just, unforgivably chip in with 'costing *me* a fortune, you mean'. She waited a second, holding her breath, but Joe didn't comment. Poor Joe, she suddenly thought, I'm almost challenging him to take the part of the villainous ex. She shifted in her seat again, grimacing at the itch on her thighs and rubbing her left leg under the table.

'What's the matter? You're fidgeting like a bored toddler,' he said.

'Tights, they've got washing powder itch,' she hissed at him across the table.

'Go down to the Ladies and take them off then,' he shrugged.

'It's not so simple,' Nina confessed, hesitating while the waiter arranged their food. She admired the pink-ness of her lamb chops, thinking that her thighs, scratched, must be about the same shade.

'Why not?' Joe persisted annoyingly.

'I've got winter white legs, my skirt's too short for showing them and we pitiful manless ladies are a bit lazy on the old leg-waxing, if you must know, OK?'

Joe laughed at her. Other diners looked around to share the joke. 'Don't tell me you *never* go out with anyone? Beautiful woman like you?'

'Beautiful, *forty-one-year-old* woman like me, you mean,' Nina corrected. 'I'm now a woman of a certain age. *Men* of a certain age, men like you, are all going out with women who are still young enough to enjoy being referred to as "girls". Besides, I'm not interested any more. I've decided all men are more trouble than they're worth, just little boys looking for over-indulgent mummies.'

'Well that's telling me,' Joe said with a grin. 'I shall make sure I don't refer to your love life ever again.'

'Good. Because I don't intend to have one. Now, can we talk about Emily? Do you think it would be a good idea to treat her to one of those round-the-world air tickets, on condition that she saves up spending money herself?'

Joe hesitated while the waiter collected plates and gave them the pudding menu. 'What about something more adventurous, like Raleigh International or whatever? Building a school up a Himalaya or something – wouldn't she like a challenge?'

'I think she's finding A-levels enough of a challenge. Come to think of it, she finds getting out of bed in the mornings a challenge. I suspect she'd like something more hedonistic.'

'Oh well in that case it's just a couple of weeks in Ibiza then,' Joe suggested flippantly. 'I expect funds could run to that. We went there once, do you remember? After you did that "Smile, how much can it hurt" poster for the cosmetic dentist people.'

'I remember. Thanks for reminding me – it was the last modelling job I did. Now I'm only fit for the "before" shot for wrinkle cream.'

'Don't run yourself down. I think, if it's any help, that you've never looked more beautiful. I remember . . .'

Nina smiled at him indulgently and interrupted, 'You keep doing that, reminiscing, whatever is the matter?' She leaned towards him, ready to be sympathetic. His face looked slightly more collapsed than she'd seen it before. It occurred to her that she would have to watch him growing older only from a distance. The lines that came, the skin that crinkled, would come as a shock to her during the rare times when they met. The monthly lunches, she felt realistically, probably would dwindle to twice-yearly, as the girls grew into women, as work intervened, or if Catherine provided a whole new family. Soon there would be cancellations, postponements. She felt sad, suddenly, as if she had lost not just her husband but a huge chunk of shared life to come. Perhaps he'd started feeling the same. Vaguely his fingers started stroking the back of her hand on the table. She pulled away gently, wondering if he'd even realized what he was doing.

'Why don't you come back to the flat for some coffee after this? You haven't even seen it yet, and I'd like to show you the room the girls have got. They decided on a silver ceiling, which looks surprisingly wonderful,' Joe suggested as Nina finished the last delicious morsel of her chocolate tart.

'*Your* flat?' she said, wide-eyed and incredulous, 'What about . . . ?'

'Catherine's gone to York to an accountancy seminar.' He grimaced and confided, 'Can you think of anything more desperately boring?'

Nina giggled, mostly at his disloyalty, 'No I can't. Unless it's a Christmas knees-up of stationery salesmen.'

'Or a quantity surveyors' outing to the Blackpool illuminations . . .'

In the taxi to Chelsea Nina felt quite drunk. 'It's

lucky I don't have to collect Lucy today, it's Megan's turn,' she told Joe.

'Megan's the new Sophie's mum, I take it. What's she like?'

'Like . . . well, she's compact. Everything small and in the right place. She's six months pregnant with twins and even that's neat and tidy and packed away properly. She makes me feel sprawling and out of control.'

'I liked you like that,' Joe said, with a sideways grin. The taxi was slowing down by the river.

'Stop it, OK just stop it,' Nina said, clambering out as soon as the door could be opened.

Catherine wasn't sprawling and out of control, not ever, not from what Nina could gather from her first view of the flat. It overlooked the Thames and was the sort of place magazines chose when they were featuring warehouse conversion homes with acres of pale wood and no visible personal possessions. It was easy to see which of the contents were Joe's choices and which were Catherine's. As Joe busied himself with the coffee-making at the kitchen end of the vast open living space, Nina paced around pretending she was admiring the river view while thoroughly checking out the soft furnishings.

Joe would have chosen the huge cream sofas, they'd have been pre-Catherine, and he'd got blown-up photos of the girls framed on the wall close to the kitchen. The plain black rug with oversized cream fringes would be one of his but Nina couldn't imagine him choosing the glass shelf-full of strange-shaped polished steel animal sculptures, or the pair of shell-pink art deco lamps. Up the steel stairs was a gallery where Joe had set up his studio, including the ancient leather sofa from home, and beyond that was the room the girls shared, together with their own shower room. The silver ceiling was pretty spectacular, she thought, though she felt strangely moved by the pair of little brass beds covered with blue and white patchwork quilts. She thought of him after they'd gone home on the Sunday nights, perhaps coming in and sitting on a bed, inhaling their girl-scent and feeling empty.

'Well what do you think? Do you like it?'

'What? Oh the flat,' Nina said casually. 'Yes, it's very . . . very you.' Joe had an amused, disbelieving look. 'Well it's almost very you,' she conceded. 'You always said you hated art deco,' she added, grinning and pointing at the table lamps.

'Yes, well. One has to make allowances, you know.'

'Yes I do know. I made lots of allowances for you.'

'Not lamps though,' Joe said. Nina laughed.

'God no, never lamps.' Sitting, half lying on the vast bed of a sofa, Nina's legs began to itch again. 'Bloody tights,' she complained, raking her legs with her nails.

'You could take them off now, there's only me to see,' Joe suggested.

'I'd only have to put the things back on again to go home,' she said.

Joe got up and headed for a doorway. 'No you don't. Look, why don't you come and choose some of Cath's, she buys them in dozens, there's loads of packs not even opened.'

Nina stared at him. 'You can't go lending your mistress's tights to your ex-wife!' she told him.

He had a naughty, sneaky grin on his face as he hovered by the door of the room in which, Nina was highly conscious, he did untold sexual adventuring with the sleek, cool Catherine. Part of her was desperately curious to follow him and have a look round. If, when she told Sally about all this at the gallery, she couldn't accurately describe their bedroom and its contents Sally would probably swear she'd never speak to her again. It was her duty to report back.

She got up and wandered as nonchalantly as she could into the room with Joe and immediately wished she hadn't. She could tell, just instantly tell, that there was nothing of the decorating of this room that was Joe's. It was all Catherine's, it had to be, this plump peach boudoir for swanning and preening, an altar for the worship of the look-good god. The atmosphere was of determined femininity with mirrored wardrobe, drawn-thread duvet cover, rose-sprigged curtains (frilled pelmets, fringe and tie-backs too) over lacy blinds. To Nina, it looked as if Catherine had decided it was already time for 1980s fabric overload to be revived; either that or she was madly compensating for Joe's cool minimalist taste. Bedside tables were draped with at least three layers of cloth, starting with chintz identical to the curtains, followed by a square of something plain and pink-fringed and topped off with white drawn-thread linen. Both were equipped with more peach-glassed art deco lamps. Joe's old gunmetal alarm clock stood like a lonely protest beneath one of them.

'Good grief, where on earth are you allowed to keep your tennis kit?' she exclaimed.

Joe turned from the drawer he was rifling through and looked sheepishly at her. 'In the cupboard by the front door,' he admitted. 'And I didn't choose the paint colour in here either, in case you thought my taste had gone seriously off. I gave her free rein.'

'You sure did. You always hated peach. But then I guess that's love for you.'

He handed her a cellophane pack containing a hugely expensive pair of velvety tights. 'Here, have these,' he offered. Behind him in the still-open drawer

Nina could just see several cardboard packs of much cheaper chain-store tights. 'Thanks,' she said, accepting. They grinned at each other.

Removing her tights in front of Joe, who sat on the bed recalling the exaggerated adventures of his own long-ago gap year, Nina felt mildly uncomfortable. There was no way the putting on of tights could ever be a dignified or attractive process, though she was willing to bet that Catherine could manage to do it prettily enough. This is ridiculous, she thought, we've shared twenty years of married life and he's seen me give birth twice. Why should I expect to look attractive or dignified to him now? Why should I want to? She sat on the bed next to Joe and started wriggling her foot into the first velvety toe. 'We're creasing the duvet,' she commented. As she turned to catch Joe's eye, a juvenile attack of giggles overwhelmed them both and they collapsed against each other, snorting and hysterical.

What happened next was almost inevitable, Nina reasoned very much later. The sex was sharp, fast and devastatingly satisfying, over before they'd even finished laughing. Nina lay back on the bed following the sponged-paint patterns on the ceiling and wishing she could stop grinning. It was such a giveaway, and so undignified. Her skirt was bunched up to her waist, her knickers were dangling from one of Catherine's precious lamps and her left leg from the knee down was still trailing the black tights. She dressed quickly, and as she put her shoes back on she found herself wishing that Joe would leave the room only so that she could bundle her own discarded tights under Catherine's pillow. It would be sweet revenge for forcing such complicated décor on so artistic a man. It was then that she caught sight of what sat on Catherine's bedside table. On top of a fat paperback novel was a chart, and a thermometer. Joe saw her noticing. 'She takes her temperature every morning,' he said, shrugging, though Nina hadn't actually asked. She didn't need to.

'What happens when it peaks?' she asked, her heart beating strangely hard.

Joe grinned, 'I either have a headache, or I work late,' he confessed.

'So far,' Nina said.

'Yeah, well, so far,' he agreed.

'Graham phoned.' Emily greeted Nina at the front door, looking pale and worried. 'It's Grandma. He said she's had a fall and she's gone to hospital and can you call him after six. I didn't know where you were.'

It was nearly that now, Nina realized as she went into the kitchen and headed for the phone. It was a classic, she thought as she pressed the buttons: here come the celestial thunderbolts, just because she had a few minutes' lapse from sense, cavorting with her ex-husband. Here comes the wrathful God with punishment. Not 'cavorting', though, she thought, tapping her fingers on the window ledge waiting for Graham to reply. That kind of instant, urgent, nailed-to-the-bed sex wasn't so lightweight as cavorting. Delicious pangs of remembered thrill ran through her body, doused by Graham's grim 'Hello?' She really must never do that again. She probably wouldn't be required to.

'Will Grandma die?' Lucy, coming into the room trailed by the inevitable Sophie, asked. Lucy had no particular expression in her voice, no fearfulness. She simply wanted to know, as if she was really asking whether Monica had got to the right age yet.

'I doubt it, God I hope not,' Nina said, trying to keep

a nervous trembling out of her voice. This was what she most dreaded, most feared. Her mother defeated, helpless and angry. Immobility, as much as ill health, would kill her. Graham had his job, she had hers, arrangements would have to be made. Panicking, she thought too far ahead as she dialled, ahead to nursing homes, builders organizing a granny extension, stair lifts. The impossibility of the two of them sharing a home. It would be like two cats in a box, she thought, waiting for Graham to answer.

'She's had a fall,' Graham, a man of only the most necessary words, told Nina at last.

'I know that, Emily said. How bad is it, where is she and what's the damage?' she urged him impatiently. Graham had always been slow to tell things, relishing the important delivery of profound news, choosing words that could require the most drastic interpretation. 'There's been an accident' had been one of his favourite childhood phrases – covering everything from the demise of an ancient goldfish to the death of their father from heart failure at the Bowls Club, with white-skirted matrons elbowing for the chance to be the one whose arms he died in.

'She fell down the stairs. One of the banisters is snapped,' he explained infuriatingly. Oh Graham, not that sort of damage, Nina thought, fighting an urge to laugh.

'And she's in the hospital, till they've assessed her. They think it's only bruising, but they're not sure about her hip.'

'She's had a dodgy hip for ages,' Nina said. 'Maybe now she'll decide it's time something was done. Those stairs, perhaps they're getting too much for her. The whole house is too, really. I wonder if this might be the time to think about moving her to somewhere smaller.'

There was a silence. Nina realized too late how insensitive she had been. Suggesting changes in her mother's living arrangements, however sensible and well intentioned, meant potential earthquakes in Graham's own life.

'We shouldn't talk about it now,' he said, his voice carefully expressionless. 'You should just go down to the hospital and see her.' He hung up abruptly and Nina felt dreadful.

'Is Gran OK? Has she broken something?' Emily looked up from her homework and asked.

'Only the banisters, according to Graham,' Nina said grimly. 'I'm more afraid it might have broken her spirit. She might get fearful now, more frail.' More dependent, demanding, difficult, she added guiltily from safely inside her head.

'Take more than falling over,' Emily grunted, turning her attention back to her work.

'They don't "fall over" though, do they, old people? They "have falls", as if it's something that *happens* to them, not something they are active enough to *do,* like children. Older people are often talked about like that as if they've gone, oh what's the word, *passive.*'

'I wouldn't call Grandma passive,' Emily pointed out. 'Anything but.'

Nina laughed. 'Too right. I'm just worried she'll decide she's actually old, and go downhill from there. She and Graham will have to do some serious role reversal, with him looking after her for a change.'

'Neither of them will know where to start,' Emily commented, laughing.

'That, Emily, is too true even to be slightly funny.'

Chapter Eight

The eight-bed ward was full of silent grey women. Nina couldn't see, at first, which one of the pearly heads dozing open-mouthed on banked-up pillows was her mother's. A soundless television was playing up on a high stand in the corner, but no-one looked at it, rather like a prattling bedside visitor who the patient wished would just go home. There was a distant smell of long-cooked food, which Nina guessed had been served a good while ago. Monica wouldn't like that, wouldn't approve of too early an ending to the day, as if they were all overtired children needing an early night.

Nina found her in a bed close to the window, sitting staring blankly out across the dusky west London skyline, her fingers playing nervously with the blanket. She looked smaller than usual, older and unnervingly frail.

'Get me out of here,' were her first words on seeing Nina.

Nina smiled gently at her and Monica scowled. 'And don't smile in that condescending way, you look like a demented lady vicar.' She started twisting around awkwardly, looking for something. 'My clothes, get my clothes, Nina. I think they're in that silly little locker thing. I can't stay here, there's no shopping done for Graham.'

'It's only for a night or two, just to make sure you're

properly mobile again,' Nina told her, getting up and trying to straighten the blankets, wondering how far she would have to go to pin down her mother. 'And Graham's fine. It's about time you admitted he was a fully grown man who can fend for himself. It'll do him good.'

'He could come to you for supper I suppose,' Monica conceded doubtfully.

'He could. Or we could all go to him,' Nina suggested mischievously.

Monica glared. 'Don't be so silly. When would Graham get chance to do cooking? He's got his work.'

'*I've* got my work, not to mention the house, two daughters, dog, cat, etc. Oh look, none of that matters just now. How are you feeling? And how did you fall? Did you get dizzy? Because if you did I hope you told the doctor. It might be blood pressure or something.'

Monica closed her eyes wearily and sighed before saying, 'I wondered when you'd get round to asking how I feel. As a matter of fact what I'm feeling most is furious. They won't even let me walk to the lavatory. They wheel in a commode, and then fuss round the bed with curtains that don't quite close. It's ritual humiliation. I'm perfectly all right and I want to go home. Or a room to myself. You'd think having a son on the staff here . . .' Her voice was rising to petulance. Nina felt sorry for her and reached for her hand. 'Just stay for tonight,' she said. 'I'll come and see you in the morning and if you're all right, maybe we can think about getting you home.'

'What about your precious job? Will you be able to get the time off? You certainly took your time getting here.'

Nina bit her lip. Sally had already done her a favour today, taking over her afternoon at the gallery. The lunch with Joe, going to his flat, that dreadful fluffy bedroom, the fervent not-to-be-thought-of sex and Catherine's thermometer – it all seemed months ago now. She could almost imagine she'd dreamed the whole afternoon, but her knickers were still damp from Joe and she was quite sure a mild scent of sex hung around her. Any second, she dreaded silently, Monica would sniff the air, nose-up like Genghis, and ask her if she'd been out making new friends.

'Don't worry, I'll sort something out,' Nina reassured her mother. 'There might be some other arrangements to be made as well,' she suggested tentatively, waiting to see if her mother had already thought of them.

'Such as?' Monica challenged, daring her to spell it out.

'Like proper care for you. If you're going to be falling down the stairs, getting a bit wobbly, maybe we should think about something to make life easier . . .'

'Like a coffin, I suppose,' Monica snarled.

'Don't be silly.'

'You're patronizing again.'

'I only meant a couple of extra handrails here and there in the house. Something non-slip for the bottom of the bath, that kind of thing. I'll talk to Graham.'

Graham sat gloomily in the pub clinging to his pint of bitter. Jennifer was opposite, her glass of cider long finished.

'She'll be all right. They're very strong, these old ladies, they're always having falls and getting better again,' she said.

'She'll decide she's old,' Graham said. 'And it'll make her angry. She's very good at blaming.'

'Well she can just blame the stair carpet then, can't she, this time. It's not as if anyone pushed her,' Jennifer said, with a note of impatience. The words *Not yet* hovered unsaid at the end of Jennifer's sentence. 'Do you want me to put another half in that glass, because I'm having another even if you're not.'

'Yeah, all right. Thanks.' Graham pushed his glass across the table and slumped back in his chair. He could see there might be changes ahead and he didn't like change, not unless it crept up very, very slowly. There was something Monica liked to say to people who asked her about living in that big difficult house with all its rooms that no-one went in, something that was just a bit embarrassing, like 'Well I've always got my great big boy to look after me.' She'd squeeze his arm and he'd feel dry-mouthed dread as if any moment she was going to take out a tiny handkerchief, lick it and wipe his face, just as she had, without fail, every morning when she'd got him out of the house to be taken, 'by hand' as she'd called it, to the infants' school. She'd say the thing as if it was a bit of a joke, really, just something you said, not meant. Everyone knew that *she* looked after *Graham*. He'd heard the neighbours sometimes, making comments like 'When's that son of yours going to go off and get married and settle down?' They didn't say it often these days though, as if at his age still being at home with a mother was like the kind of illness that you don't mention. 'Settling down' made him think of people who were much wilder than him, people on television who did mad comedy shows and then went on and did some really serious acting, or restless junkies like the twitchy skinny ones they got in A & E at work who sometimes didn't die in doorways but got better and went round schools doing talks and helping. Settling down didn't mean him: he was already settled, had never not been.

'Here, drink this, you'll soon feel better.' Jennifer's large breasts, bulging snugly in her blue cardigan, appeared by his shoulder before the rest of her did. She put the drink on the table. Just breasts and one arm, Graham could see. Breasts to fall into, that's what Jennifer had, arms and breasts to be snuggled in, smothered in. He sipped his drink fast, needing to feel cooler.

'Thanks,' he said.

'We could get something to eat, or we could just go back to . . . well there's no-one in at your place, is there?' She looked up at him strangely, a sort of sly coyness in her eyes.

Graham stared at her, not understanding. 'Home? You mean you want me to take you to *my* home?' His mother was at home; not in body obviously, but in spirit, in influence, in omnipotence and control. She was in the floral wallpaper, the kitchen smells, the bathroom bleach. A reminding hint of her lavender cologne waited for him in the hall. He couldn't take a woman there, because she'd *know*.

Jennifer bit her lip and looked pink. 'Well, not if you don't want to, of course. I mean I don't want you to think I'm being a bit forward, but we've both been grown-ups for quite a good few years now, haven't we?' He stared at her, saying nothing, feeling flustered. She leaned across the table and took his hand. 'Look, it's all right, I'm sorry. I shouldn't have even thought of it. I expect you're feeling a bit shell-shocked about your old mum. Another time. Now, are you hungry?'

'Oh God and it's Lucy's audition this afternoon!'

In the morning Nina stood in the kitchen staring at the wall calendar and willing it to swap its arrangements round so that she could fit everything in. 'Sally

116

said she'd do this morning at the gallery, but then I'm supposed to do the afternoon . . .' she muttered away to herself, watched by Emily who guzzled cereal noisily, standing up by the sink. Her schoolbag was ready at her feet, coat flung across it, just in case Nina doubted the need for a speedy getaway and asked her to do something useful.

'Why don't you get Dad to take Lucy to the audition?' she suggested. 'Or I could take her, I suppose. Depending on where it actually is, and what time . . .' she backtracked rapidly, as if making the suggestion was more than enough; thinking through to the actual undertaking would be too exhausting.

'No, it's OK, you're right. I'll ask Joe. At least it's after school so he can't complain it's a waste of lesson time. If he's not actually recording today he might be able to get there on time.' He owes me one, she thought, then corrected herself mentally, for after all it wasn't a question of who owed whom. Such brief, body if not heartfelt passion was hardly a matter of having time to trade. Only the week before Sally had shown her a magazine article called 'Sex with the Ex: Women who can't give it up!' She hoped she wouldn't turn into one of those.

'Oh and Henry phoned while you were at the hospital last night,' Emily recalled. 'He said when do you want him to do the painting, cos he happens to be free at the moment, till the end of next week.'

'Everything at once,' Nina said, looking round the room and feeling immediately defeated by the amount of clearing out that still needed to be done before the painting could even start. All the shelves would have to be cleared, all the pictures taken down, and the paintwork hadn't been washed and Henry would want the sofas and floor dustsheeted and the rugs rolled up.

She took a deep, resolute breath and started some mental sorting.

'Right. I'll phone Joe and ask him about Lucy. Megan's taking her to school and should be here any second, Henry I'll call when I get to the gallery and you, Em, are responsible for organizing supper tonight.' She thought for another few seconds, then added, 'Make it supper for four, perhaps Joe would like to stay. I happen to know Catherine's away and besides, we could talk to you about what you want to do next year, couldn't we?'

'I wondered when I was going to be consulted about that,' Emily grumbled, putting her cereal bowl into the sink. She looked up, caught sight of her mother's face and hurriedly rinsed the bowl and put it into the dishwasher. 'Sorry. I will *try*. I've got a lot on as well, you know.' Emily was doing her best to sound grand, like a stressed executive, and Nina laughed. 'You wait, you just wait. One day you'll know what having "a lot on" can really mean.'

Graham had already taken nightdresses, slippers and washing equipment into the hospital on his way to work. Nina doubted that Monica would be allowed home yet. She'd heard enough stories from Graham about the lengthiness of the Social Services' assessment procedures. Nina had only to find some interesting and heartening accessory to take to her mother that morning. She wondered about flowers, but knew Monica would take that to mean she was in for a long stay that nobody was telling her about yet. A pot plant would be even worse: she'd assume she was a terminal case. Monica loved chocolates, so Nina called in at the small food market opposite the gallery and bought some that had soft centres of kiwi and melon cream and coffee truffle at a suitably exotic price, then dashed across to Art and Soul to get some gift-wrap from the cupboard under the counter.

'You're not supposed to be here,' Sally grumbled cheerfully. 'You're supposed to be hand-holding and heart-to-hearting before it's too late and you end up in therapy dealing with eternal guilt.'

'Oh thanks a lot, Sal. Sorry to be so disappointing but she's not dying, it was just a fall.'

'Don't you believe it. They're all dying, old parents. They do it on the sly when you've just had a row and said something terrible. Or they do it while you're stuck in a jam on the M25 half an hour late for lunch with them. You're supposed to hold your tongue about anything that matters the minute they hit sixty-five. Earlier, if they're smokers,' she warned grimly.

Nina pulled out a selection of flowered paper and chose a sheet patterned with sweet peas and some lilac ribbon for the chocolates. Monica would tut about the waste but would carefully roll up the ribbon to keep for another day. She had had a dresser drawer full of such saved treasures in her kitchen ever since Nina was a child. It was probably all still there, all the neat bright rings of ribbon in the huge oak sideboard. They'd still be there after she died, Nina thought, ready for her to sort through. It wouldn't be Graham's job – he'd be too upset. Just as he was too upset at fourteen to bury his pet mouse ('Nina, you'll do it') and too upset at seventeen to go to his father's funeral ('A funeral's no place for a schoolboy, Nina').

'Haven't you got any customers you can harangue? Or what about calling up a few suppliers, give our contributing artists the benefit,' Nina asked Sally.

'No-one's around yet – it's only just gone ten.' Sally lit a cigarette and opened the gallery door, blowing smoke out to join the passing exhaust fumes. 'Isn't it today you're supposed to be taking Lucy back to that second audition for Barbados? You know you could close early and just go, though it is Friday, and . . .' It was like hearing Emily backtracking in the kitchen again.

'No it's all right, Joe's taking her. He seemed quite happy to, actually, really almost thrilled to have been asked.'

'Aha!' Sally exclaimed triumphantly. 'He's feeling left out! They do that.'

'Like parents *do* die . . .' Nina interrupted.

'Yeah but men, once you've got rid of them, they go through a phase several months later, just like Joe. I mean, he did demand that extra lunch with you yesterday. They start taking every titchy opportunity to get back in, dipping in and out now and then just to make sure they've got the choice. You should make sure he knows he hasn't. I know, I'll fix up that night out I keep promising us. Then you'll have something to torture him about.' She gave a gleeful chuckle.

Nina smiled but didn't say anything. The feeling had been creeping up on her that she almost wanted Joe to have that choice. At least, she wanted him to want to have it, which might, or might not, amount to the same thing. She couldn't tell Sally what she and Joe had done on that frilly silly duvet: not unless she wanted a lecture on wimpy weakness anyway.

'If he's going to start having another family with someone else, he won't have any choices about anything for long. He doesn't even seem to have much of a choice about that either,' she told Sally instead. Her fingers, awkwardly tying the ribbon on the chocolates, felt like sausages. Tying gift ribbon was one of those things you really need three hands for. In her head just

then she was suddenly way back, years before, thinking about changing nappies, the tricky little plastic
tapes that covered the sticky fasteners. She remembered the dexterity needed and quickly learned, of
holding down a wriggling, giggling baby while she fastened a too-big Snuggler round its tiny bottom. Then
there were all the poppers on the clothes to negotiate,
the kicking little feet in a Babygro . . .

'They were so sweet,' she murmured, finally tying
an acceptable bow.

'What? Husbands?' Sally looked horrified.

'No, babies,' Nina confessed.

'Oh God, don't say you're getting broody now. It
must be the spring weather.'

Nina pushed the parcel into her bag and made her
way to the door. 'Doesn't matter how I feel,' she said,
smiling brightly. 'l don't have anybody to feel broody
with. So it's irrelevant, isn't it?'

'Not at all. You must simply make more effort to find
someone. Have you looked in the back of the *Sunday
Times* lately? There's usually a rush of likely victims at
this time of the year. Something goes to their heads in
spring.'

'Isn't it dodgy though, meeting some stranger like
that? I mean they could be axe murderers, standing
there in some nice bar waiting for you with their neat
pink carnation and just desperate to cut your throat.'

'Don't be daft! Look, leave it to me. I've got a brilliant
idea – I promise I'll fix you up, trust me.'

'"Trust me"!' groaned Nina. 'Now why does that give
me a terrible sinking feeling?'

Monica was sitting up in her bed, looking as if she'd
been in waiting position for some time. Nina's heart
sank. Her mother didn't look any more settled in than

she had the night before. Then, Nina had been happy enough to put her impatience down to unadmitted fear and shock, but now there was no mistaking cussedness.

'They said I can't go home, not until Social Services have been round to assess the house,' she told Nina. 'It's outrageous. Aren't we always being told they're desperate for the beds? It's going to be days. I'm not even allowed to decide for myself whether I'm capable of getting around or not.'

Nina sat on the orange plastic chair beside the bed. It was too low, and her mother was looking down at her in an imperiously enquiring way that Nina recognized from childhood. Any moment she would be saying something like 'And what makes you so sure you've got all the answers, Miss?'

'There's no point letting you go home if you're in danger of falling again or doing something even worse to yourself. That way you could be occupying the bed for months. Can you get around? Have they let you get up this morning?'

'Oh yes,' Monica conceded grumpily. 'They let me get up. One minute they won't let you move, the next they're saying ghastly things like "Upsa-daisy, we don't want to go getting a nasty thrombosis now do we?" I've got these ghastly white stockings. They make my legs look dead already. I expect the rest of me will soon catch up.'

Nina laughed, and her mother's face twitched at last with humour. 'Everyone gets those in hospital now, even teenagers. It's just a precaution. You can always come and stay with us for a while, we could all take care of you between us,' Nina offered, handing her the chocolates.

Monica laughed loudly and the rest of the ward's

permed grey heads turned to listen. 'Oh heavens, Nina that would be terrible, we'd never get on. And your girls are so noisy. No, I'll get Graham to fix the stair carpet and then everything will be fine. I might even promise not to go up and down stairs while there's no-one else in the house. Anything just to get out of here. I can feel myself ageing and decaying in this bed.' She stared around the ward at the other patients, some of whom were several years younger than her, and then said in what might have been meant as a whisper, 'I'm sure it's catching, you know. I'll be as dead as they are if I stay more than a couple of days.'

'So, if you get this job, you and your mum get ten days lazing around in the Caribbean, is that right?' Joe asked Lucy as they drove to Kensington.

Lucy was sitting in the back of Joe's Audi surrounded by the essential trappings of her modelling career. Gas-fuelled curling tongs were heating and would soon be singeing the cream leather seat; her book of photos was on the floor beneath her favourite, shamingly clean trainers. Three sweatshirts were laid out beside her and the ever-present Sophie, who sat in the front next to Joe, had the responsibility of choosing which one went best with her black jeans. Sophie's role was to be an admiring observer. She was quicker at running, climbing and squirming through nettles on her tummy, but this today was Lucy's speciality and she was on the edge of being over-excited and showing off.

'We don't laze around,' Lucy declared with exaggerated scorn. 'We *work*. *Really* early in the mornings so that it isn't too hot. And I expect,' she added grandly, 'there'll be some evening shots too, because of the magnificent sunsets.' She returned to brushing her hair and dividing it into strands for curling, not meeting Joe's gaze in the mirror.

'*Magnificent sunsets!* You've been watching too many holiday TV programmes. Can't be bad though. Well lucky old you, isn't she Sophie?' Joe teased.

'Not really,' Sophie said sniffily. 'My mum and dad, they said that children doing modelling is, er . . .' she hesitated, either groping for the word they'd actually used, or suddenly deciding she needed to find a more polite one for the circumstances.

'Common?' Joe suggested, grinning at her.

'Um, I think so. Something like that,' she admitted.

'What's common mean, exactly?' Lucy asked from the back seat. Joe looked at her in the mirror. Her eyes were wide with pretend wondering. A chunk of her long chestnut hair was wrapped round the curling tongs. The ends would get split and over-dry. The finished result could make her look like something from one of those all-American Junior Miss Peanut Princess pageants. All Lucy needed now was jailbait raspberry lipstick and some heavy-handed dollops of mascara. Even though she was required to turn up resembling a normal, natural child, she, as all the other hopefuls would be doing, was pulling out all the stops. There would be nine-year-olds who'd had French manicures, tiny blondes would be blindingly highlighted and every child would already own her own bulging make-up bag. Joe felt depressed and secretly thought Sophie's parents probably had a point.

'Common means vulgar, downmarket, naff, grotty,' he informed Lucy, thinking with sad disloyalty, please God don't let her get this job. As he pulled up outside the casting studio, he regretted his plea. Worse would be the rejection she'd feel if she *didn't* get it. Either way, he thought as the three of them went inside to find Angela, Lucy's agent from Little Cherubs, Lucy shouldn't have to be going through it at her age, however much she claimed it was her choice.

Once through the hall door, the worst of Joe's fears were confirmed. Inside the rather shabby building, the air was stifling with hair spray. Lucy's loosely waved hair was of restrained subtlety compared with the flamboyant full-scale perms of some of the contenders. One poor girl with waist-length black ringlets, Joe calculated, must have spent several days having her hair ragged and curled. He was the only father, the only man apart from a couple of twittering young ones who he presumed were doing the model-selecting and who looked at the assembled dozen children as if they were loose tigers. The mothers, smartly supporting but cleverly not outshining their daughters, were mostly turned out in neat pastel sweaters or a forgettable background of navy blue. The hall, by contrast was almost dismally dingy, with peeling green paint like an early family planning clinic, and a dusty old grand piano half-covered by a crocheted blanket in a depressing shade of musty yellow. The high, paint-flaked windows were blurred with filth and there was a faint underlying smell of stale beer; Joe guessed the place was probably mostly used for theatrical rehearsals. So much for the glamour industries, he thought, looking round at the fussing mamas and their pretty poodle-daughters. 'Christ, it's like bloody Crufts in here,' he said. When running music to film for ads that featured children, he'd never considered this meat market aspect to casting. Those bright confident little faces plugging the cereal or crisps gave no hint of the horrors of mass casting.

'Lucy, darling. Over here and let me have a look at you. Got your book? Good. A touch of blusher here and here I think . . .' Angela, a vast woman in billowing purple, bustled up and gave Lucy a fast and professional up-and-down appraisal, ignoring Joe completely. She glared suspiciously at Sophie, who was looking bored and chewing a grubby nail and said, 'And who is this?'

'Sophie, my friend. She's only here because she's coming home with me after,' Lucy explained. With undisguised hostility, Angela stared at the child who, compared to the others present, looked as if she'd been sleeping rough and never seen a comb.

'Yes well, little girl, you just sit here out of the way with Lucy's daddy; and you'll be nice and quiet, won't you?' Angela ordered. Joe grinned at her, feeling a comfortable conspiracy with the scruffy, unimpressed child. Sophie's navy blue school sweatshirt had a big streak of misrouted lunch down the front of it and the knees of her corduroy trousers were baggy and ingrained with mud. Behind her was a girl in a pink and gold Versace T-shirt who would probably faint if she spilt so much as a drop of water down herself. Beside her, a curly redhead was idly picking at a leftover chickenpox scab on her bare midriff. Lucy was led away to line up next to a child in orange frilled socks, a pair of lime green cycling shorts and a yellow baseball cap. Her face, contrasting with her winter-pallid limbs, was coated with exuberant tan make-up.

'Getting into character, I think that's called,' Joe said to Sophie as together they looked at the child in amazement. One by one the girls were called behind a vast white screen where test shots of them playing with a beach-ball were taken. Each of them stepped forward confidently as she heard her name, fixing a beaming, well-trained smile as she went. Joe and Sophie could see shadows of the children on the screen, see lightning flashes as the photos were done. Bored, Joe took out his paper and started doing the crossword. Sophie, disobeying Angela's strict request, got up and wandered about. Joe glanced up but didn't call her back; after all, there was no trouble to be got into there, the place was beyond damage . . .

'I *hate* you, Sophie!' Joe was jolted out of an elusive anagram by the sound of his daughter shrieking. 'You're not even supposed to be here!' There followed the unmistakable sound of fist connecting with face, followed by a howl and a scuffle. On the big white screen, like a very early movie, shadow play of a pair of girls, one lashing out, one defending herself, could be clearly seen. 'Oh God,' Joe groaned, 'A cat-fight.'

'Out! Out at *once*!' Angela came looming from behind the screen, hurling out a furious Lucy, her curled hair flying madly and her eyes full of jealous tears. Her face was red-streaked and ugly with anger. Aghast would-be models and their fond mothers stared. Smugly, the mothers claimed the hands of their well-behaved darlings and drew them protectively close, away from the tantrum.

'I've never seen such behaviour!' Angela began, taking in Joe with her accusation.

Joe looked at her in amused disbelief. 'In this business? You must have!' he said, 'What's up Lucy, broken a nail?'

'Sophie! They've picked *Sophie*!'

Joe, fighting a disloyal is-that-all, felt sorrowful sympathy for the distraught Lucy. 'After what her parents said about modelling?' he said, then addressed Angela: '"Common, naff and vulgar", weren't they the words?' Angela, hands on hips, looked outraged. 'And Sophie doesn't even have an agent to pay, does she?' Joe couldn't resist taunting her.

127

'She'll need one,' Angela replied.

'No child of nine needs an agent. They need their childhood. Now wrap up things with Sophie and let me get these girls out of this place,' Joe said, hugging Lucy and feeling quite desperate to get her back home, to toast, Ribena, normality and Australian TV soaps.

Chapter Nine

Joe wasn't even trying to take it seriously. Nina could see quite easily that the only thing he was trying to do was keep a straight face. Megan, all flowing gentle silk and the calm smiles of the beatifically pregnant, was trying to make sense of what Sophie was telling her in the Malones' kitchen.

'They want *you* to be a model? You mean *posing* for a *catalogue*?' Her nose wrinkled in amused disgust. Sophie shoved her hands deep into her pockets and put on a don't-care face. Lucy marched to the fridge, noisily took out a can of Coke and sat at the table to drink it, pointedly offering nothing to her former friend.

'Lucy . . .' Nina warned. Lucy pretended she hadn't heard and continued drinking. Nina decided she could be dealt with later, and firmly. That made two of them to be cross with: Emily hadn't even come in from school yet, and it was after five. She'd probably claim she'd been revising in the library, pretending she'd completely forgotten she was supposed to be doing the supper.

Megan continued to look prettily puzzled, overdoing it, Nina rather thought, seeing as the situation wasn't that difficult to understand. What she was doing was acting the epitome of middle-class flummoxed, when faced with something that was tainted by possible vulgarity. In Megan's mind, Sophie was clearly only one white high-heeled step away from posing topless in a tabloid newspaper.

'I think they're getting about a thousand pounds each for this one,' Nina threw in mischievously, risking a glance at Joe. He winked back at her, understanding.

'*Really*? Heavens!' Megan seemed to have got the hang of that bit fast enough. 'Well Sophie, let's get you home and after supper maybe we'll see what Daddy says.' She turned to Joe and treated him to her biggest smile and her radiantly shining azure eyes. 'Thanks so much for collecting her from school. I'm sorry she's caused so much trouble.' Megan looked nervously at Lucy, and then back to the glowing beginnings of a good-sized bruise on Sophie's left cheekbone. 'Girls can really surprise you sometimes, can't they?'

'Lucy, isn't there something you want to say to Sophie?' Nina said.

'Only goodbye,' Lucy replied smartly.

'That wasn't what your mother had in mind,' Joe prompted her.

Lucy looked up at him, startled. His voice sounded quite hard and angry, tones she hadn't heard since he'd moved to the flat. He always talked to her and Emily as if being cross just didn't happen any more. 'OK. I'm sorry Sophie. I suppose I shouldn't have hit you.'

'No you shouldn't,' Sophie said, reluctant to end the feud. 'Should be a good bruise though, you can hit really hard,' she conceded with grudging admiration, rubbing gently at her hurt face.

'It was only one gig, Lucy. No need to take it so seriously,' Joe told Lucy as soon as Megan and Sophie had gone. 'In fact, if you're going to get so chewed up every time you don't get the job, maybe you shouldn't do it at all, because it's a hard and silly business, full of hard and silly people who won't choose you for all sorts of reasons of their own. I know, it happens to me with music all the time. I can easily spend three days coming up with a demo of swirling guitars for a client only to have them choose something by someone else that's all sickly violins. You don't take it personally, you just move on,' he said.

He took a swig of the beer Nina had put in front of him on the table. She was washing salad by the sink, turning the radio down to listen to what he was saying. She was glad they had this to talk about, one more thing that put the rather disgraceful scene of their recent sex further to the back of her mind. Joe had made no hint, not so much as a gleam of conspiracy, that he'd done anything more than simply forget about it. Nina's body hadn't – her insides tweaked pleasurably and she tried to concentrate on Lucy's behaviour.

'It isn't so much that she minded about not getting it that I object to,' Nina joined in. 'But the dreadful way she's treated poor Sophie. Now *that* was awful. How could you have walloped her like that? It was hardly her fault . . .'

'Was,' Lucy grunted, 'She did it on purpose. You should've seen her.' Lucy strutted about, miming being Sophie. 'She took her hair out of its ponytail and fluffed it all out, like *this*, and then started wandering around, you know, like waiting to be noticed. And then they did. Notice her, and call her in. You wouldn't believe her, going "What, me?" all pretend surprise.' Then Lucy grinned happily. 'Anyway, her mum and dad won't let her do it so it doesn't matter really.'

'Well there you go then,' Joe agreed, but looking at Nina. She too had her doubts that Lucy was right. Megan would probably love a paid-for mid-pregnancy break in Barbados. Who wouldn't? She looked at the clock – quarter to six. 'Where's Emily?' she asked vaguely, wondering if she should be worrying properly by now or should just carry on blaming teenage unreliability. Emily was, after all, supposed to be the one at the sink washing lettuce.

Emily had had a terrible day. What should have been the stuff of fulfilled fantasy, the unexpected meeting with Simon in the road outside school, was a complete nightmare. Bloody Nick, bloody bloody Nick she chanted to herself as she cut across the edge of the Common from the bus stop. She was really late, all that hanging about in the library waiting for thick dumb slapper Sadie Phillips to finish with the French poetry translations. From the many and confusing hours that separated now from morning, she recalled something about promising to do supper. That was something else she hadn't got right, and Mum would be really furious, going on like she always did about it being a household of three perfectly capable women, well, two and a half, so why should *she* be the one who had to do *everything*.

As she strode furiously, she kept tripping on clods of grass broken up by ponies from the riding school. Some she kicked angrily, wishing each one was Nick's shin, some she stamped hard into the ground, wishing it was his possessive, bad-timing head. She shifted her heavy bag from one shoulder to the other, regretting that she hadn't stuck to the main pathway where it was easier to walk. It was a miserable gloomy early-darkening day like a throwback to winter, matching her mood. She thought of Glaswegian Mrs Keiller pointing this out with great excitement in Eng. Lit. as a 'classic example of *pathaytic farlacy*'. Bloody Nick choosing that very moment, that moment full of

132

glorious potential, to come bounding across the road and pick her up and swing her round as if she was some sort of cuddly toy that he owned. There they'd been, she and Chloe, just getting to the bus stop, just slowing down at the bit where the hedge hid them from school and you could light a cigarette with nobody seeing, and there was Simon in his car. He wasn't driving anywhere, he just sat there on the double yellow line, waiting.

Emily marched over the Common huddled into her coat, remembering the lurch inside her as she recognized that it wasn't just a coincidence: *Man-Date*'s instructions actually *worked*. 'With subtlety and guile, it is easy to let a man know where you'll expect him to come and find you, etc.' She'd managed quite easily to drop the name of the school into the conversation when she'd met him. She hadn't had to resort to subtlety and guile at all. It had been one of those silly teasing things, him treating her like a little girl in front of her dad, 'And which school do you go to then?' and she'd told him, and he'd said, 'Oh well I'll have to come and meet you at the gate some day, carry your books.' She'd thought by the end of his sentence he'd probably already forgotten what she'd said, even though she'd been craftily specific, making a joke about the cigarette hedge. And bloody Nick, stupid brainless Nick, had come racing up, just as she was getting close to Simon's window and he was winding it down and smiling and something that really mattered and would always be remembered was going to be said. Nick had grabbed her from behind and swung her up and kissed her ear, kissed her in that way that must have looked like she *wanted* him to do that, that he *usually* did it. She'd shrieked like someone of, oh God, she groaned miserably, like someone of *Lucy's* age.

Simon had probably thought she was totally pathetic and just as juvenile as Nick.

She stopped walking and shook her head from side to side, hard, like Genghis when he'd got grass seeds in his ears on his walk. She was trying to get the hot damp feeling of Nick's breath out of hers. The path was even darker now, this last bit where all the overgrown shrubs were. Everyone complained that the blackthorn never got cut back properly from the path. No-one walked there at night, not ever, except once a march of cross women claiming the right to be wherever they wanted to be. Even they'd been in a safe pack of about ten. Emily didn't care where she was. She cared only about where she wasn't, which was in Simon's car. Now *his* mouth somewhere near her ear (like all over her neck) was something to think about, even if it wasn't going to happen today, if ever now. Off he'd driven, with a sly little I-can-see-how-it-is grin, which was just so unfair, because he *couldn't*. And she wouldn't hang around and wait for the bus after that because it would have been humiliating, standing there with Nick going 'And who was *that* then?' and daring to look stroppy.

'Hey girl, come here.' Emily was dimly aware of a man's urgent, muffled voice hissing into her thoughts. *Fuck off* was her first mental reaction, angry at being intruded upon. She was in a mood for being alone and brooding, not for conversation of any sort. The blackthorn shuffled and shook and out into the path stepped a tallish man in a long coat, with his hands in his pocket, giving Emily the immediate impression of a coffin-shape. Emily almost giggled, so like the classic flasher did he look. If he'd appeared like that in a movie, she and all her friends would have sneered and yawned at the cliché. He wore a knitted black

134

balaclava helmet, the sort the little boys at Lucy's school wore to play SAS games in, and a long brown riding mac, all flaps and buttons and so many pockets that nobody needed. She waited for him to speak, a look of bored challenge on her face.

'Play with this?' he mumbled softly, the hands in his pocket pulling his coat open. Emily stood still and scarcely breathed, staring at the scarlet penis, straining stiffly from the opening in his trousers. It didn't look like Nick's, which was cool and pale and almost inclined to be aloof. This looked angrier, frantic, hot. For a silly muddled second, she thought it was just a stubby painted stick, false party-trick flesh like those hands that people shove up their sleeves to drop on the floor and astound their friends with. The man's right hand now gripped it and pulled harshly at the skin and a low sound rumbled from him. Emily stood still, watching and waiting. Her mind was as frozen as her body, but clamouring to get in was the thought that perhaps she should run, scream, shout, anything.

'Touch it, come on, touch it,' the man pleaded. She stared at the black wool where his face should be, looking for clues that he might have some soul. 'Just look then, bitch, just *look, look*,' he demanded, breathing hard and stepping nearer. The gripping hand was working so fast it seemed blurred. Emily started to back away, but then he was there, breathing on her, his hand gripping her arm and clutching her against him and trapping her against a tree. She could smell stale cigarette-breath, and the waxiness of the coat. Her back could feel every ridge of oak bark scraping as he pushed against her. She kicked out as hard as she could but her legs felt like pieces of foam rubber, incapable of making an impact. Then it was over, wetness like a slug trail glistened over the surface of her

135

skirt but there was fresh cool air between Emily and the man. He looked smaller then, somehow collapsed and feeble, backing away, fumbling and stumbling.

'You fucking stupid *wanker*,' she yelled to him angrily. 'You wouldn't even have cared if I'd been some little *kid*, would you? Selfish, evil git.' She turned then and ran, racing off the path and crashing through brambles and hawthorns to get to the road. 'Don't follow me, don't let him be following me,' she pleaded to whatever deity was listening. She didn't feel the scratches of the branches, or the misshapen roots twisting her feet off balance. She felt nothing but the need to run till she reached her own road and dashed past a surprised Henry on his way home. 'Hello Em, seen a ghost?' he quipped, flattening himself against his gate as she hurtled past.

'Drop dead!' she yelled, with the last breath she could spare from her aching lungs.

'Hello darling, where on earth have you been, we were starting to—' Nina began as Emily flew into the kitchen. She and Joe and Lucy watched as Emily, still gasping for breath, hurled off her stained skirt and tights and threw them out of the back door. She started to tremble and then to cry, falling onto the sofa and curling herself tight into a corner, her head down among the cushions.

'Whatever's happened?' Joe sat beside her and tried to gather the sobbing girl to him. She wrenched herself back quickly and cringed away, further into the corner. Lucy instinctively moved herself out of the way, over to the door and stared, a thumb that hadn't been sucked for five years finding its way to her mouth.

'OK Joe, let me. You could make her some tea,' Nina suggested quietly. She knelt in front of Emily and took

136

one of her hands. It felt stiff and cold. Nina was frightened, scared for whatever Emily had been through. She coaxed her gently, 'Come on Em, tell me, has someone hurt you?'

'No,' Emily muttered. 'But on the Common there was just this man.' She lifted her head and stared at the floor. Nina waited, and Joe clattered about with the kettle and cups, things falling over out of control as his own hands shook.

Gradually Emily told just enough of what had happened and was persuaded of the need for the police to be called.

'Let me, I'll get them!' Lucy said, reaching for the phone.

'No. I'm doing this,' Joe said, unwrapping her fingers from the phone. 'Thanks,' Nina said, looking up at him. There were tears glistening in his eyes, something she hadn't seen, she was sure, since the day Lucy was born. I do wish he still lived with us, the spontaneous thought came into her head, the words as clear as if she'd stood alone in an empty theatre shouting them out loud.

Graham was very tired. Every patient on the shift seemed to have weighed at least twenty stone. The nurses had all been snappy and rushing. One very old man had fallen asleep and gone sideways half out of the wheelchair while Graham was finding out whether it was the fracture clinic or just normal orthopaedic to take him to, and it had taken three of them to load him back in again. 'If it wasn't Fracture before, it will be for sure now,' the young Irish charge nurse had muttered humourlessly and Graham had known it was all his fault.

No-one had asked him how Mother was, and

Jennifer had gone home early the night before saying she had tights to rinse out. She'd had that hard-done-by look that Mother liked to put on when he'd forgotten some little thing, like not putting the cups the right way round on the hooks or the time he'd brought home that bread with the little bits of dried tomato in. He'd liked it but she'd said it wasn't good and that foreign flour tasted odd.

While Jennifer was off home washing her under-wear, he'd got into bed with hot chocolate and his aircraft log, quite glad to have the chance to catch up with some recent numbers that he hadn't had the chance to put in. Sleep was tricky with no-one in the house to blame for the strange little creaks and squeaks. The cat, like him, had its own unshakeable routines and slept in its kitchen basket. It wasn't allowed upstairs. Graham kept waking and thinking there was someone on the stairs. 'It's just the house set-tling,' Mother used to say when he was little, and he lay in the dark thinking about her saying that, and thinking about how back then he used to clutch the satin cuff of her dressing gown and rub it between his thumb and his bottom lip. Social Services were send-ing someone round soon, to check for enough stair rails and that there was something non-slip for the bottom of the bath. Graham had got it all organized.

His shift, the early one that he preferred, had fin-ished now but Jennifer's hadn't and he wondered about going up to the ward and seeing if she fancied something to eat when she got off later. Apart from visiting Mother, he didn't like going to the wards unless he was actually working. He hated that spare-part feeling, hanging around by the nurses' desk waiting for one of them to stop bustling and ask what he wanted – you couldn't just go wandering about looking for the right one, everyone in the beds stared. Jennifer might be doing the bloods, or the teas or some very personal tending behind a curtain. He took his jacket out of his locker, extracted a 2p coin from the pocket and flipped it. Heads Jennifer first, tails Mother. Mother won (nothing new there, he thought vaguely) and he set out for the Care of the Elderly department. They used to call it Geriatrics, he recalled as he went, which he considered a word of some distinction. Then there'd been the phase when everyone pretended that old people were exactly the same as everyone else: if you'd had appendicitis, it didn't matter whether you were seventeen or seventy, it was the same illness. Except that it wasn't. When you were seventeen and went home, your mum looked after you and you got better in a week or so. If you were well over seventy like Mother, then after hospital you were a weak and unreliable convalescent and never quite the same again. He'd heard enough patients' relatives muttering that next time it was likely to be the last, curtains, all that.

Monica now ruled the ward. Over the dawn-light breakfast she'd terrorized the young assistant who brought round the food and tried to distribute it as silently and stealthily as possible. She was terrified of Monica who kept a beady critical watch over her and grumbled as if the eggs should have been prepared by Albert Roux.

'Why give us eggs at all?' she demanded of Graham, complaining at full volume that she'd been faced with something that may have had only three minutes boiling but had been almost fossilized in the hot trolley. 'We're forever being quizzed about our bowels. Eggs like that sabotage one's entire system. Why do they ask if we've "been" as they so coyly put it, when they serve

139

up food that guarantees the answer "no" for a good four days? And that woman over there – ' She pointed across to the bed opposite to a sleeping lady whose complexion was the colour Graham usually noted in the patients he transported to the mortuary – '*She* can't take anything that hasn't been liquidized, so do you know what they did?' As usual she neither waited for nor expected a reply. Conscious of the rising volume, Graham felt his shoulders hunch in an attempt to be invisible. 'They shoved her egg through a sieve and then down her throat. Almost choked and died.' Monica looked highly satisfied with her complaints. The rest of the ward's occupants shuffled their magazines and adjusted their headsets.

'Social Services are coming as soon as they can fit us in,' he said carefully, trying to put off the moment when she'd discover how vague they'd been about exactly which day. He hoped Nina would have to deal with that one. 'I'm organizing another rail for the stairs and they might say we need some in the bathroom too. We could put a shower in,' he suggested tentatively.

'A shower? We've got a shower, a perfectly good one,' she sniffed.

'That's in the bath. I mean one you walk into with its own door, no stepping over big ledges where you could trip.'

'There's nothing wrong with my eyesight,' Monica retorted, 'I don't have any trouble seeing where the side of the great big pink bath is. What do they think I am, totally decrepit?'

Not yet, Graham thought to himself with dread, but it was a good idea to prepare. Further ahead – how far or near exactly? – was the prospect of much more intense looking after. Nina should be doing that, he thought. Daughters were for the personal things. He did personal things at work, portering those of unreliable bladder, those who reacted badly to coming out of anaesthetic. He didn't want it in his off-time as well. He would never be without a mop. He felt depressed. After he'd quietened her down with talk of the cat and the garden, Graham set off for home. He felt the need for fresh air, great gasping lung-fulls of it. He left his car for later and set off striding across the Common, head down against the scudding wind, staring down to where only the sprouting grasses and the dog-stained bases of trees were properly in focus.

'Oh. *You're* here.' Henry walked in through Nina's back door and found himself in the unusual presence of Joe. No-one else seemed to be around.

'Hi Henry, glad to see you making yourself so much at home,' Joe replied.

'What? Oh, yes, well. It's just the neighbourly way in,' he said, looking back at the door as if expecting it to say something in his support. 'Must be my Northern upbringing.'

He sauntered over towards the sofa but then hovered around awkwardly, inhibited by Joe's rather off-putting presence. Joe looked grim; normally he'd point out and laugh at Henry's display of tactlessness. He wanted to ask where Nina was, as she was obviously who he'd come to see. All that sympathy and support he'd given to Nina over the past difficult year and Joe was allowed back in to make free with the house as if he was perfectly welcome. Henry didn't approve of civilized separations. Marriages that ended, particularly this one, should be a proper battlefield, then everyone knew where they stood. He resorted to polite niceties. 'How are you all anyway? I saw Emily earlier, running like the hounds of hell were after her.'

Joe leaned against the sink and studied Henry, unsmiling and silent. Henry put his hands in his pockets and stared back, wondering what he'd done. He felt like a bad schoolboy about to be told by a furious headmaster: 'Of course you know why I've sent for you.' Perhaps Joe was calculating just how close he'd got to Nina since the divorce. Gleefully, Henry prepared to torture him a bit, hint that there was more going on than the odd drink and movie together. Joe, though, had a miles-away look about him, so he might not even take it in.

'I've just come to ask Nina about the paint. Whether she wants me to get it or will she,' he started explaining, feeling annoyingly flustered.

'I don't know anything about it. Sorry Henry, I assumed you'd called in because you'd seen the police car outside and couldn't resist nosing in. Do you fancy a drink?' Joe opened the fridge and pulled out a can of beer and a bottle of white wine that had been opened previously. He pulled the cork out and took a sniff. 'I don't know how long she's had this but it smells more or less OK.'

'Er, no thanks,' Henry told him, perching nervously on the arm of the sofa. 'I didn't see any police, but what *were* they here for? If you don't mind telling me, that is.'

'Out on the Common, there was a fucking flasher – he had a grab at Emily,' Joe told him, concentrating on pouring the wine as he said it to keep his voice under control.

Henry gave a nervous burst of laughter. 'A flasher? Oh! I thought you'd been burgled or something dreadful like that . . .' The words were hardly out of his mouth before he felt his head connect with the floor and his body lose all sense of which way up it should be. Joe had, in one staggeringly swift movement, put down both bottle and glass and hauled Henry into the air and down to the ground. He stood over him now, his foot against Henry's throat like a hunter showing off a shot tiger.

'I used to think you were just a bit of a prat, Henry,' he said, his voice trembling with fury. 'Now I know you're a *huge* one. You think it was funny? You think some harmless saddo just waved his limp little dick from a nice cosy distance? You think that would have sent Emily into a life-fearing panic?' He wandered back to the sink and continued pouring the wine as if nothing had happened. Henry stayed where he was, rigid with shock and feeling a ridiculous sense of embarrassment. Clambering up from the floor would only draw attention to the fact that he had been so forcefully (and easily) put there. Joe looked down on him with disgust and emptied his wine glass over Henry's paint-encrusted chest.

'Oh just get up and go home, Henry. Go home and play with your fucking paints.'

Chapter Ten

'It's nothing to do with sex, it's about physical domination. It's all about power,' Sally was saying to Nina at the gallery.

'Yes I know all that.' Nina didn't want to talk about it. She sat on the floor, unpacking a box of glasses, taking rolls of bubble-wrap from each one and polishing meticulously before placing it on a shelf. She'd worked up a soothing rhythm to the work, smoothing out the bubble-wrap and laying it out flat on the floor, cleaning each glass the same way, starting with the bottom, twisting it clockwise and ending with a brisk wipe round the rim. The rims were different colours, a glimmering ring of sapphire or ruby or citron. They'd soon be sold – a set of six would make a good wedding present and it was coming up to that season.

Nina was immersing herself in the routine, shutting out thought. She rather wished she hadn't told Sally about Emily and her encounter on the Common, but then Sally walked her dog there just like most of the other residents and it was only fair to warn her. Emily had pleaded with her that if she really had to say anything, then just to say it was a flasher, nothing more. She felt tainted by being touched, and as if that feeling would be increased with each person who knew. Sally, never short of an opinion, inevitably contributed well-meaning interpretations. To her, as to Henry, exposure was just one of those nasty little occurrences that one could expect – the sort of thing men with nothing better to do went out and did. No big deal: practically every woman you met had come across a flasher. It was thought of as one of life's unpleasantnesses, like treading in dog-dirt and just as easily forgotten. In fact Sally had been dangerously close to finding it funny. It was easy to imagine her thinking that *she* wouldn't have run home hysterical from seeing a man wave his penis at her, that she'd have given him what for, told him she'd seen a bigger dick on a dachshund, or that he should do that sort of thing in the privacy of his own bathroom. Emily, a week ago, would probably have said she'd have done exactly the same, but then that didn't account for the element of danger and threat and the awful aloneness. And he'd touched her, which made it real assault. Nina could have made it into a joke, said something like, 'Guess what, Emily met a *flasher* on the way home from school. Poor girl didn't know where to look!' But then that would both be untruthful and a betrayal of Emily, who was outraged and devastated that someone could so thoroughly and unexpectedly call up terror. It didn't even begin to figure as something that could be laughed off, it was a wicked invasion.

'I wish they wouldn't call them "flashers",' Nina came out of her trance and said. 'It almost makes it sound glamorous, sort of sequin-studded and joky, as if they're just one of life's little eccentricities and no more dangerous than a marauding fox out there in the bushes.'

'Are they really any more dangerous though? Don't they get their kicks just by *showing*?' Sally asked. 'I mean, all little boys wave their equipment around from the first day they can get their hands on it.' She laughed, 'I remember Daniel only ever wanted to pee out on the street against someone's hedge. I always used to ask him if he wanted to go, just before we left the house, and every time, after about a hundred yards when we got to where the shops and people started, there he'd be, unzipping and looking around for an admiring audience. I guess some men simply don't move on.'

'They can start with that, according to the police, and then some of them carry on pushing for more thrills right up the scale towards rape or even murder. Emily is really traumatized, all the fight's knocked out of her and that's saying something. She's stayed in the house for three days now. She doesn't want to go out at all. Joe's offered to drive her to school and pick her up after but she says she's not going back this week, she's so angry that she can't cope.'

Sally's perfectly pencilled eyebrows rose up her forehead in surprise. 'Joe? Is he back home with . . .' Nina laughed; trust Sally to pick up on the Joe situation as a priority – and that was even without being told what had happened at the flat. 'No he *isn't*!' she told her, putting the last glass on the shelf and turning her blushing face to the floor as she gathered up the squares of bubble-wrap. Rather than chucking them straight into the bin, she put them carefully on the counter next to the till, ready for safe hoarding, amused to realize that without question she was turning into her own mother.

'Joe's just spending a lot of time visiting and making sure that Em knows he's there for her. It's really useful, seeing as Mother's *still* in hospital.'

'How kind,' Sally grinned knowingly. 'Next thing you know his bathrobe will be hanging behind your bedroom door again.'

'I don't think so. In fact I'm *sure* so,' Nina said. 'For

146

one thing Catherine's bought him a disgusting peachy coloured one to go with the walls. Whatever happens, and nothing *will*, I'm not giving that house-room.'

'You could take it down the garden for a ceremonial burning and then replace it, without saying a word, with something gorgeous like those navy blue waffled ones from Conran, or something cashmere,' Sally suggested.

'Absolutely not!' Nina dismissed the idea. 'I shall never again be responsible for the purchase of any of Joe's clothes. I never was, actually, come to think of it. I think it was one of the things he minded about. Catherine probably buys him silk socks from Muji and pretends they're actually a present, when really she's just being mumsy.' She shuddered. 'Oh never again, what bliss.'

'Protesting too much again,' Sally warned as the gallery door opened. Nina looked up, prepared to welcome a customer and saw that it was Graham. 'Oh hi, how are you?' she said, 'Coffee?'

'No thanks. I just came to talk about Mother. They're coming to check the house later this morning and then she can come home.' Graham had always been one for getting straight to the point, frill-free conversation, but this sounded like an accusation. Nina felt irritated. She hadn't told Graham about Emily and the man on the Common, because he'd pass on the story to Monica, who would worry and fret and keep harping on about it for months, long after everyone else had forgotten about it. So Graham probably thought she'd simply lost interest in Monica now that she was clearly well on the mend – she hadn't been to see her for two days, though she had phoned Graham and made sure that neighbours and the entire bridge club would be in attendance.

'Yes I do know. Do you want me to collect her? You'll be at work then, won't you?'

Graham stood looking too big and awkward with his hands in his pockets. He looked around, eyeing the gallery's stock nervously. Nina noticed how he hardly turned his head but somehow flicked his glance around furtively, as if it wasn't for him to express any interest in this sort of thing. She thought of the arty knick-knacks her mother had collected over the years, the usual Dresden shepherdesses, the Staffordshire dogs, Meissen porcelain, all locked into display cabinets where the dust, the cat and clumsy fingers couldn't get at them. Graham, as far as she was aware, had never in his life bought anything of artistic interest. It had simply never been his role. She wondered if he minded about that, if he'd ever felt he'd missed out on home-building. It was tricky contemplating asking him, in case he then started to brood on something he'd never given any thought to.

'She might need help getting dressed.' Graham addressed the floor and Nina recognized this from childhood: the avoidance of eye contact when he was asking for more than he was saying.

'Are you sure?' Nina asked. 'She seems just the same as usual, apart from furious that she's been kept in so long. She *says* she's absolutely fine, can't wait to get home and get on with life.'

'Well she would, wouldn't she? She wants to be at home,' he persisted. 'But she shouldn't be on her own. That's what they said at the hospital.'

Nina sighed, picked up a sheet of the bubble-wrap to fidget with and popped its air sacs one by one. The little explosions seemed to fill the hollow air of the gallery like gunfire. It was a satisfying noise. 'What exactly are you saying, Graham? I have offered to have

148

her to stay with us for a few days, but she says she won't come because she wants to be back in her own place and back with you. What else can I do?'

'All you *can* do is take her home, give her some supper and leave her to it, I should think. She's got the telephone,' Sally contributed briskly. Graham's body became even more hunched and defensive, now faced with two of them. He glared at Sally and waited in a sulky silence to bring out the words he really wanted to use. Eventually he said, 'You could come and stay at the house with her.'

'What? Oh Graham that just doesn't make any sense. I'd still have to go out to work, just like you do. And what about the girls? They'd have to come too.' Nina gave an explosive laugh. 'She doesn't need two of us to look after her, she's got you and all her bridge and Townswomen's Guild pals. She'll be fine, Graham, don't worry so much. I'll call in whenever I can. Promise. If you're really worried, perhaps we could organize one of those alarm things that she could wear round her neck. In fact I'll do some phoning and talk to her about it this afternoon.' She reached out and patted his arm. He looked stiff and wary of the gesture. 'Don't *worry* so much,' she told him. 'Be careful you don't undermine her independence and turn her into an invalid. That's the last thing she needs. Look, I'll meet you at the house later this morning for the social worker visit, will that help?'

Graham left, and the gallery seemed full of unexpressed resentment. 'Why *is* he so worried, do you think?' Nina asked Sally. 'I mean those two have been rubbing along all these years without exactly overwhelming affection between them. So why is he so terribly concerned now? She's fine, she insists she is, though she says no-one believes anything you say once you're past sixty. They'd have let her out after twenty-four hours if they hadn't got to make sure she was going home to suitable stair rails and stuff. It's like conditions for parole.'

'You've really got no idea, have you?' Sally said, looking at Nina in wide-eyed mock amazement.

'Well no I haven't. Tell me.'

'It's not *her* he's worried about being properly looked after. It's himself.' Sally went and opened the door so she could light a cigarette. 'It's a possibility of role reversal and he doesn't know how to deal with it. All these years your besotted mother has taken care of her beloved little boy's every need and now he's wondering who is going to grill his sausages for him just the way he likes them.'

'It certainly isn't going to be me,' Nina declared. 'If he can't grill a sausage at the age of thirty-nine . . .'

'I know and you know. But you'll have to keep reminding him that he's a big boy now or you'll end up with two households to run and a very large extra child. Trust me, I do know. When you've got boy children it's hard to stand back and let them do *anything* for themselves. You so desperately want to be needed. Your mother has done such a thorough job of making herself indispensable that your great big baby brother can barely wipe his own bum.'

Emily lay in bed listening to the distant sounds of Radio 4 drifting up from the basement. Henry wasn't like proper painters they'd had in the house, the ones who whistled along tunelessly to whatever came up on Capital and left coffee cup rings all over the table. Henry brought his own favourite Charles and Diana porcelain mug for his tea, liked listening to *Gardeners' Question Time* and argued out loud with the panel about when to mulch delphiniums and how to build runner bean wigwams. Emily usually enjoyed having him around, feeling that in the great war between adults who'd long ago taken every exam they'd ever need and teenagers who had them to come, Henry was on the teenage side. He'd admitted taking his own French A-level with a raging hangover and 'borrowing' someone else's art portfolio to try to get into college – an attempt which had failed since the someone else's name was written neatly in the bottom left-hand corner of each drawing. Henry still kicked his shoes off and left them where they could be tripped over, had a fondness for Marmite on toast and only read newspapers that he could describe as 'fun'.

Emily was starting to feel hungry and wanted to get up, eat Weetabix and watch Richard and Judy in the kitchen. Henry would be jolly (not because he wasn't sympathetic, but because he was convinced, despite being done over by Joe, that a good laugh fixed everything) and she wasn't sure she could face that. The TV would be under a dustsheet or even stored away in the big cupboard under the stairs. Every time Nina painted a room things got put into that cupboard, and only half the things came out again because Nina then had a splurge on obliterating clutter. 'One day me and Lucy will be in there,' Emily said to herself as she climbed out of her bed. 'I'm surprised that's not where Dad ended up.'

She went and showered, then searched around for clothes to face the day in. They had to be all-covering, all-enveloping. 'How can you wear all that when the weather's getting warmer? You look like you're going walking up a mountain or something,' Lucy had said the day before when Emily had come downstairs in jeans, boots, a polo neck jumper and a snug fleece. 'It

151

wasn't your fault you know,' her mother had pointed out with crass obviousness. 'It wasn't a matter of what you were wearing, just a matter of where you happened to be at the time.' Emily knew all this, deep down inside. Truths like that raged round in her head tangled with the anger. Right now it was a question of keeping her body, her legs, even her hands private for her viewing only, just for a while.

The phone rang as Emily was trailing slowly down the stairs. She didn't dash to answer it as she normally would, even though she immediately worked out that at school by now it would be morning break time and that the call was probably Chloe or Nick (stupid bloody Nick, so much was all his fault). Eventually she heard Henry booming 'hello' down the phone in the kitchen. She sat on the top step of the basement, listening while Henry chatted up Chloe, asking her how her love life was going. There were long silences when Chloe was presumably telling him. People did that with Henry. Every now and then he gave one of his big laughs, the sort that made you quite sure you'd just said the funniest thing he'd heard all day. It was a deep rumbling laugh, lovely but not as lovely as her dad's. She wished it was him painting the kitchen. She sneaked down the stairs till she could see Henry, lolling back in the big deep armchair (squashing its shroud of old sheet), with his feet on the kitchen table. He was wearing one blue sock and one black one.

'Are you colour blind or just a poser?' she asked him, interrupting rudely as she came into the kitchen. Henry didn't move, just grinned at her over the top of the phone and continued listening. 'The Princess has just come down, do you want to talk to her?' he said. 'Of course she bloody does, you don't think she'd be calling *you*, do you?' Emily tried being rude to him, but couldn't resist smiling. He was so like one of those out-size soft toys that people buy for babies, which they can't play with till they're far too old to want to. 'And don't listen,' she hissed at him, taking Henry's place in the chair and shoving her own feet onto the table. Pulling a face, Henry tugged at an imaginary forelock and returned to his ladder.

'Chloe? How's things? What have I missed?'

'Nothing. What's there to miss?' Chloe grunted. 'Though I think you might have used up your sym-pathy quota because I overheard a mention that your *La Peste* essay might be getting done while you're at home. Is it?'

'What do you think?' Emily laughed. The essay had actually been done the day before, swiftly and angrily finished in a burst of mind-numbing concentration that effectively shut out any humiliating thoughts of the man on the Common.

'I think you've done it and I bet it's brilliant,' Chloe replied, impressing Emily with her perception. 'It's ter-rible when we have to work to take our minds off things, isn't it?'

'Suppose so,' Emily agreed, feeling depressed.

'Nick sends love. He thinks you've got flu.'

'Fuck Nick,' she said. 'Though actually no, I don't recommend it.' As she said this, Emily could sense Henry up his ladder turning to look down on her in wonder. She looked up at him and frowned. 'I should have taken this call upstairs,' she said to Chloe. 'There are some very big ears flapping down here.'

'I'll come and see you after school – I'll bring a sur-prise, a nice one I promise.'

'Lovely, just so long as it's not Nick,' Emily ordered, putting the phone down. She lay back in the chair and gazed up at Henry, who sensed her eyes on him again and smiled at her.

'What?' he said. 'Wondering if I'll tell your mum what you've been up to with this Nick?'

Emily looked suitably scornful. 'Stroll on, she'd be worried sick if she thought I was actually still a good little virgin. My mum's a Seventies *swinger*, or whatever they were called, don't forget. I expect you were a Sixties one,' she added with calculated cruelty, watching with satisfaction as an expression of mock pain crossed Henry's face. He sat down on top of the ladder. 'Must rest the ancient aching legs,' he said. 'And yes, I was that Sixties swinger. If it moved, you shagged it. One is not necessarily proud of that.' She laughed: he looked so weary it was hard to imagine him in active and hot pursuit of some short-skirted, plum-lipsticked girl.

'What about now?' she asked quietly, wondering as she said it what she was really getting at.

Henry stood up and turned his attention back to the ceiling and started painting with care and concentration. 'What a question! So rudely personal. *Now*, I've come to an age where discretion is all. A gentleman never tells.'

'You mean, this gentleman isn't getting any,' Emily concluded with teenage brutality. Losing interest, she clambered out of her chair and started rummaging in cupboards for Weetabix. She made coffee for the two of them, then took herself off up the stairs to indulge her need to watch daytime TV in the sitting room.

Only half listening to a sofa discussion on how less than perfect bodies could find a way to wear translucent dresses that summer (don't even *think* about it, that's how, was Emily's damning conclusion), she continued thinking about Henry. She felt safe alone in the house with him, but wondered, in a detached way, whether she should. It could have been anybody out there on the Common. That muffled voice and wrapped-up head could have been anyone at all. It could have been Henry or Simon or that new Paul man from across the road or Mr Clements from primary school. She tipped Weetabix off the spoon, halfway to her mouth, feeling slightly sick. At least it couldn't have been her dad: he was with Lucy, hauling her off that little sneaky brat Sophie and bringing them home. In theory, though, in nauseating, actual puke-inducing theory, it could be any man on the planet and every one of them. They'd all got that power to intimidate, to terrify, to *subject*. Just suppose they really spent all their time having to be careful to keep under civilized control, with the urge to break out only just under the surface. She looked at the TV screen where three over-groomed women sat chatting and smiling in sublime happy confidence, blithely advising women on how to make themselves look seductive.

'You could be next,' Emily waved her spoon to the middle one, a slim bossy woman with streaked red hair and a brave pink suit. 'You could leave that studio and out by the car park there might be A Man who wants to treat you like scum. Don't ever forget it, because I bloody won't.'

Nina arrived at her mother's house at the same time as the Social Services inspector and they squashed through the gate together, awkwardly. Rather to Nina's surprise, while she was laughing an apology, the social worker bossily pushed her way ahead up the narrow, lavender-fringed path, leaving Nina, amused, in no doubt that the woman was more than sure of her own importance. The woman was probably, Nina would guess, no older than she was, but had taken on the tight grey curls and faded large blue spectacle frames that she perhaps thought might give her the authority of someone older.

Graham opened the door before they reached it, looking anxious, worried, Nina assumed, in case the rapid modifications that had been done in order that Monica could be allowed home might not be adequate.

'It's like not being allowed out of prison till the probation arrangements have been set up, isn't it?' Nina commented cheerily as Graham stood aside to let them in. The social worker – 'Call me Julia,' she instructed by way of abrupt greeting – did not smile.

'You wouldn't believe how many hospital beds are occupied by people who could manage perfectly well at home if only the right arrangements would be made. The Council can only do so much, you know,' she said rather crossly as if the last thing she needed was to be putting up with someone lacking suitable seriousness.

'The council had nothing to do with it,' Nina told her, feeling waspishly defensive. 'We used Yellow Pages and folding money. *And* it was all done and finished three days ago. We've been waiting for *you*.' Graham was frowning, his eyes imploring Nina not to get on the wrong side of this person who seemed to have so much power.

'Yes, well. That shows initiative,' Call-me-Julia approved grudgingly.

Nina stood behind her in the hallway while the stairs were inspected. Julia had a no-nonsense body, solid and firmly encased in a firmly belted navy blue mac. She had, Nina thought, a very businesslike bottom, broad, firm and flat. It would not swing round during a tricky blanket bath and knock things off a table. As Julia stood above her on the third stair, tugging at the new rail that was fixed opposite the banisters, Nina fought a terrible urge to prod at the efficient derrière, like the woman in the Beryl Cook painting of the three bowling ladies. 'Is it all OK?' she enquired instead.

Julia was giving nothing away, turning to face them as she made a cryptic note on her clipboard. She clasped that firmly to her bosom, which was also firm though not flat, as if she was secretly making notes on their suitability, not just the house. Graham sighed. 'Would you like some coffee?' he offered, heading for the kitchen.

'Ah the kitchen.' Julia followed him and he increased his speed, alarmed. 'Kettle? Plugs? How much dangerous leaning, how accessible?' She looked around swiftly, taking in instantly Monica's pristine grey and white kitchen. She stared at the floor tiles, weighing up their slip-rating, quickly looked at the cordless green translucent kettle and murmured, 'Yes, good. Now upstairs.'

Nina and Graham followed. Nina looked at her brother, trying silently to express how like a child she was feeling, like a nervous Brownie about to win or lose her badge for Age Care.

'Hmm. Oh, and a child! Where . . . ?' Julia had opened the wrong door, Graham's.

'No, no that's my room,' he blustered, pushing past and closing the door swiftly. His face was pink. Nina had caught sight, very briefly, of the model aircraft, swaying from the strings in the rush of air from the opened door. She recognized his embarrassment and sympathized. His room was no-one's business but his. There was no call for Julia's clipboard comments on that. '*This* is my mother's room,' she volunteered, swiftly taking over as leader.

She went into Monica's room and inhaled its faint papery scent of old-fashioned roses, her favourite flowers. The wallpaper was patterned with bold deep pink and scarlet full-bloom roses and their fresh bright green leaves, vivid against a white background, with scarlet, green and white striped curtains. She thought back with guilt to the bedroom at Joe's flat, the peachy washed-out bud-sprigged fabrics, the drenching of all surfaces in exhausting cloths. She might have been lying on that bed while her poor mother lay upside down on the stairs. Nina hadn't been inside her mother's room for, oh years, she thought. It seemed to be an intrusion, standing there, uninvited, inspecting the furniture for traps to floor the unsteady. Her bed-side table, though, and the dressing table and the old green velvet chaise-longue remembered from child-hood stood massive and unchallengeable: they stared back at them all, somehow collectively asserting that it would take more than one wobbly old lady to knock these gleaming polished pieces sideways. They stood as ever, firm and friendly, and even Julia appeared diminished beside them.

'The bed's a bit high . . .' she attempted, but without conviction.

'Mother is quite tall. We all are. She'll be all right, and I'll be here,' Graham countered, gaining strength from the surroundings.

'And there's a phone right here beside the bed, and Graham's only across the landing,' Nina added.

'Hmm. Yes, well, with the new handrails in the bath-room I don't see any *real* problems. If you've made the arrangements, I don't see why your mother shouldn't come home today. Doctor permitting, of course.'

'Of course,' Nina agreed, biting her lip against a grin. Nina could just imagine Julia's cowed deference in the presence of a medicine man. Perhaps she even became quite coy and twittery in the Presence.

'I'm so glad she's gone,' Graham said when he had closed the front door. His skin glistened with the perspiration of tension. Nina felt sorry for him. 'I'll make us both a cup of tea,' she said, 'to celebrate. Though you know, well better than most of us, that they really don't want people like Mother to stay in the hospital, because they need the beds. There wasn't much doubt really.'

'I'm not so sure,' Graham said, following her to the kitchen and leaning against the door frame. 'I expect they worry about being sued. I mean, suppose she came home and slipped in the bathroom the very next day?'

Nina concentrated on the cups and the tea, vaguely aware of the sound of the cat flap behind her. A horrible choking noise suddenly filled the quiet air of the kitchen and she and Graham watched with interest as the grey striped cat sicked up a barely digested mouse on the floor, neatly and carefully, so it seemed, selecting a white tile. Nina looked at Graham and together they dissolved into helpless giggles, of a sort they hadn't shared in years, not since as small children they'd stood together behind their wildly ranting mother as she'd declaimed to whatever gods were listening that she deserved better.

The cat sat looking at them, licking its lips clean, narrowing its eyes in satisfaction, and then delicately curled a pale front paw and began washing.

Chapter Eleven

Catherine sniffed cautiously at her bedroom air like a cat suspecting there might just be something interesting to find if only the right scent could be selected. Joe lay sprawled in the cane armchair watching her, comfortably guilt-free (old lovers, particularly old *wives*, couldn't possibly count), and waited for her sensitive nose to tell her whether he'd left a fermenting sock under the bed or that the water in the vase of tulips was slightly less than fresh. He discounted entirely the possibility that she could smell Other Woman. Nina's presence had been several days ago now, and so fast and furious as barely to leave an imprint on the duvet. He shouldn't be thinking about it, not now Catherine was back, but the memory still gave him a secret smile and a joyous lurch in his blood pressure.

Catherine liked to take a long and decidedly unspontaneous time to get ready for sex, which at first he had thought was some kind of seduction technique that she and perhaps a dorm full of girls at her boarding school had concocted as being a terrific tease. Now he knew better – she just liked titivating herself; it was some sort of solitary foreplay. A less lazy man than Joe might wonder if the process was almost insultingly masturbatory. She dressed and made up one way for work, another for bed, simple as that. It wasn't psyching-up time she needed, like athletes going for the hurdles final, it was simply that she prepared thoroughly for sex, thinking about what to wear as if it was a tricky business meeting. Did that make him a client? Dressed and anointed, he thought, that's how she presented herself on a bed, like an elaborate dinner-party main course. Sometimes, mid-coitus, her hand would stretch out, not in blissful languor, but to pluck a stray pillow back into place.

His fingers twitched on the arms of the chair and he watched her slender round bottom as she bent to put shoes in their appointed pocket of the hanging rack in the wardrobe. Suppose he jumped on her now? Fondled her from behind, wrenched off her silk knickers and simply pinned her to the bed. Maybe just this once she wouldn't give him that sultry over the shoulder wait-for-it smile as she slinked into the bathroom with a teeny handful of Agent Provocateur purple lace, feverishly running the shower and shaking out the perfumed oils. It must have been something she'd read somewhere, he decided, 'Smell sweet, keep him sweet', or worse, 'Treat your body as an altar, he will worship you.' They were living together for heaven's sake, not first-dating, he couldn't care less whether her French knickers were the same mint green as her bra and properly ironed before they were slithered out of and abandoned to the floor. Nina had had a compelling scent of warm busy human, something so profoundly arousing that he wondered why no-one had yet bottled and patented it.

'You've changed the duvet cover. How sweet of you,' Catherine said, looking at as much freshly laundered froth of pink beribboned easy-care poly-cotton as could be seen under the many frilled silky cushions.

Joe shrugged, eyeing the marshmallow bed without interest. Like the rest of the bedroom, it did not feel as if it was his, simply somewhere he was expected to visit Catherine. He felt rather more comfortably at home the nights he crashed out on the old black leather sofa up on the studio balcony when he'd worked late on a piece of music, often finishing only hours before recording. He'd done that often enough back at the house and the sofa was the only piece of furniture he'd taken away, something to curl up with, cosy, grubby and home-scented like a security blanket. Bedwise, his own taste ran to plain white cool Egyptian cotton, of the sort he and Nina had collected over the years from various Heals sales. In the back of his mind he could still hear the echo of his mother-in-law warning Nina 'You're letting yourself in for years of ironing', and looking at him with dark hostility as if she suspected him of deliberately setting traps designed to keep Nina chained to sweaty domestic tasks while he swanned about womanizing.

That bit at least wasn't so terribly far from the truth, he now thought vaguely to himself, remembering how ridiculously, childishly, excited he'd always become whenever some gorgeous, breezy and independent young ad-agency woman, keen to make her mark in the business, had made it known that she and her body just might be available for the price of dinner and some easy flattering assurance that her career path was sure to be meteoric. Not that Nina had exactly been chained to the sink, he reasoned, any more than Catherine was. They were both the sort who sent bedlinen to the laundry.

'So what did you get up to while I was away? Did you go out to play with lots of old girlfriends?'

Catherine drifted around the room, hanging clothes in the wardrobe, taking worn underwear through to the laundry basket in the bathroom. He smiled but didn't answer, slightly irritated that she was treating him like a wayward ten-year-old when he'd been out and earning his own living since she was playing kiss-chase in top infants. He watched her many reflections swinging to and fro as she moved the mirrored wardrobe door and noticed how Bambi-thin her girlish legs were. Nina's were still slim but they had a re-assuringly solid womanliness to them. Catherine's legs reminded him of Emily's and Lucy's. They were so young and fragile they could only mean *responsibility*. He missed Nina then, quite achingly and he tried to evict the feeling from his brain, only to find that that wasn't where it was lodged: it seemed to be stuck like indigestion in the region of what would pass for his heart if he believed in that sort of thing. Logically, he tried to reason that he wouldn't be feeling at all like this if Catherine happened to have solid, head-prefect, school-hockey legs. Equally logically, he acknowledged that he wouldn't be sharing this hellish cosmetic bag of a bedroom with her if she had.

Catherine, sublimely unaware of his disloyal thoughts, pulled a pair of unworn tights from her brown leather Mulberry holdall, rolled them up and went to put them away in their drawer. She hesitated and frowned, her fingers picking their way through the neat plastic dividers that separated the different deniers and colours.

'I'm sure I had a new pair of black velvet Calvins in here.' She looked up, puzzling at her own reflection. Joe watched coolly, waiting to see if her imagination would come up with an interesting explanation for their disappearance. It wasn't likely, he thought, depressed. And he was right.

* * *

Monica suddenly didn't like fish after a lifetime of claiming it as far superior to meat. Nina and Graham had been raised on what Monica had referred to as the brain's building bricks (green vegetables were scaffolding) right from the time they could do their own bone-extracting. Nina had grilled her a large and juicy plaice, bought that morning from the man with the van who parked by the pub twice a week and who plied a brisk and expensive trade based on his assertion that he'd just come straight up from the coast. 'He probably has,' Sally once said cynically. 'He probably lives in Eastbourne and drops in at Billingsgate on his way up.' The fish was moistened with lemon, delicately drifted with pepper and dill and parsley. Nina thought it looked delicious.

'Aren't you eating?' Monica asked, as Nina laid a tray with an embroidered linen cloth and Sunday cutlery.

'No, it's a bit early for me. I'll eat with the girls later,' she said. 'I'll just stay with you till Graham gets home. I've left him another fish in the fridge. All he has to do is grill it.'

'Ye-es, maybe.' Monica sounded doubtful. 'I suppose you couldn't just . . .'

'If you're going to ask me to stay on and cook for Graham, no I couldn't,' Nina told her, laughing. 'You shouldn't expect so little of him, he must feel quite insulted! Come on, into the sitting room, you can eat this in front of the News for once.'

'All this fuss and I've gone right off fish. They gave us slabs of it in hospital but it didn't taste real. Fish doesn't come in neat oblongs,' Monica complained, but she walked ahead of Nina, slowly making her way across the hall to the sitting room where the fire blazed comfortingly and the cat waited on the sofa.

Nina followed with the tray, watching how her mother placed her feet more firmly, more deliberately on the carpet than she used to. This, only a few years ago, was a woman who'd won the local drama cup for her energetic performance as Lady Macbeth. Now she looked down as she walked, not up and ahead in her usual rather stately way, making sure that her feet were exactly where she thought they were. She's more nervous than she'll admit, Nina realized, suddenly feeling more qualms than she'd so far allowed herself about the time her mother was accustomed to spending alone. 'Alone' wasn't a problem when you were active and capable and when going out or staying in was a matter of simple yes-or-no choice. Worried, she foresaw Monica gradually deciding that visiting friends, the bridge club, the Guild, the garden centre were in turn becoming just too much trouble. She could become more and more isolated, perhaps over something that pride wouldn't allow her to admit like the slippery dangers in unswept autumn leaves, or a wobbling kerb-edge at the crossroads by the Common.

The house seemed to be full of traps too, in spite of the bleak new stair rail which stretched pale and offensively modern opposite the polished oak banisters. Monica's beautiful old silky embroidered rugs suddenly seemed to consist only of threadbare, shoe-catching edges. The elegant lamps on the tables at each end of the sofa looked spindly and insecure, their wiring treacherously looped on the way to the plug sockets. Even the supremely placid cat seemed a danger, waiting to choose its moment to plait itself among Monica's unsteady legs and topple her, head zinging into the sharp wooden door frame or shattering through the glass display cabinet.

'Graham and I wondered if we should get you one

of those alarms,' Nina suggested, settling the tray on the low table in front of her mother. Monica's face wrinkled with distaste, though whether at the unwanted fish or at her suggestion, Nina chose not to ask. 'You see ads in the Sunday papers for them,' she went on. 'You can be linked to a council helpline, wear the bleeper round your neck and then if anything happens you just press it and you've got someone to come and sort you out.'

'Who, some stranger? Poking about in the house? I could be lying there helpless while they burgle.'

'No, a neighbour, me, Graham – whoever you decide to give a key to. Suppose next time you fall over you're nowhere near the phone. You could be lying there till Graham's shift finishes, or longer if he goes out somewhere.'

Nina watched Monica's fork playing with the plaice. She was eating it, but grudgingly. Nina stopped talking. It might be enough just to plant the idea; Monica could mull it over and decide she'd been the one to think of it for herself some time later. While she was eating probably wasn't the best time to conjure up awful images of her lying helpless on a floor, getting cold, bleeding heavily, immobile. Monica's own nighttime imagination could be relied on to supply those pictures, Nina was sure.

'The food wasn't actually *that* bad in the hospital, considering,' Monica commented, cutting a Jersey Royal potato into eight minuscule bits.

'You'll think about the alarm later then, won't you?' Nina said quietly, going to clear up in the kitchen. From the doorway she heard her mother saying, as if to reassure herself, 'But Graham doesn't go out. Hardly at all.'

* * *

166

Graham was looking forward to getting home. There'd be Mother back again, someone to shout 'Is that you?' as he came in, in the way that told you she wouldn't want it to be anyone else. It wasn't the same, just having the cool grey cat waiting there, sitting on the stairs being aloof but rubbing round enough when it came to tin-opening time. Cats didn't ask you about your day, didn't sympathize when you told them about that cow of an A & E sister who refused to help with the dodgy lift doors because that was Maintenance not Medical. Mother made all the right noises, the cat just licked its paws and blinked and looked superior. On the other hand, it would be trickier to get out of the house at night now, popping out to see Jennifer. He'd have to think about inventing some more owl activity on the Common, or wait till Mother was safely in bed, nice and early with cocoa and a Catherine Cookson. It wasn't a good time to unsettle her with the truth. In fact, when was?

Jennifer was just passing as Graham reached his car. He didn't wonder what she happened to be doing wandering through the staff car park, didn't think to calculate that the dusty acre of scrubland tucked away beyond the mortuary wasn't on the way to or from anywhere.

'You'll be glad to have her home,' Jennifer said, coming to stand next to him as he unlocked the Fiesta door. They were squashed together between his car and a scarlet Passat. When Graham opened his door there seemed to be even less space. She was very close.

'Yes. She didn't like it much in there,' he told her, grimacing towards the buildings behind him.

'So I heard!' Jennifer laughed. 'Mary on the ward told me she certainly had them running about.' Graham frowned and she put a hand on his arm. 'I don't mean like room service in some hotel,' she re-assured him. 'I mean she seemed to like everything just *so*, all efficiency.'

'She has very high standards,' Graham said, defensively. 'She just likes things done properly. If she sees that someone's been left stranded on a bedpan for half an hour, calling for help and not getting any, then I think she's right to make a fuss for them.'

He made a move towards the car, but Jennifer's pillow of a bosom seemed to form a barrier. Her breasts loomed between him and the car seat. He'd have to rub his ear against them if he wanted to get inside. Usually this was the kind of thought that helped him get to sleep at night but just now he simply wanted to get away, get home, be Monica's son, not Jennifer's – what was he? – boyfriend? partner?

'Sorry love. Look, don't be so serious! Get your mother settled in and maybe we could go for a drink. Not tonight, that wouldn't be right – but maybe tomorrow? What do you think?'

Graham thought that would be all right, especially if agreeing would mean he could get into the car. And she was now showing something like proper respect. 'If I can get someone to come and sit with Mother, then yes, tomorrow might be fine. Or perhaps after the weekend might be better, so she's feeling safe,' Graham conceded. Jennifer moved away at last and he sighed, feeling as if her breasts had been squashed into his chest preventing his breath from coming out properly.

Driving along the road, away towards the Common, he allowed himself to think about those breasts again. This time he imagined them naked, big and firm, the same ballooned shape as they were when she was dressed. He knew some big women drooped terribly when all support was removed, but somehow Jennifer looked as if she didn't. Unclothed she would still be rounded and mountainous but soft and warm at the same time. His hands sweated on the steering wheel and he was glad of a string of red traffic lights to give him time to compose himself before he got to the house. Nina had said she would buy plaice for supper. He liked that.

'I'm back! Has anyone who isn't me thought about food?' Nina shouted as she walked down the stairs to the kitchen. She stopped at the doorway, amazed. 'Good grief, it looks wonderful! You've transformed it!' she said. Henry, at the sink washing brushes, turned round and grinned, pleased. 'Well I thought I'd just get as much done as I could while it was quiet. Is it all right? I mean we can go over the walls with any colour you like, it doesn't have to stay white.'

'No, no it's fine, I love it all fresh and pure. It looks twice the size. I really like it all empty like this.' She walked around, enjoying the feeling of clean space. Joe's flat was like that, all open and uncluttered, apart from that awful strangling bedroom. Henry had moved the dustsheets from the sofa and chairs, there was a crowded vase of cornflowers and white stocks on the table and someone had taken all the books out of the cupboard and put them back on the shelves.

'There's just the windows and doors and skirtings to do now, all the eggshell bits. More white?' Henry asked.

'No,' Nina decided instantly, looking at the flowers. 'Blue paintwork. A really rich, Caribbean sea blue. And the curtains can all go to the jumble. I don't think I want any.'

'What? Just empty windows? You can't.' Emily came into the room, catching the end of what her mother was saying. 'People will be able to see us, we'll be spied on.'

Nina laughed, 'Who's going to look and from where?' Emily came across and glared out of the window, her face daring anyone even to think of glancing in. 'Look! See that? That new man across the road up in that room, he's looking, he can see right *in*!'

Nina followed her gaze. 'Oh that's only Paul. He's set up an office in that small bedroom. I don't suppose he even gives us a glance, really.' He *was* looking though, Emily was right. She waved up at him and he waved back. Probably he couldn't see more than a couple of feet into the room. Equally probably he wondered what kind of woman she was, gazing out and up at him like that. 'Perhaps you're right,' she told Emily. 'OK, a plain blind at the front window, but no-one passes round at the back, there's only the garden.'

Emily shuddered. 'Well that's even worse than people passing. Someone might climb in and start looking *on purpose*. You just wouldn't know, because you couldn't see them from inside when it's dark. They could be pressed up right to the window and you wouldn't know.' She slumped onto the sofa and curled up, hugging her arms round her body. 'You're just so innocent, Mum, you'd never think anyone *evil* might be out there. Lucy would probably hope there *was*. Anything for an audience.' Nina went and sat next to her, taking her limp, unresponsive hand.

'Goodness, I'm sorry Emily, it was just a frivolous suggestion really. Of course I want you to feel safe and private. I should have thought before I spoke. But you know you really mustn't let this incident on the Common blight your spirit. That way, the man will have won, made you a real victim.'

'I know, I know. And he didn't really hurt me, I

know all that. But he could have, he might with some-one else.' Emily picked at the edge of her sweatshirt. The ribbed band was coming apart from the rest of it, and Nina wondered how long she'd sat that day, just brooding and picking. Emily continued in little more than a whisper, 'I just feel depressed because men've all . . .' and here she looked up from under her fringe and glanced across at Henry '. . . all got that strength, deep down packed away in case they really want to use it. And when they *don't* use it, they're just being polite, aren't they? With that strength they know they can just get their own way any old time. I hate them for it. I hate them all.'

'Er . . . I'll see you in the morning shall I?' Henry, the brush-washing completed, stood in front of Nina, his hands on his hips and the zip of his jeans at her eye level. Any amount of primitive stirring might be going on behind the denim. Perhaps only deliberate distract-ing thoughts of say, England's last test defeat, keep most men from pouncing whenever the urge takes them. Emily's almost right, she thought, looking up at him, but, get real, only almost. Henry was waiting, grinning and looking untidily boyish. There *were* Nice Men.

'Henry, I'm sorry, all that hard work and I haven't even offered you a drink,' she said, getting up and heading for the fridge.

'Oh *God*,' Emily declared angrily, hurled herself off the sofa and out of the door.

'Now what have we done?' Henry asked, looking perplexed.

'I've been nice to a man,' Nina said, by way of ex-planation.

'Oh and that will never do,' he teased.

'Not in Emily's book, not right now. Oh and I've

forgotten Lucy! She's over at Megan's. Look help yourself to a beer and I'll just dash across and fetch her. Won't be a sec.'

'No, I won't stay actually,' Henry said, collecting up his brushes and stowing them upside down in a jam jar next to the sink. 'I've got a hot date with a take-out, a video and a blonde. See you tomorrow?' He and Nina went out together through the back door, and parted at the front gate. Nina crossed the quiet road in which a black cat sat washing its back leg and waiting to cross someone's path for luck. 'Come on puss, over here,' she called to it, but the cat didn't move, simply gave her a sly glance and went back to its cleaning.

'Hi! Come in and see if you can find your daughter!' Megan greeted Nina. Behind Megan was a wall of sound and fury: gunfire, shrieking and squeals. 'Well obviously the girls are on speaking terms again!' she said, following Megan through to her steel and white kitchen.

'Shouting terms, more likely,' Megan yelled above the din. 'They're being SAS heroes kidnapping some world-threatening monster. They've tied Sam to the banisters up on the landing but he doesn't seem to mind.'

'They probably wouldn't care if he did,' Nina said. Paul, perched on a kitchen stool and leaning against the worktop, emerged from behind a large newspaper. It crossed her mind that if he could see into her kitchen, he might also be able to keep watch via her sitting room window and possibly even see into her bedroom. He slid off the stool and greeted Nina with a kiss on each cheek. 'Hello Paul, how are you?' she said.

'Fine. How is your mother? Lucy said she was due out of hospital today.'

Megan slid a glass of wine into Nina's hand.

'She's fine. Well, so far. My brother lives with her so he'll be there to keep an eye on her.' Nina sat on a stool next to Paul and watched Megan chopping vegetables. She did it with surprising clumsiness, considering how neatly she moved and how delicately expressive her fingers were when she spoke. Large uneven slabs of carrot, hacked leeks and shredded celery piled up on the board beside her and were then hurled carelessly into a vast blue Le Creuset cauldron. Nina would be willing to bet though that something sumptuously appetizing would somehow be the result. It had to be, to match this perfect nuclear family. The Brocklehursts, attractive devoted parents, pair of pretty children and the blessing of the third pregnancy, were what Joe would call an advertiser's wet dream.

'So he's not married then, your brother, or is he divorced or whatever?' Megan asked.

Nina laughed. 'No! Graham's never got round to leaving home. Mother made him much too comfortable! I don't suppose he ever will now.' Paul and Megan exchanged glances, which Nina speedily interpreted.

'I don't think he's gay, if that's what you're thinking. He's just not bothered either way,' she told them.

'Oh come on, everyone's bothered, one way or another, surely!' Paul said. 'It's only natural. He must have some secret vices!'

Nina felt slightly aggrieved. It was none of their business. However had she got into talking about this? 'Well he's happy enough, so what does it matter?' she sipped at the wine, but found it sour.

'Classic sex crime profile,' Paul commented casually, leaning forward and looking as if he was only pretending to be serious.

'What is, exactly?' Nina asked, daring him to spell it out.

'Mother's boys. Men who've stayed too long tied to Mummy's apron strings. It's the first thing the police look for when there's a nasty murder. You know, you must have read it countless times,' he said simply, with a taunting grin.

'Oh Paul, stop it! I'm sure Nina's brother is a perfectly nice man who just happens to prefer home cooking to living in a bedsit on beans and take-outs.' Megan attempted peacemaking.

'Yes he is.' Nina put her glass down, appalled to find that her hand was trembling. 'And I'm sure that when the police catch the man who's been molesting girls on the Common, they'll find he's a *perfectly nice* man with a saint of a wife and some perfectly ordinary children. Now, where is Lucy – I really must take her home.'

Chapter Twelve

'Are you sure you want to go? I'm sure Joe will understand if you'd rather just stay here.'

Nina pushed aside a pile of Emily's clothes (clean and awaiting drawer space, or overdue for the laundry basket?) and sat on her daughter's unmade bed. From beneath it, the sleeves of a grey jumper could be seen splayed across the floor like a murder victim. The air of chaos made Nina's fingers twitch with the urge to start sorting. Like a child told off for fidgeting she sat on her hands, determined not to pick up so much as one grubby garment. For that way lay the thwarting of a developing independence by heady parental control: Nina refused to be tempted to emulate her own mother, who was still fondly picking up, sorting and washing Graham's dropped socks.

Emily was selecting more clothes, some from a drawer and some tugged out of the piles, and shoving them into a pair of Sainsbury's carrier bags. She seemed to be covering all social possibilities: from a night of minimal dress in the gluey heat of a club to a freezing sulky walk along the wind-blitzed Thames. Late on Sunday night they would all be brought home and tipped carelessly out to join whichever heap seemed appropriate at the time and the bags would float softly across the floor, wafted by the breezes of Emily's to-and-fro presence until they graduated to becoming the overflow for her rubbish bin. In between now and Sunday night the house would be agonizingly quiet, just the metallic click-click of Genghis's claws on the kitchen floor, his snuffling by the door, the spooky night-time whirring of the hamster's wheel.

Nina shivered. She wished she wasn't going out, wished she hadn't promised Sally. It wasn't the being out, or the lightly surfing chat with a table full of strangers that troubled her, nothing beyond the normal laziness that went with the effort of getting ready and actually getting to the restaurant; it was more the gloominess of coming back to a house that sounded of nothing and no-one.

'I do want to go. I want to see Dad and it's some-where else to be. And it's near really good shops,' Emily said. She hauled out the grey jumper and sniffed at it. 'There's another day in this I think,' she decided cheerfully, cramming it into the bag on top of a pair of emerald green boots.

'There, that's everything,' she said, picking up the bags and heading for the door. 'Is Lucy ready? Can we go now?'

'What's the big hurry?' Nina asked. It was on the tip of her careless tongue to add *It's only your dad.* Not so much of the 'only', she reminded herself.

'Oh I don't know, I'm just ready to go out. I've been in for ages, like some kind of invalid. Only I'm better now. Well nearly, I think.'

Nina followed her down the stairs. Lucy was waiting at the bottom, her little cat-face looking up at them anxiously. 'If anyone from Little Cherubs rings, you will call and tell me won't you, Mum? Promise?'

'Of course I will,' Nina told her. 'Whyever wouldn't I?'

'Whyever should they ring, you mean, after you beat up Sophie and screwed up your audition. I bet you're

176

off their books for good. I bet you're blacklisted, no-one employs troublemakers,' Emily taunted her sister. Lucy's eyes filled with tears. 'You are such a cow, Em.'

'Oh look don't start a fight now, not when you're off to spend the weekend with Joe. He doesn't need you two turning up in awful moods.'

Though why *not*, Nina thought as she picked up Lucy's bag and hauled it out of the front door and into the car boot. Why should he only get them on best behaviour terms? She made a quick wish that in his presence (and Catherine's, oh especially Catherine's) they should have at least one vicious (but quick) row and that they should absolutely not clean the bath after use. In addition, one of them should suddenly become vegetarian and the other might accidentally stumble heavily against the biggest shelf-load of the art deco elongated ladies. More cheerfully she went on, 'I'm sure having the odd tantrum has never stopped most models from working. People have very short memories in that business, so don't worry. Though I think you could write Angela a note, apologizing. That would help – you should have done it days ago really. Tantrums are one thing, but there's no excuse for bad manners.'

Lucy brightened and leapt into the back of the car. 'I'll do it at Dad's. On his computer.'

'No, by hand. More personal and more as if you mean it,' Nina said.

Emily swung all her bags into the back of the car, clutching them in front of her as if scared all her precious possessions might be taken away at any moment. Nina looked in the rearview mirror and noted that none of the bags' bulges seemed to be book-shaped.

'Homework, Em?' she suggested tentatively.

'No chance. I've been doing nothing else for days. Give me a break,' Emily growled.

'It's your life, your A-levels,' she conceded as she backed the Polo out of the drive.

'Exactly.'

'I'm not going to do any exams,' Lucy stated.

'Oh yes, and how come?' Nina asked.

'Hey, if *I* have to, *you* have to,' Emily growled.

'Well I'll be so rich and so famous I won't need them,' Lucy said seriously.

'Look, you're only *pretty*. It's no big deal. It doesn't get you that much in life. Only the more shallow and stupid of men,' Emily said with exasperation. 'And you probably won't be pretty for that long, so what then?'

'I'll marry a mega-rich movie star man. And then I still won't need exams.'

'Give me strength,' Emily sighed. 'Mum, where did you and Dad go wrong with her?'

Nina laughed. 'Don't know. Lucy my love, you seem somehow to have absorbed some very dodgy values from a whole other age. I know, this weekend, tell all this to Catherine and see what she has to say about it. If she's going to keep living with Joe, maybe it's time she put in some effort towards the other aspects of his life. He doesn't come just as one lone person.'

'You make us sound like heavy baggage,' Emily said quietly.

'No, no you're not baggage, never that, but you are responsibility.' Joe knew all that, Nina thought as the car crawled through the Friday evening Fulham traffic. He'd never, not once, shown the slightest sign of *not* wanting to take his full share in caring for the girls. Not once in the past year had he said 'No, not this week-end, I've got something on.' If he'd only been half as good at husbanding as he was at fathering . . . A Fiesta cut in in front of her and she slammed her foot on the brake. 'Bloody stupid sod!' she shouted, over-reacting furiously.

'Chill, Mum,' Emily said, emerging from her doze against the back window.

'It's OK, I was thinking of someone else,' Nina murmured.

'So, what would you like to do this weekend? Any ideas?'

Catherine looked at the two girls as if they were strange exotic animals with dangerous habits. She stood awkwardly in front of them, close to the front door as if she might need to bolt off into the night, and her arms were wrapped round her body as if she didn't quite know what to do with her hands. Joe wasn't home yet; he'd phoned from a difficult recording session with apologies.

Catherine's shaky discomfort made Emily feel enormously happy. It was something to do with pecking order, as in who, exactly, counted as the guests in Joe's apartment. She was also pretty sure she hadn't been forgiven for the early morning phone call. She and Lucy, cruelly recognizing someone in victim mode, looked at each other, which was a mistake because it sent their faces into contortions of suppressed giggles.

'We don't need to do anything special. We'll just hang out,' Emily told her, thumping across the polished ash floor and collapsing, with her bag-lady possessions around her, into the cream sofa. The cushions sighed gently as she settled deep into the seat and she smiled contentedly. This flat was very comfortable, very sleek, her friends would love it.

'If you and Dad ever want to go away, you know, like

for a few days' romantic trip or something,' she said, a sweetly radiant smile, hinting at willingness to please, beaming from her face, 'I could stay here with just my friend Chloe and look after the place for you. Keep the burglars out. It's so peaceful here, we could get on with some exam revision.'

'Well that would be very . . . er, kind.'

'Really, it's no problem!' Emily shrugged. Lucy giggled treacherously and Emily glared.

'I think I'll go and unpack my stuff,' Lucy decided and Emily got up and followed her upstairs to the room they shared at the back of the studio balcony. Below them, Catherine was carefully rearranging the squashed cushions and brushing teenage dust off the fabric. Emily trailed her fingers along the back of the ancient grey leather sofa that used to live in Joe's studio back at home. Her nails traced the grooves where the cat's claws had wreaked damage.

'I used to lie on this when Dad was working. I used to tell him which tunes I liked most and when I thought it was all rubbish,' she said.

'I did too,' Lucy added. 'It was me who told him which was the best sound for that advert where the car drives across the desert and straight up the mountain. *He* chose something that sounded *squishy*.'

'Hopeless,' Emily agreed, opening the door to their shared room. 'I wonder how he manages without us?'

'He isn't without us though is he, we're *here*.'

'Yes but *he* isn't,' Emily said, throwing her collection of bags onto the blue and white patchwork-covered bed. 'Which reminds me . . .' She dashed out through the door and leaned on the balcony rail, looking down to where Catherine was now perched on the edge of the sofa, flicking quickly through a magazine and looking about as relaxed as if she was waiting her turn for some serious root canal work.

'Catherine? I was just wondering . . .' Emily smiled down at her, her long hair flopping forward and obscuring her expression. She shoved it back impatiently – it was important that Catherine saw her being 'nice'.

'Yes?' Catherine said tentatively, looking tense.

Emily continued smiling, enjoying Catherine's upturned face, a picture of nervous anticipation.

'How is your brother, what was his name? Steven, or Simon, was it?'

Catherine smiled, clearly hugely relieved. Emily wondered what possible terror any request she was likely to make could have held. Perhaps she'd thought Emily was about to demand access to her condom collection, or had chosen this moment to confess that she and Lucy were determined to make her life such hell that she'd take off for ever and leave their dad alone.

'He's fine. He could come over if you like, he lives very near. I know he's more your age than I am.' She bit her lip, looking worried as if she'd inadvertently confessed to her hopelessness with Young People. As if we can't tell, Emily thought, leaning on the rail and enjoying her superior moment. 'I don't mind if he comes. Or doesn't,' she shrugged, knowing that by the time she'd gone back through the bedroom door Catherine's perfectly French manicured finger would be halfway through pecking out his number.

'I've got nothing to talk about. I mean what have I done lately? I've seen a couple of films and chosen a bit of paint colour,' Nina complained as she and Sally sat in the taxi on their way to the restaurant for their rendezvous with the Knights Out singles dinner parties agency.

Sally had chosen this particular one in great excitement from an ad in the evening paper, aspiring to at least a baronet but dreaming of a duke. When Nina had pointed out that it was obviously the shining armour kind of knights that were on offer rather than the very few available other sort it had been Sally's look of enormous disappointment that had made Nina agree to go along and try her own luck. She was wearing her blue silk suit and the skirt was feeling just slightly uncomfortably tight. It would ride up across her thighs as she sat at the table. She could only hope for a generous amount of tablecloth to avoid giving whichever man she was put next to the wrong idea. Or the right one – perhaps she should be more adventurous. 'You never know . . .' Sally's favourite going-out-in-hope phrase came to mind.

'I mean, I've done *nothing.* It's all been taking care of the girls, the gallery, my mother, Henry while he painted and a measly lunch with my ex-husband. Hardly riveting stuff for a potential life partner to get to grips with.' The steamy aftermath of the 'measly lunch' with Joe came quickly to mind and was banished – she hadn't even told Sally about that one, so she was hardly likely to chat up a strange man with 'No, I don't do a lot, just sex and Sainsbury's.'

Sally was looking at her in such amazement that Nina almost believed she'd been voicing her thoughts. 'Good grief, what's the matter with you? Surely you don't intend to go out with a whole bunch of strangers that you'll never clap eyes on ever again and spend the evening telling them about your aged mother? For all they know you could have spent the last week bungee jumping in Nepal or fondling dolphins in the River

Tyne. Make something up! I always do – that's part of the fun. You can bet your uplift bra that they will. It's as much about fantasy as it is about the love-search bit, that's why it's called Knights Out.'

Nina giggled, 'Terrible name, it made me think about jousting. But then I suppose that's what relationships are. I know, I could pretend to be training to be the new Mother Teresa.'

'No you couldn't,' Sally countered smartly. 'Not if you're hoping to pull.'

'Oh. OK, then I could be a retired ice-dance champion, writing a book on the definitive triple salchow.'

Sally sighed. 'No idea, have you? Look, last time I did this sort of thing I was a jewellery designer – I know plenty about that because of the gallery. And the time before that I was an erotic novelist; I couldn't resist that one, it went so well with my leopard-print shoes.'

'You don't know anything about erotic novels,' Nina said. 'Or maybe you do?'

'Well of course I do, everyone who's ever had sex does. And besides they had a publisher on Richard and Judy so I'd picked up a bit of the vocab. Use your imagination, choose your profession! It's so easy!'

The cab turned into a narrow street off the Fulham Road and slowed down. 'We'd better get out round the corner, we're not supposed to know each other. No-one is,' Sally said, leaning forward to talk to the driver. Nina ran her tongue over her nervous, dry lips and prayed for the evening to pass swiftly. Sally looked at her as the cab stopped. 'If you're hoping for anything to come from this evening, pray not to be put next to a BBD.'

'What's a BBD?' Nina asked suspiciously.

'Some poor sod who's had a bloodbath divorce. One

they just can't stop telling you about. That way lies pure and utter boredom. OK, into the fray, may yours be a rich pussycat and may mine be a stallion.'

Recording studio staff seemed to be getting younger, Joe thought as he took a mug of tea from the tray that the tape operator had brought in. He looked like a fifth-former on a fortnight's work experience – skinny, large-footed and mottled with rampant acne. Joe didn't want the tea, he wanted to be home with his girls, all three of them, taking them out to eat at the Café Rouge round the corner and coming home to watch a video and sprawl on the sofa scattering popcorn. He looked at his watch and found the time had moved on only ten minutes in what he'd assumed to be the past hour. The studio was in a gloomy basement and like all such places had no windows and no feeling of fresh air and reality. The frankly sordid control room, with its musky smell of stale cannabis and cold coffee and long past their best ginger suede-and-steel chairs, could only truly appeal to young and impressionable rock musicians who'd assume this was Doing Success. To jaded Joe it felt just claustrophobic and he was pacing the floor with the urge to escape.

'Run it once more, Kev,' the girl from the agency requested. She looked at Joe and smiled, a slow and confidential just-between-us smile. He grinned back at her then sipped at his fourth mug of tepid tea. She didn't interest him, not even slightly. With detached speculation, just to see what was stopping him, he inspected her, the slim and shiny suit with its aren't-I-*gorgeous* short skirt, the sassy blond hair with its carefully asymmetrical parting and expensively cut untidiness. A year or two ago he'd be asking her if she fancied a drink after, just so he could watch those long legs curling themselves round each other on a bar stool. Now he didn't care. As the track ran and the singer tried once more to fit the lyrics to the melody, he tested himself, trying to work out whether he was feeling just too old, asking himself how he felt about that.

'Drink after this? I think we deserve one,' the girl was saying, her smile confidently expecting a 'yes'.

'Sorry, I'd love to but I've got to get back. I'm late for the family,' Joe heard himself saying. She pouted and turned away, blushing rather appealingly. The detached part of his head, where he kept the old juvenile Joe, jeered at him but there was no wavering, no contest.

As he left the studio, going down to the car park in the lift, he wondered about Nina alone that evening in their – no, *her* – house. He thought of her curled up in the soft lamplight on the sitting room sofa with the TV on and Genghis snoring softly on the rug. When she kicked her shoes off they always landed upside down. Or she might be upstairs wallowing in a scented bath, indulging in some serious body-pampering. He tried not to think of her giggling over a bottle of wine with Henry in the kitchen or brutally discussing All Men are Bastards with the flimsy new woman from across the road. Not once did it cross his mind that she might not be home at all.

Nina sat at the large round table and pinned her name tag to the lapel of her jacket. She felt as if she was at a primary school social where people she had been seeing at the gate for the past few years would come up and say 'Hi . . . er . . .' swift-look-at-label, '*Nina*' and they'd both pretend the label wasn't necessary, not at all.

For a Friday night the restaurant didn't seem to be particularly busy, and their table, away in an alcove slightly apart from the main room, reminded Nina of taking the girls for a birthday treat at a burger bar where large parties were safely roped off out of range of trouble. She shifted uncomfortably on the cane chair: she'd been right about the skirt, which was already riding up and would only stay put if she kept her knees virtuously still and together, defeating, she thought with a smile, the unspoken object of a Knights Out evening.

She looked over to where Sally was sitting on the opposite side of the table, already with a large drink to hand, her eyes swivelling round to check out the other, what were they, customers? punters? Sally's lower half, which no-one could see, was wearing a pair of sensibly comfortable stretchy trousers but her top half was a stall laid out: a low-cut blouse of something semi-transparent, blotched with scarlet roses which reminded Nina of her mother's bedroom wallpaper. Big tumbling frills of the same fabric fell across her bolster of a bosom and a necklace of silver leaves (from gallery stock, Nina noticed) nestled in the folds of her cleavage. Her thick, streaky blond hair was fluffed out like the fur of a cat that's spoiling for a fight. Nina hoped that among the six men on offer, who so far all looked discouragingly like corporate lawyers on their way home from the office, Sally would truffle out a true Knight for herself. To Nina, so far, they were simply a collection of dull grey suits and safe ties. There were four other women: two in safe black but sporting something bold in terms of jewellery, and one with jet-black long hair who wore a scarlet high-necked Chinese-style dress that clung to her slim body and what she and Joe used to call shag-me shoes, high, gold and open-toed with double ankle-straps. Nina sipped her spritzer and imagined Joe muttering comments in a restaurant along the lines of, 'Pity she can't just put them on the table and let them do the talking', as he'd be sure to do if he was with her. She wished she was at home, suddenly, with him and the girls and a Friday night video, Genghis and the cat scavenging on the carpet for spilled popcorn . . .

'Welcome to Knights Out,' Scarlet Dress suddenly announced. 'I'm Belinda, I'll leave it to you to make your own introductions as the evening progresses. For those of you who haven't joined us before, this is simply dinner with friends. The only difference is that you'll be friends by the end of the evening, rather than at the beginning.' Her audience tittered softly and some of the braver sets of eyes started to seek out someone round the table to be sharing the joke with. Sally grinned across at Nina and winked, raising her glass. Her eyes and head slid sideways to indicate the man sitting on her right and Nina forced back a giggle as Sally made a being-sick face across the table, hiding behind her menu.

'Hi, I'm Lawrence,' the Grey Suit on Nina's left spoke. 'Have you been to one of these things before?' It sounded like an echo, because, Nina quickly realized, this seemed to be everyone's opening line.

'I'm Nina. And no I haven't actually. And you?' He looked all right on close inspection, she thought, tall, athletic and with very clean hands. Add a Good Sense of Humour and he might be anyone's Lonely Hearts column dream man. Surely, by definition, the sort of man who shouldn't need to be doing this.

'Yes, once or twice. I prefer it to one-to-one dating and for very good reasons. Can I just ask, are you divorced or widowed or what?'

'Divorced, actually,' Nina lied, feeling that if she said 'separated' she might be outed as a Fake Single and marched from the premises. She wondered which profession to select when he inevitably asked. Lion-tamer came to mind.

He smiled, rather sadly. 'Ah, then you'll understand. You see with my wife, well I had a terrible time. The wrangling in the courts, you wouldn't believe it, absolute bloodbath . . .'

'I am *not* watching bloody *Watership Down*. Not on a Friday night and that's final.' Emily faced Lucy in Blockbusters and wondered how disgracefully sad she looked, arguing with her sister about the best way to spend a night *in*.

'OK, what about *Clueless*.'

'Seen it twice. Look Luce, it's *The Saint* or *Evita*. I don't feel in the mood for anything with heavy sex or violence.'

'Had too much of both this week?' Simon's voice behind her, too close to her ear, flippant and careless, made Emily jump with nerves and she swung round angrily.

'You *fuckwit*, what would *you* know?' she hissed rudely in his face. Simon's smile still beamed, but his eyes looked as if he'd been smacked. He backed away a few steps, alarmed.

'Hey, sorry. Whatever I said wrong, I didn't mean it.'

Emily tried to collect her wits, tried to smile back at him but her treacherous lip trembled. She felt a complete fool for over-reacting, but men really shouldn't creep about startling girls like that. Lucy crept up next to her and took her hand, patting at it with soft fingers, doing her best to soothe. Simon was looking perplexed. He had his hands shoved far down in the pockets of his jeans just like boys at school when they were embarrassed by a teacher's thoughtless sarcasm. He tried again. 'Er, look – Catherine rang and told me you were in here choosing something to watch. I just thought you two might be wanting a bit of company, that's all. I'll go home again if you like.' He grinned: 'Actually I think she's a bit scared of being on her own with the two of you.'

'Yeah, well I'm not surprised,' Emily confessed. 'I'm really sorry, I'm not usually such a bloody Rottweiler, I've just had a dreadful couple of weeks.'

'Oh I remember it. A-levels,' he shuddered. 'Your degree finals somehow aren't as bad.' Emily let him ramble on, happy enough that he'd so misinterpreted her idea of a bad time. He didn't need to know it had all started with him. If he only hadn't given up so easily outside the school and driven away after Nick turned up . . . She looked at him, trying to see him with newly attracted eyes. She felt nothing, only numb indifference. He was still the best-looking thing she'd seen that year, the man that if she had to give marks out of ten to would easily rate a score of twelve and a half. He had Catherine's slim pale features, eyes the colour of chocolate cake-mix and the kind of foppish blond hair that Nick would probably slag off as 'fucking public school'. It seemed a pity, she thought from this new chill sex free distance, that she felt no zing of attraction. She'd work extra hard that evening on feeling better.

'So can we have *Star Wars*?' Lucy was saying to Simon.

'Yeah, if you like. OK with you, Emily? Have you seen it?'

She shrugged. 'I don't mind. Lucy hasn't seen it.'

'And my big sister will hate it.' Simon grinned at her. Emily smiled with weary politeness. I really do hope I wake up again in the next couple of hours, she thought. Otherwise it really will be the most terrible wicked waste.

Chapter Thirteen

Main Course Man (Lawrence) was now, thankfully, at the far end of the table repeating to one of the Black Dress women the miserable details of his divorce. Nina knew he was doing this because the poor woman was sneaking a glance at her watch behind her glass and looking as if she was trying to make up her mind between faking sudden nausea or the need to make a phone call. In a quiet moment, Nina could just catch the words 'absolute bloodbath'. The poor man probably thought his sad story made him somehow appealing. Perhaps he'd read somewhere that the fastest way to bed a woman was to get her to feel sorry for you. Or maybe he just wanted someone to tell – and tell and tell. He'd be better off in counselling, she thought as she turned to size up the man she'd been allocated for the next course.

Pudding Man, labelled Mick, was studying the menu very carefully, from which she gathered that his priority seemed to be food before seduction. She looked at his face and could see his lips moving slightly as he read. Generously, she trusted that he was simply savouring the words as if they were edible. He had not yet spoken to her, merely managing a barely polite shy smile. On her left, a stocky Welshman was explaining to an eager big-eyed redhead the importance of the rugby throw-in and his large splayed thigh twitched up and down with nervous excitement, jiggling Nina's chair.

Nina didn't particularly want anything more to eat. While Lawrence had given her the uncut version of his divorce, she had stolidly munched her way through a vast plate of guinea fowl stuffed with *foie gras*, *boulangère* potatoes and a wigwam of French beans. There'd been nothing else to do, for she'd quickly realized she was not required to converse or even comment beyond the occasional 'How dreadful' and 'Poor you', just to show she was still awake.

'Well Nina, what are you going to have? Anything nice and gooey taken your fancy?' Mick suddenly turned to her and grinned.

Not you for a start, was her immediate reaction. Then she took a closer look. He wasn't just a Grey Suit. He was an Armani grey suit with dark brown hair cut neatly in a style that reminded Nina of old photos of Mods. His blue eyes were framed with sun-ray laughter lines and his teeth were so beautiful she could hardly believe they were British. His hands were craggy and worn from some sort of hard manual work, which had Nina vaguely weighing up how pleasurably abrasive they might be on her skin. At the far end of the table, Sally was winking shameless encouragement at her. She bit her lip to stop a giggle. 'I wouldn't mind a *crème brûlée*,' she admitted, wondering if this could be construed as a double entendre, and also whether she cared if it was.

'Mmm. Sweet and creamy. Delicious,' Mick purred suggestively, then as if recalling some kind of behaviour rules, said, 'I'm more of straightforward pie man myself. Apple, pear. Lemon tart at a push.' He looked confused, rather sweetly embarrassed as if he'd realized he was rambling and didn't know how to stop.

Nina wanted to give him a hug, tell him it was all right, he was doing fine.

'I'm a plumber,' he told her, looking wary and eyeing her carefully to get her reaction.

'Well that's useful,' she enthused. 'Such a change from all the helpless musicians and artists I usually meet. I mean you rarely find a pianist who can even so much as bleed a radiator, do you?'

'No thank God, or I'd be out of work. Each to his own talents, I say, and then we might be on the way back to full employment. What do you do?'

'I parent, I run a gallery with a friend and I worry a lot,' she told him.

'But we won't talk about our other halves, OK?' he said, grinning and indicating Lawrence, hunched forlornly over the table, snivelling into his wine glass, his eyes glinting with drunken tears. He was muttering to himself and a photo of his family was propped up against a bottle of Perrier. The Black Dress beside him was chatting happily to the woman on the other side of him, and the two of them shouted across him, having discovered a shared interest in salsa classes.

'My friend Sally told me that it's the best thing about these dinners, the women you meet rather than the potential partners,' Nina commented, then rapidly added, 'Well sometimes, not with everyone, I mean . . .'

'Hey, don't apologize, I agree with her,' Mick laughed. 'I've met some great women. Sorry if we men aren't up to standard. I'm told we very rarely are.'

'Someone's given you a hard time. Sorry, I know we're not supposed to talk about it,' Nina said.

'Makes me sound like something with big sorrowful eyes in Battersea Dogs' Home. Don't waste too much sympathy on men, trust me, that's playing right into their hands. Sympathy leads to sex,' Mick said with a smile.

'OK I'll keep that in mind. I shall remember to be callous and cruel so I don't give the wrong impression.'

The crash at the far end of the table was shattering and wonderfully loud. Lawrence had reached the point where alcohol and misery had obliterated his balance and had tumbled off his chair to the floor taking bottles, glasses and plates with him. The entire restaurant fell into inquisitive silence, necks craned; some people were standing for a better view. From a nearby table there came a ripple of applause.

'Oh bloody hell, I just knew he was going to be a sodding disaster,' Belinda, the team leader yelled. She scrambled out of her chair and tottered round on her delicate gold shoes to see what damage the stricken Lawrence had caused. The Black Dress he'd been attempting to bore with his divorce details was wiping tears of hysteria from her eyes and scooping Mississippi Mud Pie from her cleavage at the same time.

'I just hope he doesn't think I'm going to let him lick this lot off,' she spluttered through her laughter. Lawrence lay groaning, tangled in his chair and broken crockery.

'We could make a quick exit, what do you think?' Mick grabbed Nina's hand and was already steering her towards the door. 'Unless you want to hang around and wait for him to throw up all over Belinda's gold shoes as well?'

'No, you're right,' Nina said, looking round for Sally, 'I'm ready to go. What about paying?' As she said it, Mick was showering £20 notes in the direction of Belinda, who gave the departing pair a sharp and speculative look. 'She looks like she'd be thrilled if we all disappeared,' Mick commented. 'What a bloody fiasco.'

'Poor man,' Nina said as they walked out into the chill air. 'He's going to feel terrible about this later.'

Mick squeezed her hand hard. 'Now I told you, don't waste your sympathy.'

'Nina! Where the hell are you going?' Sally, panting for breath and with her bosom heaving impressively under its frills, caught up with them as Mick was flagging down a taxi. 'Are you *mad*?' she demanded. 'You can't just go off with the first bit of tasty rough that grabs you with his hairy paw, you don't know what could happen.'

'Yes I do, but nothing will. Not with my luck,' Nina told her. 'But you're right, really, I know. We're just going for a drink, somewhere public I promise, and then I'll go home, all by myself and safe, OK? I won't even give him my address.'

'OK,' Sally agreed grudgingly. 'Be careful.'

The taxi sped off down the Fulham Road and turned into Beaufort Street. Nina sneaked a look at her watch. It was already past eleven and she suddenly felt very tired and not at all in need of another drink. She felt safe enough, in spite of Sally's warnings. But if she had to pin down her lack of anxiety, there was nothing more to go on than that Mick smelt reassuringly of baby soap. Making an effort was called for, she decided, if she was ever to get back into the swing of this dating thing again.

Out on the King's Road, it was still as busy as in the middle of the day. Young twined couples laughed into each other's faces on their way home to bed. They made it look so easy, so normal. She yawned gently and thought about cups of tea and her warm soft duvet.

Being single was very wearing. As the taxi sped past Designers Guild she caught sight of a solitary girl leaning against a shop doorway, her arms huddling round her body and her face turned down towards the pavement, like someone who was trying to disappear. There was, in the paired-off street bustle, something curiously still and lonely about her. A mane of tangled hair hid her face but her body and long thin legs could have been Emily's. I wonder what the girls and Joe are doing, Nina thought, only half listening to Mick being amusing about plumbing disasters.

Well it was his fault. Simon's fault. 'Come round any time, whenever you want,' he'd said. Probably he didn't mean just an hour after he'd left, but she couldn't do anything about that, not when she was up against instinct.

Sitting next to him, their matching denim thighs touching, while they watched *Star Wars* she'd felt her body sizzling. This was what came of concentrating so hard on getting back to feeling like she used to. Her feelings had started to creep back, and then just kept coming like an unstoppable tide. She could hear his munching teeth as he chewed the popcorn and she felt maddened with the need to have those teeth on her skin. In the air were faint traces of his shampoo and she became faint with the effort of trying to keep the scent in her nostrils. If she talked to him about the man on the Common, told him all about it, made herself tearful, he'd have to comfort her. He'd have to wrap her body up in his, show her that not all men were like that, not all men, not him. He couldn't do any of that with Lucy squeaking and bouncing on the rug in front of them, with Catherine looking icy in a chair with her silky legs crossed, waiting for Joe to stop falling asleep on the opposite sofa and take notice of her.

Emily wished she'd taken her coat out of the flat with her, but then Lucy would have seen, would have asked loud questions and they'd have stopped her going out. The King's Road was crammed with people, as if there was a big party going on just round the corner and everyone was invited except her. She kept looking into the faces of passing men. They were all smiling, all with arms round women, or holding their hands, leading them along like pets. She shrank back into a shop doorway, pretending to be looking at the swags of fabric in the window. There were too many people, too many men. Statistically, there must be some out there, right next to her even, who had done to other women something terrifying and violent, just as that man on the Common had done. Perhaps they'd done something worse, or perhaps they'd only thought about it. One of them might suddenly break out from the crowd and crush her against the doorway, hands fumbling for her breasts.

Emily breathed hard and tried to control the need to scream. She looked again at the piece of paper in her hand. The address was only two streets away, it wasn't that difficult, there weren't any unlit alleys that she had to go down. 'Come and see me, come any time. Soon as you like,' he'd whispered as he left. Well he hadn't whispered, not if she thought about it, not if she was honest, and she was only almost sure that when he'd said the soon as you like bit he'd meant *now*. It was just that only an hour on, she'd started doubting her own interpretation. In truth, Lucy had heard: she'd even thought he meant both of them. Catherine had probably heard. Both of them would laugh if she let them think he'd only meant *her* when he'd said it. She turned the last corner.

Plenty of street lights, lights on all over the block where he lived. If she only knew just which one was his flat; it had just crossed her muddled mind that he might not have gone straight home. He might have gone on out somewhere, a club or a bar. He might have friends he was meeting and he might be laughing with them about this silly schoolgirl who he'd so easily made fall for him, just with a few soft words and a little touchpaper spark to the vulnerable back of her neck. They'd be laughing about her green pleated uniform skirt, her squealing with a boy that day outside the school.

If Lucy woke up now she'd be worrying. She'd sit with the light on waiting for Emily to come back. Emily wouldn't come back and Lucy would go to their little bathroom and rattle the door handle quietly, careful not to make Catherine come out to see what was happening. She'd know Emily was up to something and want to tell Dad but be too scared to in case they weren't allowed to come to the flat again.

Emily shivered outside the mansion block and looked up at the few lighted windows. It was nearly midnight. She checked the piece of paper, squinted at her reflection in the glass door and rang the bell marked 34.

'I don't expect you to come straight home and have sex with me, so please feel free to relax.' Mick handed Nina a large freezing glass of vodka and tonic and smiled at her.

'I'm relaxed enough. I give my own expectations priority over yours, so please don't worry about me,' Nina said primly.

Mick laughed. 'If I knew what the hell you were talking about, I'd probably say "OK yeah, fine",' he teased.

'Either way, I guess I'm being put in my place, so I apologize for mentioning the "s" word. Can we start again?'

Nina laughed, he looked so contrite. He also looked rather uncomfortable, squashed into a small frilled chintzy armchair with not enough room for his legs in front of the gilt and glass low table in the Athenaeum hotel bar. He reached across and picked up the dainty pink bowl of cashew nuts. 'God that restaurant, not enough food to fill a cat. Are you still hungry? Do you fancy a sandwich?' Mick looked around for the waiter, who handed him a menu of bar snacks. 'How about a round of smoked salmon? I could murder it.'

'Actually I ate loads. My first-course companion was the one who passed out, and believe it or not at that point he had plenty to say – I think I could, under hypnosis, even tell you the name of her lawyer and their children's birthdays.'

'Yeah, I know. It's terrible how some people never get over it. Still at least the poor guy was trying, making an effort to get out. For every one like him there's a hundred sitting lonely in a grotty bedsit eating beans out of the can and flicking through the wedding photos. Believe me, I've been there.'

'I always thought men who were halfway presentable were snapped up by lone women the minute they'd assembled a laundry bag full of dirty underwear.'

Mick pulled a face and chuckled. 'You've got to be joking. If a man even looks as if he doesn't know one end of an ironing board from another these days, most self-respecting women run a mile. They've usually just escaped from all that.' The waiter brought a vast silver platter piled with smoked salmon sandwiches. Mick picked up one in each hand, clearly as starving as he'd claimed to be.

'I've got a brother who's never so much as plugged in an iron,' Nina told him. She picked up a piece of watercress and chewed on it, savouring the hard metallic taste.

Mick guffawed, 'What? Well in that case he's either sending laundry out or he's still living with his doting mum. Which is it? Can't be the mum though, not really.'

'It is, actually. They seem to like it that way. She looks after him in exactly the same way she has since he was a small boy, and he lives there still sleeping in his childhood room, going to the pub now and then and still having plane-spotting for a hobby.' She felt disloyal suddenly, and wished she hadn't said any of this. It was private, it wasn't even any of her business, let alone his. Mick was a stranger though, never likely to be seen again, so as in a confessional it felt safe to say it all. What Paul had said about criminal psychological profiles still rankled in her mind. I'm just testing, she concluded, picking up a sandwich that she didn't really want, just probing at more and more of this stuff to see if Mick will come out with something like Paul's opinion.

'I bet she wouldn't have let *you* stay home and be pampered like that,' he commented. 'I expect you were brought up to go out and do all that for some husband.' He looked at her admiringly. 'Lucky old him, if you don't mind me saying, you don't get many wives like that to the pound these days. Where is he now? How did he let you get away?'

Nina's laugh sounded brittle even to her own ears. 'He's worshipping at the feet of some young blond gorgeous thing who thinks the only place for a kitchen is at the back of a restaurant. No seriously, I never did go in for the cossetting and skivvying that Mum does for Graham. I think I had some kind of allergic reaction to it. If I ever lived with the kind of man who actually asked "Have I got a clean shirt?" I'd probably strangle him.'

Mick sighed, 'The first woman I married wouldn't even let me into the kitchen to make a cup of tea. Hand and foot she waited on me till I felt like a helpless baby. Then one day she got radical and went off to live with another plumber. A female one this time. You can't believe how liberating it was for someone like me, filling my own fridge.' He hesitated for a moment then added, 'Lonely though. All those meals are always for one.'

'Whichever way you look at it, it seems none of us can get it quite right,' Nina sympathized.

'Too right,' Mick agreed. He raised his glass: 'Here's to muddling through!'

'I've got to be home by midnight. There's a friend of Mother's from the bridge club in babysitting,' Graham told Jennifer. He couldn't be late, he'd said he was going owl-watching again and Mother had given him a look. Jennifer glanced at her watch and pursed her lips, calculating. 'Doesn't give us much time, not if you don't want to turn into a pumpkin. Perhaps we should make a move – it's nearly closing time anyway.' She was already out of her seat, collecting her handbag from under the table.

The pub was full of raucous groups of men who seemed to be celebrating a late season football win. Graham, this year, couldn't even remember who was going to be in the Cup Final, hadn't felt involved in reality enough to take any notice, not since Mother's accident and Jennifer. For all he knew, Accrington Stanley could be back in the league and up for transfer to the premier division. He picked up his jacket from the back of the chair and put it on, carefully holding onto his shirt cuff so it didn't get rucked up inside his sleeve. 'Where are we off to then?' he asked Jennifer. 'Do you want me to run you straight home or do you fancy a stroll by the river?'

She was giving him a very odd look. When Mother looked at him like that he had to spend a good few minutes working out what he'd done wrong. Usually she told him before he'd decided.

Jennifer didn't say anything, but took his arm and walked him out into the cool night air.

'We'll go back to mine,' she told him. 'We've got nearly an hour. That should be enough.' She was smiling, her eyes looking as if there was a secret. Graham blushed, thinking of her breasts again bursting though her uniform overall. He hadn't had a lot to do with sex, but that didn't mean he spent less time than anyone else thinking about it. Lads at work would be winking and nudging now if they could see the look in Jennifer's eye. They'd be leering and yelling that he was in there, was on a promise. They made it feel like a dirty thing, but then that was the strange thing about sex: it was no fun if it wasn't.

Graham fumbled with the car keys and they clambered into the Fiesta. It smelt of Murraymints. His hands were clammy on the steering wheel and he looked at Jennifer's legs as she arranged herself on the seat beside him. Stretched inside their shiny black tights her knees were round and soft and gleaming pale through the nylon. Most men took this for granted, had wives and girlfriends they could feel like this with whenever they wanted. He wondered, for the first time, what it would be like to have a woman who was *not* his mother to come home to every day, to share a home and feel comfortable and snug with. Would there still be the thrill of the sinful about sex, of something that was not allowed? Or would it become just another thing you did, a hobby like plane-spotting or something dull and day to day like eating or even going to the bog?

Jennifer lived on the second floor of a block of flats on Nina's side of the Common but in a street where the shops were battened down under metal awnings after closing. No-one was around, just a skinny dark cat running across the road and sliding under a broken garage door and the sound of a large dog barking nearby.

'No lift I'm afraid. Let's just hope the stairs don't wear us out,' Jennifer said, unlocking the main door. Inside, the stairs smelt of disinfectant as if someone at least made an effort. 'It's a bit small but it's all my own, which is nice,' Jennifer told him. 'Though I wouldn't mind moving on if I got the chance. Round here you need three locks on the door.'

Graham wondered what he was supposed to say. He sympathized about the need for security. He and Mother had window locks; he assumed everyone had. At least Jennifer wasn't on the ground floor where prowlers could look in through her bedroom window while she dressed, or worse, watch her sleeping and she'd never know. He sat awkwardly on the small grey corduroy sofa, watching Jennifer fussing over coffee through the kitchen door. He wondered what she looked like asleep, wondered if he'd ever have the chance to be there in the morning when she woke instead of what he could tell he was going to be doing tonight, dressing in the dark while she dozed, creeping home, and sneaking back to his own room to take his clothes off all over again.

'You could come for tea. Meet Mother,' he found himself saying.

Jennifer appeared at the kitchen door, two mugs of coffee steaming in her hands. Her face was split by a beaming smile. It was just as if he'd given her a present.

'I'd like that,' she said. 'I could bring a cake, that is if your mother wouldn't feel affronted. Some people do, in their own homes.'

'I'm sure she wouldn't. Not if it was a chocolate and walnut one anyway.'

Jennifer hesitated with the coffee, looking at a door beside the bookshelves. 'We'll take this through there then, shall we?' she said, a small nod indicating that Graham should open the door. He stood up. He didn't know if it was the cake, or the invitation or what was going to happen on the other side of the door, but he felt that something important was settled.

'You're freezing! What are you doing out on the streets at this time?'

Did he need to ask, Emily thought angrily. Did he want her to spell it out?

'Have you had a row with Catherine and stormed out?' Simon grinned at her, leading her through a large curved doorway into his room. The walls were painted deep pink – Vulva Pink, she found herself thinking. A giggle burbled in her throat as she thought of it on one of her mother's hand-made top of the range bloody fancy paint charts, labelled exactly that. It could be darker than Foreskin and lighter than Nipple.

'What's so funny?' Simon asked. 'She hasn't thrown you out has she?'

'No. Anyway how could she? It's Dad's flat, not hers,' Emily said, resorting to stroppiness to cover embarrassment. What *was* she doing there? Or at least what was she doing there that might sound convincing. She'd assumed it would all be extremely easy, that he'd know the script. Also, according to Chapter 6 of *Man-Date*, she was doing this all wrong. She shouldn't be throwing herself at him, but waiting for *him* to throw himself at *her*. She should be tantalizing him with cool distance – carefully being the first one to end phone calls, refusing dates that didn't involve vast cash outlay. Unreal.

She perched neatly on a saggy purple sofa and scuffed her feet on the stained maroon carpet. A previous owner must have had a leaky dog, she thought, looking at the series of smudgy stains. Or maybe Simon just had lots of wild parties.

'You said I could come. Soon as I like, you said,' she told him, her voice full of accusation, looking up at him and trying to seem bold and sure of herself. It seemed a better option than looking demure and vulnerable (as per Chapter 1). He sat sprawled in a cane armchair inspecting her. He looked amused, as if she was a funny little flown-in creature that he didn't quite know what to do with.

'Perhaps I'd better go.' She stood up and shoved her hands into the pockets of her jeans. 'It wasn't a good idea.'

'Oh I don't know,' Simon said quietly. He offered her a cigarette. She took it and sat down again, looking at it carefully before putting it to her lips, not trusting herself to put the right end into her mouth. He leaned across with his lighter and put his hand to her hair as he came close with the flame. She felt the pressure of his hand on her ear. It was just a hand, she told herself, just a male hand no different from Nick's except Nick's would be inside her bra by now. His mouth was now beside his hand, close to her neck and breathing gently on her skin.

'Come to bed,' he said, then he sat back and smiled at her. 'After all, it's late.'

Chapter Fourteen

'Is Nina coming today? What time is she coming?'

Monica sat at the kitchen table turning the pages of her newspaper too quickly to be able to read anything properly. Graham put the shoe-cleaning box back in the cupboard under the sink and looked up at her. She'd asked two questions. The second one implied that she already knew the answer to the first one. But if so, why did she ask it? He wondered if she was losing her mind a bit. How much, was the big question, and how quickly. Perhaps she wasn't losing it at all, but was just too impatient to listen properly. That would be like her. He hoped, deeply hoped it was that. She'd never been patient, never seen the point of waiting for the green man to show at traffic lights before crossing the road.

'Look at that,' she'd say, watching some careful soul obediently hovering on the pavement edge, staring at empty streets, just because the pedestrian light hadn't changed from red. 'You'd think people could use their own common sense at a road junction.' He'd always liked her busy spirit. She was a woman who got things done. Got things done for him, of course, come to think of it. Got his food cooked, his laundry done, his life smoothed out. That couldn't be denied.

'I wanted her to take me to Sainsbury's,' Monica said. There was a small, new whine to her voice, as if she more than half expected Nina and the whole world to let her down. The note had been there ever since she came out of the hospital, the tone of a woman who assumes she'll be disappointed.

'I'm sure she will take you, if you ask her. It's her day off, the gallery's closed on Mondays. Perhaps she'll take you out for lunch as well. You'd like an outing, wouldn't you?' Graham didn't like the sound of what he'd just said. It felt as if he was talking to one of the patients in that soft soothing way that all hospital people did. Sometimes there were sharp ones who glared when he did this, and said something about not being in their dotage yet, but even they didn't seem to mind when their pain got worse.

Monica didn't reply. She was now absorbed in reading her horoscope as content and passive as if the conversation had never begun. Graham opened his mouth to speak and then thought better of it. If he spoke, this might be the dreadful moment when her mind really did blank off all they'd been saying and he was forced to face an awful truth.

He was ready to leave for work and didn't want to face anything but the pre-rush peace of the A & E department before Outpatients opened. It was still only 7.30. His mother didn't need to be up yet and at first, when she'd come out of hospital, he'd expected her to be exactly as she was before, full of 'Don't Fuss' and 'I'm Perfectly All Right', quite content to carry on being argued with about her insistence on getting up in time to cook his breakfast, then going back up to bed with the paper and a cup of coffee for an hour. Now she was fully dressed, bathed and ready for the long day downstairs.

She sat at the table like a good child, letting Graham make toast for them both. He refilled the coffee machine and set it up ready for her mid-morning drink.

'What time is she coming?' Monica asked. Graham couldn't remember if that was exactly what she'd asked before. It sounded like it; he should listen more carefully. Perhaps the not listening was something in the blood. At work he'd got into the habit of only half listening. Really it was all he needed, that and enough calming phrases to reassure the patients on their journeys round the hospital. The ones lying on trolleys were usually only half there anyway, absent in their pain or shock or anaesthesia. The ones in the wheel-chairs were talking to the space in front of them. He had time for his own thoughts, time to dream about what might turn into a future with Jennifer if he only had the nerve. There seemed to be a sequence of steps in a relationship that he hadn't quite got the hang of in the same way other people had. When he observed other couples, just sitting together in the hospital café, or strolling on the Common or shopping, it was like watching a ballroom full of people dancing something complicated and Latin American and making it look as if it was the easiest possible thing.

'Time for me to go, Ma,' he said, bending to kiss the white-whiskery face. For the first time he noticed how lined her skin was, neatly and evenly crazed like a drought-stricken African riverbed.

'Well I don't suppose she'll be long,' Monica said, looking at the clock. It said 7.45. Perhaps she thinks it's the evening, Graham thought, feeling horribly alarmed.

'No I don't suppose she'll be long,' he agreed.

'I'm going back to school today,' Emily announced, appearing in the kitchen with her bag of books and wearing clothes without holes in them. Nina glanced up at the clock and back to Emily. 'You must have got

209

up incredibly early,' she said. 'It's not even eight yet and you've washed your hair.'

'Oh thanks,' Emily replied, dropping her bags onto the sofa. 'I actually thought you'd be pleased, glad that I'm all out of victim mode and *back to normal* as they say.'

Risking the usual early morning rebuff, Nina got up and went to hug her. Emily was unusually relaxed about it, allowing her mother to touch her for a full five seconds before shrugging her off and reaching across to the cupboard over the sink for a mug. 'Sorry Em. Of course I'm pleased. I certainly don't want you to fail your A-levels just because some man—'

'Some *bastard*,' corrected Emily immediately.

'All right, some bastard . . .'

'Yeah, yeah. Don't go on about it. I don't need reminding. I've had enough of all that from the police. That sergeant woman, she keeps asking me if I want Victim Support and counselling and all that. I just think the longer I drag it out, the more he'll have possession of my head.' She took her coffee and sat at the table, opposite Nina. Her eyes looked less confident than she'd sounded.

'I am right, aren't I? Mum?'

'I expect so. Only you can know that. You are if that's what you think. Have you talked it over with Joe?'

Emily grinned. 'I didn't see that much of him over the weekend. Not by himself anyway. He was working Friday night, and then on Saturday he took Lucy to see Fulham get creamed by Sheffield Wednesday. And then there was Sunday. He cooked a mega lunch by the way. Catherine's always there and I'm not talking to *her* about *anything*.'

'Oh yes, Catherine,' Nina murmured, thinking of the thermometer again. Perhaps this weekend there'd been a peak on the temperature chart and that was why Joe had worked late on Friday night. She imagined him skulking in a bar till he could make a reasonable guess that Catherine would have lost interest or gone to sleep, and then sliding into the flat with his shoes in his hand like a teenager terrified of being grounded. Why, she wondered, had he not simply tried telling her he didn't want any more babies and laying in a supply of top-quality condoms? She would ask him next time they met.

'Do you know she doesn't like proper roast potatoes, not the way Dad does them in goose fat?' Emily was saying. 'When I say doesn't like, I mean she doesn't *approve*. She says they should only be done in olive oil with rosemary otherwise we'll all die of clogged arteries. Then Dad told her, he said, "We sometimes did them like that *at home*." You should have seen her face!' Emily got up, rinsed her cup and picked up her schoolbag. 'Got to go, meeting Chloe at the bus stop,' she said, heading for the door. 'Are you taking Lucy and Sophie today?'

'Yes I am, why?'

'Just wondered.' Emily was fiddling with her hair, looking shifty, Nina suddenly thought. 'What's Lucy likely to tell me when you're not around?'

'Nothing. Nothing at all. Did I even suggest it? And if she does, she's making it up, OK? It was just a strange dream she had. See you later.' And she was gone.

Nina shoved cereal bowls into the dishwasher, quickly wiped over the worktops and went out into the garden to see what was growing. The ceanothus, which was reaching out so far from the fence that it almost blocked the side gate, was about to flower. Pots of pink tulips had reached their last stage of appeal, with their petals thrown open to the sun and their elongated pale stems stretched like pleading. From an open window far upstairs she could hear Lucy singing along with the radio, putting on a voice that was supposed to sound sassy and American. Lucy was probably singing to the mirror, with her toothbrush as a pretend microphone, posing sexily like something out of *Baywatch*. It reminded her of Megan and Sophie's forthcoming trip to Barbados, which everyone had seemed to decide not to mention. It was probably soon – much later and Megan would be too pregnant to be allowed on a plane.

'Morning! Any coffee going?' Henry appeared through the side gate, shoving aside the ceanothus and wandering casually into the garden. 'Your delphiniums are coming along. They're going to need staking, though.' He marched across the terrace and started poking at the stems, weaving them together. As soon as he let go they collapsed again.

'Sorry Henry, no coffee right now. I've got to do the school run. I'm just about to go and collect Sophie from across the road.'

Henry looked disappointed for a moment and then immediately cheered up. 'I'll come over with you. See what the lovely Megan looks like first thing in the morning!'

'Oh she'll be really thrilled to see you, I'm sure. All women just love a surprise visit from a man before 8.30,' Nina told him with knowing sarcasm. 'Come on, I don't want to make these girls late.' She walked through the kitchen, picked up her bag and called up the stairs: 'Lucy! Time to go!'

'You'd better lock this gate out here,' Henry said, pointing back to the garden. 'I came to tell you, there's been another girl attacked on the Common. Late on Saturday night apparently. This time he had a knife and made her hand over her underwear. Didn't do anything else though. Strange.'

Lucy thundered down the stairs and met them at the front door. 'What's happened, why are you looking so serious?' she demanded.

'Another girl's had some trouble with a man on the Common. Like Emily did,' Nina explained calmly. It was pointless to keep it from her: it would be all round the school by the end of the morning. At the gate, parents would be muttering to each other and hiding the facts under half-sentences and meaningful looks and their puzzled children would make up their own lurid versions. Lucy's eyes glowed huge and round. 'Wow that's really horrible!' she said, already halfway out of the door longing to spread the news. 'I'll just go across and knock on Sophie's door!' she yelled back to them.

Nina shuddered. 'God, I hope they catch him soon. There's nothing worse than not feeling safe. Ridiculously, it hadn't occurred to me that the thing with Emily was anything more than a one-off. I take it they do think it's the same person?'

Henry shrugged. 'Not sure. I was just in Mr Patel's picking up a *Mirror* and heard someone talking.'

Lucy was bouncing with the excitement of being the bearer of news and Nina could hear her imparting the gossip from across the road. The words 'exposing' (which Lucy thought was a rather grand and grown-up technical word) and 'knife' could be heard quite clearly, given loud and dramatic emphasis. Megan, stunning in loose black trousers and a flowing pink linen shirt, was looking pale and tight-lipped. Her arms were folded firmly across the baby-bulge as if protecting it from hearing. Nina waited at the gate for the two girls to come out but Megan beckoned her in

213

and she and Henry strolled up the path.

Megan gave Nina a cool look. 'Girls, go and wait by the car, will you. I just want a word with Lucy's mummy.' Her smile, Nina thought, would freeze rivers.

'What's the matter? Is Sophie all right?'

Megan's head tipped prettily to one side and she beamed at Henry before turning to Nina. 'Look, I don't want to be difficult, but we do try to shield Sophie from the nastier side of life. Without being unrealistic about things, you understand. It's just that she'll come across all the horrors of the grown-up world quite soon enough, thank you.' Nina felt as if she'd been told off for talking in class. If she'd had hackles, they'd be rising. Megan was standing, still with her arms folded, a picture of self-righteousness.

'Well I'm sorry if Lucy was a bit over-eager to pass on the news, but don't you think Sophie needs to be just slightly aware that it's not all Disneyland out there?' Nina said. 'I mean she's nearly ten. It's not impossible that she could take it into her head to trot off on her own to make a camp in the bushes on the Common.'

'No she wouldn't do that. I've told her not to.'

'Told her there's witches and bogeymen out there, have you?' Henry cut in. 'That'll really do the trick.'

'Henry, please. That doesn't help,' Nina said. 'Look Megan I'm sorry but a real girl was attacked, there is a real problem.'

Megan sniffed. 'What on earth was a girl doing strutting about on the Common late on a Saturday night anyway? Quite honestly she's only got herself to blame, if you ask me. It was simply asking for trouble.'

Nina sighed and gave up.

'We'd better get going,' she said, looking at her watch. 'Lucy's got an early recorder lesson. I'll see you later, but I can't do this afternoon, I have to go and see my mother.'

'Oh all right, sorry.' Megan looked flustered. 'Look I'm really sorry, you're probably right. Don't take any notice of me.' She smiled and patted her swollen stomach. 'It's probably just hormones or something. I'll pick the girls up.'

'Hormones, buggery,' Henry sniffed as they reached the car. 'She's scared, that's the truth.'

'I don't know why, she never goes on the Common, not as far as I know. They don't even have a dog.'

Nina opened her car door and threw her handbag across to the passenger seat. As she climbed in, Henry's face came close enough for her to smell soap, sweet powdery baby soap. 'Dog or no dog, believe me, she's scared enough. By the way, did either of us actually mention to her that it was late Saturday? I don't recall. I guess she must already have heard.' He shrugged, 'Bye now, have a nice day.'

'Tell me about your weekend then.'

Emily sat in the cloakroom with Chloe, hidden behind coats, feet up on the shoe racks. They were skiving assembly and knew that if any staff came checking for stragglers they'd stop at the door, glance lazily over the floor for feet and if they saw none, stroll away again.

'My weekend?' Chloe looked at the ceiling and pretended to ponder. 'My weekend by Chloe Ellis,' she announced, then giggled, 'Well it was so boring, I might as well have had a straight run from Friday through to today with no gap. I slept and watched TV and worked. To prove I did nothing more exciting than French revision I could recite you the subjunctive of the verb *être*, or I could just give in and say, "OK Emily, go ahead and tell me about your weekend." I can see you're almost exploding to.'

'I got him,' Emily said simply, watching Chloe's face for a satisfying reaction.

'Got him? Who? Nick? I thought you could have him any old time you wanted. So did he.'

'Sod off. *Simon,* the one I told you about.' Why did even your best friend do that? she wondered: pretend they've forgotten everything you've had most on your mind, everything important and special that you've dumped on them, just so they can spoil the moment.

'Oh him. When you say "got", do you mean, like, bed-wise?' Chloe's eager eyes betrayed her interest. She was gleaming for details and Emily felt duly satisfied. She hesitated. 'How and when and what etcetera,' Chloe finally demanded.

Emily amazed herself with what she left out. She wouldn't admit to the fear-feelings of being out in the Saturday night crowd. Couldn't admit to terror that Simon would laugh at her and march her straight back to Joe's. Skilfully, she glamorized the night, told of a secret midnight arrangement, lied that he'd sent a taxi to wait round the corner while she made sure Lucy was sleeping and slid like a hunting cat out through the door. Sometimes truth crept in. 'We haven't done it,' she confessed. 'Not yet. It'll be all the more exciting because of the wait.'

Chloe looked confused. '*Why* haven't you? You went to all that trouble and then didn't do it? What *did* you do, have a nice cup of tea and a biscuit and then go home?'

Emily giggled, 'Well actually, more or less that.' Chloe looked doubtful. 'It's not because I'm younger, it's not that,' she insisted. It was the man on the Common, that was what it was all about. Lying on

Simon's bed, feeling his warm breath and his fingers stroking the soft tender skin of her stomach under her shirt, she'd curled herself up, away from him, protecting herself in case he suddenly turned animal, tore off his own clothes, confronted her with unstoppable violence that was nothing to do with sex.

She'd told him about it, after he'd coaxed and persuaded. She'd muttered her story into the pillow, not much caring whether he really heard or understood. Later, he was kissing tears from her face gently like a cat tending a sleepy kitten, but his hand was reaching for the phone, calling for a taxi.

'But next time,' she grinned at Chloe. She crossed her fingers and stroked the wood of the bench beneath her. Let there *be* a next time. He hadn't actually said.

'Yeah, keep them waiting, make them pant,' Chloe agreed.

'I think he's up to something. He's got a secret,' Monica told Nina in the chic French coffee shop overlooking the pond. The au pairs were out there again on the benches like match substitutes who just know they're not going to be asked to play, smoking desperately and glaring at their toddling charges.

'What, Graham? What sort of secret?'

Nina wondered, as she had before, about Graham and sex. It surely played some part in his life; he wasn't neutered like his old grey tomcat. Whatever private affairs he was up to, she couldn't blame him for not letting on to Monica. She remembered, with horrible pitying clarity, when Graham at seventeen had, after much brooding and courage-building, asked a girl called Helen to go to see *The Italian Job* with him. Helen had been meek and blond and had a Saturday job at the sweetshop on the corner. As soon as Monica knew what Graham planned, she'd made a point of going in for a box of Quality Street and a chat about Graham's favourite chocolate centres. 'Your Helen' she was referred to in the house, as in 'Why don't you invite Your Helen round for tea on Sunday' and 'I had a nice chat with Your Helen at the bus stop today'. Monica couldn't resist involving herself. She would have called it taking an interest, looking out for Graham, making sure he didn't get hurt. Quite soon, Helen was seen on the back of a motor bike, legs and arms wrapped round a new and more thrilling love in her life, one whose mother probably didn't even know her name. Monica, air of disappointment and told-you-so to the fore, referred to her for long after Graham's pride had recovered, as That Helen.

'Perhaps he's met someone,' Nina suggested. 'Is he out a lot?'

'Not so much out, not out like saying he's going somewhere special.' Monica's fork was dissecting a slice of chocolate gâteau into bite-sized pieces. 'He says he's going out to watch the owls on the Common. He takes his balaclava thing, you know, the one I knitted for him when he first went plane-spotting and used to get earache. So he's camouflaged, he says. Then he's out for hours.'

'Oh right, I see. Well he's always liked owls, hasn't he? And planes of course, anything that flies.' Nina laughed.

Monica's fork started mashing the cake, as if she couldn't really recall how it should be eaten. It reminded Nina of a child with a lost appetite, trying to hide the food by making it look smaller. She wanted to say something gentle like, 'If you don't want that cake, just leave it,' but the words stuck, they sounded too parental, as if the two of them were subtly swapping roles. She hoped she wasn't the only one who wasn't ready for that yet.

'Sometimes he takes an extra coat, too, as well as his old waxy one. A good one, as if he's really off to somewhere else. He smiles a lot,' Monica eventually said.

'Oh does he?' Nina was interested. 'Then perhaps he *has* met someone. That would be a good thing wouldn't it?' she encouraged her mother. 'Don't you think it would be nice for him to have someone to go out and have some fun with? After all, it's been a long time coming.'

Monica went silent and started shoving cake into her mouth. She didn't stop till it had all gone, coughing occasionally on the dry crumbs and finally sitting looking sulky with chocolate smeared on her lips.

'He's all right as he is. *We're* all right. No need for things to change,' she said at last. Nina decided not to pursue it.

'Look – let's go off somewhere,' she suggested. 'How's the hip, can you manage to stroll round Harrods? You always used to take me there when I was little and needed cheering up.'

Monica frowned. 'The hip is fine and I don't need cheering up,' she said. She was taking her time to think and consider. There was the beginning of a smile in her eyes, so Nina knew she was pleased at the idea. 'All right, if that's what you'd like, we'll go. Just let me go to the Ladies.'

She stood up and made her way to the back of the coffee shop, smiling regally at other customers. Nina had a quick look in her bag to see if she had enough cash for a taxi. Fine or otherwise, she didn't think anyone whose body had taken the battering that Monica's had should have to stand around in a bus queue. 'Whyever didn't you tell me?' Monica suddenly appeared in front of her sounding furious. 'Why didn't you tell me I'd got chocolate all over my face? What I must have looked like, walking past all those people. They must have thought I was senile!'

Nina laughed. The fury was profoundly reassuring.

Joe liked department stores. There was a cosy sameness about them all. The ground-floor cosmetics palaces smelt just like all the world's girls on hotel and office reception desks. The furniture departments all stocked the same outmoded sofas that no-one under sixty would ever buy. Menswear always had an apologetically small range of designer suits as if making a concession to the so-you-think-you're-trendy market. The stereotype only rang true outside central London, though. Here, as he got off the tube at Knightsbridge, the choice was Harrods or Harvey Nichols. He hesitated for a moment on the platform and then took the Brompton Road exit for Harrods.

Harrods had the pet department.

Nina could tell that Monica was feeling very pleased with herself. She'd bought an elegant Italian suit in teal blue which would be perfect for the bridge club annual dinner. Nina was carrying the bag for her, but Monica kept glancing at it as if expecting Nina to put it down at any moment while she looked at clothes and wander away carelessly without it.

'I wonder about a hat . . .' she said. 'Then if there's anything formal in the day some time, I've got a suitable outfit there all ready.'

'Like a wedding, you mean?' Nina suggested mischievously.

'What wedding?' Monica looked alarmed. 'You don't mean Graham? Has he said something? It would be just

like him, going and telling you first. And it would
be like you, too, not to be able to keep it secret.'

They were in the middle of the carpet department
where Nina was hoping to find a new rug to go with
her basement repainting. Monica sat down heavily on
a pile of tufted Berbers.

'He hasn't said *anything* to me, I promise,' Nina said.
'And anyway what's got into you? Graham used to be
the one who could do no wrong. Now he can't get anything right. What would be so awful about him getting
married? I'd have thought you'd like the idea.' She
didn't think that at all and they both knew it. Nina was
simply trying, as she so often had, to shift Monica's
view of Graham from small, vulnerable child to grown,
capable man. It was hopeless, she should have given
up years ago. Perhaps she should have quit back at the
time when she'd visited the house, she remembered it
vividly, with Lucy still baby enough to be in a sling,
and found Monica at the kitchen table, carefully filling
in Graham's application form for the job at the hospital.

Still slumped dejectedly on the pile of rugs, Monica
had the air of someone who'd settled for the day. A
smooth young male assistant, sensing that this was not
an imminent sale, strolled by and looked at them. 'If
Madam would like the Ladies Rest Room . . .' he
suggested.

'No Madam bloody wouldn't,' Monica got up suddenly and bellowed at him. The astonished young man
took a step backwards and tripped over a carpet edge,
tumbling gently onto a stack of Assyrian silk one-offs.

Nina and Monica dissolved into giggles. 'Quick, in
here before we're chucked out,' Nina said, grabbing
Monica by the arm and steering her through the doorway into the Pets department. In front of her, staring

into a glass tank containing a pair of tiny tortoises, stood Joe.

'Hello! What on earth brings you in here?' she asked him. She felt quite shaken by how alone he looked, gazing at the two shambling little creatures as if he almost envied their paired-off captivity. 'Oh it's you,' Monica greeted him with less enthusiasm.

'Yes it's me,' he agreed jovially. 'And actually I just popped in to see if they've got any hamsters.'

'Hamsters?' Nina repeated. Monica wandered off tactfully to watch a large blue parrot carefully picking at its claws. Nina was under no doubt that she'd remain just within earshot.

Joe laughed. 'Hey, you used to complain about me doing that, repeating words as if I'd never heard of them. Yes, hamsters. I was wondering about getting one for the flat.' He shifted his feet around a bit. Nina remembered him doing that when he was being evasive. She grinned and came closer to him, saying in a half-whisper, 'Is it because I so nastily suggested getting Catherine a kitten instead of letting her have a baby? Because if it is, trust me, a hamster doesn't even come close.'

Joe was laughing now. 'Nothing to do with her. It's for Lucy actually, so she's got a hamster in both places. She likes to have pets and I quite miss them too, believe it or not.' He patted his front. 'I can feel the lack of Ghenghis to drag me out for walkies.'

'You can walk him any time, feel free. Just come round,' Nina told him. He looked over her shoulder to Monica, who was now inspecting a brood of lop-eared rabbits. He grabbed Nina's arm and pulled her to the corner where fancy rats groomed their fleshy pink tails in a big glass tank. 'It's not just the pets I'm missing, you know. Will you come out one night next week for dinner? I'd really like to see you. What about Friday?'

'More discussions about Emily's gap year?' Nina teased.

Joe grinnned. 'No. I don't want to talk about the girls this time. I'd like to talk about us.'

Nina frowned. 'But Joe, there isn't an "us".' She wished she hadn't said that. It was unnecessary, just a petty dig. He was looking very unhappy. A year or two ago, when everything was hurting, she'd simply have thought to herself that it served him right. Those feelings had long gone. 'I'll come out with you some time soon,' she relented with a smile. 'But not on Friday.'

'Oh. Something special?'

'Possibly. Someone,' she told him, and then wished she hadn't said that too.

Chapter Fifteen

Mick was phoning at least twice a day. Sometimes he left messages on Nina's answerphone, quite cheerful ones but with an edge, such as 'Missed you yet again! Call me if there's a spare moment in your busy life!' He always sounded, Nina thought, as if he didn't really expect her to be able to find one. Although she resisted it, she felt responsible and resented it. She didn't want to be in charge of whether he had a happy time or not. Although she'd agreed to see him again, and she was happy enough to go out for a no-strings drink or to a film, these calls put her off ringing him back.

Sally was furious. 'You really shouldn't have given him your number. That was crazy. Even if you thought you might want to see him again you should just have taken his. Now you never know, he might turn up at the house. He might turn out to be a stalker or a mad axeman.'

Nina laughed, 'You can talk! You've been out with more strange men over the past year than most people rub up against in a lifetime of rush-hour tube travel! And anyway I only gave him my number, not the address. And we are ex-directory.'

Sally wasn't convinced. 'OK but just suppose he's got a dodgy mate in the telephone business? He could have got hold of your address already. He might be lurking under that great thick wistaria that you never got round to trimming next time you come home late at night. He could be one of those men who carries one of his dead mother's old stockings in his pocket in case he feels the need to do a bit of strangling. You really should take more care, especially with people like that loony on the Common hanging around. Perhaps he *is* that loony.' She grinned. 'Anyway, what did you get up to after that Knights Out disaster that made him so desperate to see you again?'

'Nothing! Absolutely nothing! We went to a bar, put the world to rights over a drink like you do and then I took a taxi home. And before you ask, I didn't tell the driver where to go until I'd got safely in and shut the door.'

Nina and Sally were in Art and Soul early in the morning before the gallery's opening time, sitting on the floor unpacking boxes of greetings cards. The cards were hand-painted watercolours of beaches, with tiny shells and little fragments of striped fabric stuck on them. Quite a lot of the bits of decoration had fallen off, leaving a gritty heap at the bottom of the box.

'What do you think these bits are meant to represent?' Sally asked, holding up a square inch of blue and white fabric.

'Deckchairs? Windbreaks?' Nina suggested. 'Titchy little hankies, the sort that men in cartoons tie on their heads in the sun?'

'I think I'll just stick some back on at random. No-one'll notice.'

'No-one but the artist. She's bound to come in and check what we've sold. They always do.'

'That's true. It's as if they can't quite let go, a bit like driving a hundred miles to drop in casually on your child when he's gone off to college, and then being surprised when he isn't overjoyed to see you.'

'I hope I don't feel tempted to do that when Emily goes. She'd probably pretend she didn't know me.'

'You won't, don't worry. It's mothers of boys who do that sort of thing. You know what we're like, we just can't believe our little soldiers can actually work a launderette or open a packet of biscuits without Mummy's help.' Sally was laughing, but then became more serious. 'But then you see, they seem to be so much more loving than girl-children. They don't insist they don't need us and battle for their freedom from the day they're born like girls do. So it's rewarding and you just carry on letting them need you for as long as they'll let you.'

'Just as well I only had girls then,' Nina told her. 'I don't honestly think I'd treat boys any different, and then they'd blame me for ever for getting it wrong.'

Sally looked thoughtful. 'It's more to do with the way they treat you,' she said. 'In the end you have very little choice in it, you just take your cue from them.'

'My mother, she thinks . . .' Nina began, then hesitated, trying to recall exactly what it was that Monica *had* thought. What had she been most worried about, Graham's moonlight wanderings on the Common or the possibility that he was meeting someone?

'Thinks what?' Sally prompted gently, putting the cards down and rearranging her large legs on the gallery carpet.

'I *think* she thinks Graham's seeing someone secretly. At least, he goes out at night looking shifty and says he's going bird-watching out on the Common,' Nina told her.

Sally chuckled, 'Well I won't say "What do you mean 'secretly' at his age" because I know what their set-up is. But why does she think so and what is she planning to do about it? Send a private detective out to have him followed? Give him a clip round the ear and keep him in for a couple of weeks till he comes to his senses?'

Nina stood up and stretched her stiff limbs. 'No idea,' she said, going through to the back room and filling the kettle. She felt slightly queasy, which she put down to having only had a half-ripe pear for breakfast, and in immediate need of a cup of milkless tea. 'I think she should simply mind her own business.' She stood in the doorway and looked back at Sally. 'And I'm going to tell her to do exactly that.'

Sally laughed, 'OK go ahead, Graham will be right behind you!'

Lucy seemed to be feeling strangely benevolent towards Sophie, considering the way Sophie had stolen the Barbados modelling job from her. On the evening before Sophie and Megan were to leave, Lucy wanted to go across the road to deliver a carefully wrapped goodbye and good luck present.

'You don't have to come, I can go by myself,' she insisted to Nina, fending off any threat of being accompanied. Nina was busy hanging up a new emerald and sky blue blind at the front window of the basement, standing precariously on a chair and wishing she'd remembered that it was quicker and easier to attach all the cords before the final hanging, not after. She felt vaguely conscious of being watched as across the road, up at his study window, she could just make out Paul working at his drawing board. There were quick pale flashes as his face turned this way and that, so he might well be having a proprietorial stare up and down the road as he worked, just as Emily had thought. He probably thinks I'm watching *him*, Nina decided, climbing down from the chair and looking for her shoes under the sofa.

'Sorry Lucy, but I'm coming with you – and I will be till they've caught that man,' Nina said, heading her daughter off at the back door.

'But we're miles from the Common, and if you stay here and watch from the window you can even see me every bit of the way!' Lucy protested.

'We're not miles from the Common, it's just yards. Metres, if you understand that better. And besides, whoever it is has to use the streets to get there so he could be anywhere. So I'm coming with you.' Lucy scowled and Nina became acutely suspicious. 'What exactly is this present you've got for Sophie? Can I have a look?' She reached for the package but Lucy snatched it out of her way. 'No! Don't, it's fragile!'

Lucy hid the package behind her back. Nina had caught sight of the label which read *Not to be opened till you're on the beach* in multicoloured ink. Lucy had clearly spent some time working on this. The wrapping paper was hand-made too: pale blue paper painted with palm trees and sandy islands. Nina would have felt touched at her daughter's generosity of spirit if Lucy wasn't looking so decidedly shifty. They stood together at the door glaring at each other, Lucy with the gift still firmly protected behind her back.

'OK.' Nina relented, for whatever it was it was surely private between Sophie and Lucy, some giggly secret that was none of her business. 'Let's just take it over to Sophie and give it to her then. I want to wish her and Megan a happy time too.'

Halfway across the road Lucy suddenly stopped. 'Mum?' she asked tentatively.

'What is it darling? Come on quick, we'll get run over.' Nina took her hand but it was like dragging at Ghenghis's lead when he'd got the scent of a rabbit in the opposite direction. Feeling foolish, wondering if Paul could still see them from upstairs in his study, Nina allowed Lucy to pull her back to the pavement. 'What is it, Lucy?' She put her arms round the girl and pulled her gently against her. 'Are you still feeling a bit upset that it isn't you who's going? Because if you are, it's not so terrible. It would take a saint not to be the teensiest bit jealous.' Especially, Nina thought privately, as Lucy had not been offered so much as an audition or a quick go-see since the day she'd behaved so appallingly.

'No honestly, Mum it's not that.' Lucy pulled back and her large blue cat-eyes gazed up wide and wondering. 'I was just thinking, I hope I can really trust Sophie not to open this present as soon as I'm out of the door. What do you think?'

Nina laughed, 'Good grief Lucy, only you can know that, she's your friend. If you don't want her to open it why are you giving it to her?'

Lucy pouted. 'I just *am*. Come on then Mum, let's just go.' Nina took note of the pout. Lucy, in a mood, looked alarmingly sexy. It crossed her mind that the word 'jailbait' was an ugly and badly thought-out term, as if any man perceiving sexual allure in a child was an innocent party, cajoled and tempted. If Lucy really wanted to continue modelling, she decided, it would have to wait till she was old enough to be doing the choosing about how seductive or not she could be.

Megan opened the door looking unusually flustered. 'Oh it's you,' she said rather rudely as if she was expecting someone else and was disappointed.

'I'm sure you're busy, we're just here so Lucy can give something to Sophie,' Nina explained. Paul clattered down the stairs towards them. 'Don't keep Nina out on the step!' he admonished Megan, 'Come in Nina

229

and have a *bon voyage* drink!' Megan glared at Paul but smiled at Nina. 'Yes, do,' she said. 'I'm sorry, I've got my mind on the packing. Sophie seems to want to take all her army kit and I've got to find a moment to sneak her camo sweater and boots out of her case while she's not looking.'

'At least you've persuaded her she won't be needing her woolly balaclava,' Nina commented, noticing it hanging with coats.

'Oh, yes, after a struggle. She'd only gone and wrapped Paul's Swiss army knife in it and hidden it in her bag. Can't you just imagine the fuss at the airport?'

Nina followed Paul and Megan through to their kitchen where an opened bottle of wine and two glasses were already out on the table. Paul fetched another glass from the dresser.

'Not for me, thanks,' Megan said, pulling a bottle of mineral water out of the fridge. 'He doesn't seem to take any notice of this!' she said to Nina with a grin, patting her round stomach. 'He just thinks life goes on exactly as usual and then it's born, magic! Even Sam sometimes asks me if I'd like a rest and pats the sofa cushions for me.'

'That's very sweet of him,' Nina agreed. 'Does he mind you going away with just Sophie?'

Paul handed her a glass of Chardonnay. 'Oh he won't mind,' he answered for Megan. 'Sam and I will just hang out and do boys' stuff.' Megan made a face. 'Like stay up too late, guzzling pizza in front of the box!' she said. 'Henry's already been round, discussing the big-screen football that's going to be down at the pub. They've promised to let Sam come with them to watch an afternoon match. All that smoky atmosphere and puddles of beer.' She shuddered. 'Still, you can keep

230

an eye on them for me, can't you? See they don't starve?'

Nina laughed, sure she was joking, but Megan looked anxious for some reassurance. She couldn't be serious, surely? Did she honestly imagine one grown-up male couldn't be trusted to manage alone with his own child in his own home? Paul sat smiling in-scrutably into his glass, looking rather like a teenager with plans teeming in his head for when the parents are away. Nina wondered what those plans were. Possibly they were like the ones Joe used to have, something to do with while the cat's away . . .

'I'm sure everything will be fine. After all, it's only ten days,' Nina told her. 'You just go and enjoy yourself and don't waste time worrying whether Paul's cut his finger opening a tin.'

'So what was the present? Can you tell me now?' Nina asked Lucy as they went back across the road to home. Lucy was smirking, which wasn't a good sign. 'Just suntan cream,' she said, her eyes still sus-piciously wide with false innocence. Nina allowed herself to feel relieved. Somewhere at the back of her mind she'd had a horrible feeling her thwarted daugh-ter might have bestowed on her unsuspecting friend a cute little box containing something disgusting – Genghis-shit maybe, or a couple of gift-wrapped slugs from the garden. Something, anyway, that would ensure her opinion of this trip didn't go unrecognized.

'What did you think I'd given her?' Lucy's voice rose and she stopped and faced her mother as they reached the gate. 'Something horrible, I suppose. Do you really think I'm like that? That's so unfair! I hate you!' Lucy dashed ahead into the garden and round to the side gate. It was locked. Emily must have gone out after they'd left and bolted it from the other side.

'Sorry Lucy,' Nina said, catching up with her and leading her back towards the front door. 'You can't blame me for wondering, after how upset you were.'

'Yes I can. You don't trust me. Families should trust each other. *Dad* would have trusted me,' Lucy raged. Inside the house she stormed into the sitting room and switched on the TV. On her way down to the kitchen Nina could see her through the open doorway, stiffly upright on the sofa, arms folded belligerently and a scowl crumpling her pretty features. One foot was swinging angrily to and fro like the tail of a cross cat, and her toe was making provocative contact with Genghis's ear as he lay dozing. She suddenly wished Joe was there to witness this display, Lucy's first serious pre-teen sulk. He was going to miss an awful lot of 'firsts', and for him, or possibly for her, she found that she minded quite a lot.

In *Man-Date* it said, in Chapter 8, that you should never follow up on a date by ringing the man. You must wait for him to call, the idea being that he was so grateful for your delightful company that he would be sure to ring up and thank you. Problem was, it seemed you needed a man who'd either read the same book or had natural inbuilt wondrous manners. The book didn't cater for any other type – they were the ones you were supposed to dump.

Emily lay on her bed surrounded by school books and shoved her fingers hard into her ears so she wouldn't hear whether the phone rang or didn't. If she was going to revise the path to Othello's down-fall she would need to get earplugs to cut out all distractions, or the sad lack of them.

Chloe kept asking if Simon had called and now Nick had got the idea and started having digs about her

Older Bloke. It could only have been Chloe who told him, the two of them seemed to be ganging up sometimes, giggling together in the lunch queue, sharing their geography notes and making gruesome plans for the field trip that involved lots of vodka and midnight visits to each other's rooms. When Nick talked to Chloe he laughed a lot and got very close to her and she sort of leaned on him at the same time. They were so close, Emily noticed, that Chloe was brushing *his* dandruff off *her* shoulders. It was her own fault – if you fight people off for long enough, in the end they get the idea.

Jennifer had changed out of her uniform. Graham almost walked past her as he pushed open the A & E main door, thinking she was a patient's relative, hanging about outside for fresh air or a cigarette.

'I thought your mum would be sick of the sight of nurses, after staying in here,' Jennifer told him. She looked nervous, her fingers flicking at the front edge of her sky blue linen jacket and checking the buttons on her pale pink blouse. Graham grinned at her. 'You look really nice. She'll like you,' he said simply. He was nervous too, deep down, but he didn't want her to know. This one mattered, this one mustn't be frightened off. He felt excited about something he'd discovered that morning as he went to work: the realization that if Monica made a big scene and forced him to choose – go on living with her in the home he'd had since early childhood or go off to be with Jennifer – it would have to be Jennifer. The thought made his stomach tighten. He'd caught up with real people, at last, decided something that most people deal with at twenty-something, if not sooner. He just hoped that, leaving it this late, there wouldn't be any unpleasant hostilities. Monica would need looking after, that much he knew, but something could be worked out.

'I brought the cake,' Jennifer said as they climbed into the Fiesta. 'Coffee and walnut, like you said.'

'*Chocolate* and walnut, you mean,' he corrected. 'That's the one she likes, remember when I told you?' His mouth twitched into a smile, recalling what had happened that night after they'd talked about the cake. Like a thrilled schoolboy he'd driven home with silly, juvenile phrases running though his head: *Doing it, shafting, shagging, screwing, fucking, having it off.* He'd evoked a satisfying feeling of mild dirtiness, naughty secrecy, shameful thrills. He'd kept pulling the feeling back whenever he had a quiet moment.

'Doesn't she like coffee flavour then?' Jennifer's anxious face was turned towards him. She was wearing grey eye shadow which made her eyes look huge and vulnerably young. 'I could always just leave it in the car I suppose.'

'Don't worry, I expect she'll like it. She'll be pleased you went to the trouble. That's the kind of thing she likes, doesn't really matter too much about what flavour.' It wasn't completely true, but reassuring Jennifer was very much the most important thing now. If she chewed her bottom lip much more, all her careful lipstick would come off and stick to her teeth. Mother would think that slovenly.

Monica had expected some young flighty blond thing, something like that Helen from years ago. Even though he'd mentioned that Jennifer was in her forties, she'd still pictured a skirt too short, hair too brassy and a small but aggressive bust. It was quite a shock when Graham introduced Jennifer, it shook her off her stride.

'Oh. Hello,' Monica squawked, startled that Graham was bringing to her sitting room someone large, not frumpy but undisguisedly middle-aged and who might, at a push, even be a grandmother herself. It made her realize sharply that Graham was no longer a boy bringing home a shy date.

'Nice to meet you, Mrs Dyson. I work at the hospital with Graham,' Jennifer said, offering her nurse-clean hand to be shaken. 'We've become friends,' she added, and the smile faltered as if she'd perhaps gone too far, or at least said something stupidly obvious. Monica was pleased by this, it showed suitable nervous defer-ence and she pulled herself up to her full majestic height, glad, in her suit of imperial purple, to feel at an advantage once more. Now she could smile and bestow kindness. Graham hovered uncertainly, his hands scuffing at the back of the sofa, clenching and unclenching as if he didn't know what to do with them.

'Do sit down, and do call me Monica,' his mother said with a regal smile, and Graham sighed, relaxed. It would be all right.

Monica became very pleased with Jennifer. Here was a woman who asked about health and who sym-pathized over hospital food. She was a doer, not a sitter. When Monica got up to go to the kitchen and make the tea, Jennifer was on her feet instantly, insist-ing that there was no need for her to stir, she would find her way around. Graham sat looking stolid, watch-ing them both as if he was on the edge of a dance floor observing the action. Jennifer gave him a look, a really amused what-makes-you-think-you-can-just-sit-there look.

'Oh leave him,' Monica laughed, reaching across and patting his knee. 'He's been at work since seven this morning.' Something guilty stirred in Graham's face. 'So's Jennifer,' he said, hauling himself out of the chair

235

and going with her to the kitchen.

'Well there's a turn-up. Nina should be here to see this,' Monica said to herself. She could hear them murmuring across the hall in the kitchen. There were comfortable sounds of the kettle, the rattle of crockery, sounds of home. She felt relaxed, almost sleepy. She'd not felt like that with any of the others. Not with that Helen, though she was so many years ago she didn't really count, or a skinny brittle-haired mousy thing called Susie who'd worn jeans so tight she'd gone pale as she sat down, and not with the sulky hairy one who'd taken up so much room on the sofa with her voluminous hand-crafted patchwork skirt and orange sandals. She'd had very dirty toes but hadn't taken up Monica's whispered offer of the use of the bath.

'Here we are,' Jennifer announced. She was carrying a large cake, held up importantly in front of her as if this was a birthday. Graham was behind with the tray.

'So you two work together. How interesting,' Monica commented as she poured tea.

'Well not exactly together,' Jennifer told her. 'I'm up on the wards of course, but we do run into each other from time to time, don't we?' Monica's quick brain supplied the word 'darling' at the end of Jennifer's sentence. She didn't look quite like the frippery sort who'd actually say it, but something like it lingered in the atmosphere. So she'd been right all the time, Graham probably hadn't seen an owl in months.

'Do you enjoy bird-watching too? And looking at aeroplanes too?' Monica enquired mischievously.

Jennifer didn't even look puzzled,which was a small disappointment.

'Well I can tell a Concorde from a Jumbo and a sparrow from a thrush, that sort of thing. Graham's promised to show me some more exotic species later in

236

the summer. In Norfolk, didn't you say, Graham? We thought we might go for a long weekend.' Jennifer blushed slightly, and Monica was delighted that she'd given so much away.

'What a good idea. Graham hasn't had a holiday for ages. And so many air bases out that way too, I gather. Perhaps while you're away I could go and stay with Nina for a few days . . .' her voice quavered slightly. Graham looked at her quickly. 'Well yes you could,' he said, 'She did ask you when you were in hospital if you wanted to go there. It won't be for long anyway.'

Monica sipped her tea rather sulkily. 'Or you could come with us,' Jennifer suggested brightly. Graham glared at her. 'What's wrong?' Jennifer asked him. 'Don't you think that would be fun?'

Monica took a large bite of her cake and a sharp intake of breath at the same time, which was a mistake. Choking and spluttering, she felt hot and out of control, fighting for air and starting to panic. Her vision blurred by unfocused fear, she didn't even see Jennifer leave her chair, just felt her big capable hands circling her, hauling her up and squeezing her ribcage hard. Cake particles flew over the rug where the grey cat sneaked up immediately to investigate them, and Monica realized the moment she started worrying about the mess that death wasn't an option this time.

'There. All better,' Jennifer said, settling Monica back in the chair and handing her a box of tissues. Monica leaned her head against the chair's embroidered wing and sighed. 'I do rather prefer chocolate cake to coffee, you know, dear,' she murmured weakly.

Nina didn't want to cook supper. Just the sight of the pale dead chicken made her feel sick. It looked, to her nauseated eyes, like a piece of sculpted lard. 'It's free range, it's probably had as good a life as a hen gets, but even the sight of it's making me feel really sick,' she told Henry as she looked in the fridge to see if there was any alternative that she might feel better able to handle. Henry took a leisurely swig from his bottle of Becks. His eyes roved round the room, inspecting his paintwork for blemishes. 'Missed a bit in that corner,' he said, waving his bottle towards the front window. 'I could pop in some time tomorrow and touch it up for you.'

Nina started cutting a cucumber and eating a couple of the rings. They felt cool and fresh, just bearable. 'No don't worry about it, just think of it as the Islamic tradition, that nothing can be perfect unless it's created by God.'

'That leaves only plants. Oh, and people if you could call them perfect what with humans having a hand in making them,' he said looking puzzled. 'Perhaps that's what's wrong with you, about the chicken and feeling sick,' he suggested idly. 'Perhaps you're pregnant.'

Nina put the knife down and turned to stare at him. She laughed. 'Oh heavens, Henry what a ridiculous idea. Now you've made me feel quite faint!' Teasing him, she did a bit of theatrical swaying, clutching the edge of the sink.

'Are you all right? Sorry, whatever I said I was only joking. OK I'll leave the paint.' Henry was anxious and beside her now, arm round her, clutching her tight. He was doing 'reassurance', Nina recognized, and something more. She struggled free, punching him lightly to make sure he knew it really was just fun.

'I'll make you a cup of tea shall I?' he offered. 'You look like you need one.'

'Henry I really was just playing. Though the queasiness is real enough. I expect it's something I ate. Tea

238

would be lovely though, thanks. Weak, no milk. I'm afraid that's something else that makes me feel a bit peculiar.'

Emily threw *Man-Date* across her bedroom and decided rules were for breaking. She would phone Simon. If she hadn't got an essay to finish, she would have done it from a payphone as close as she could get to his flat. Then, when he said something like 'I wish you were right here, right now,' she would be. Home or out though, she wanted to feel as good as she could about herself while she did it so she rolled off the bed and went across the landing to the bathroom. She would shower and put make-up on and wear something that made her feel sexy. He'd just have to sense it down the phone. If she wanted him to imagine her as irresistible, it would be useless for her to be still in her sweaty school shirt and the deadly bottle-green pleated skirt.

The aroma that hit her as soon as she opened the bathroom door reminded her of hot holidays. It was suntan lotion, lots of it, slapped on for some serious absorbing of the rays. It had to be Lucy who'd got it out; only the two of them ever used this bathroom. She's so bloody messy, Emily complained to herself.

There were towels all over the floor and the cupboard under the wash-basin was open with all kinds of things pulled out as if Lucy had been searching for something in a big hurry. Emily bent down and started putting away a split bag of disposable razors, two spare cans of deodorant, a travel pack of clothes-washing liquid and a four-pack bag of loo-rolls. She couldn't find the Ambre Solaire bottle, though there seemed to be quite a lot of lotion spilled all over the sink, and she assumed Lucy had taken it off somewhere with her. 'What's the little sod up to?' she murmured as she tidied. There was something gooey all over one of the pale blue towels too, something pale that didn't smell too good. Certainly isn't the suntan stuff, Emily thought as she sniffed at it. It smelt like old milk, something forgotten at the back of the fridge and accidentally poured onto cereal. 'Ugh!' she said, putting the towel to her nose and taking a tentative sniff. She looked around but only Lucy's school shoes and a sweatshirt were left on the floor. In the bin was a white carton with a torn blue lid. Double cream? With a best-before from some time last week? Emily puzzled. Whatever was Lucy up to?

Chapter Sixteen

'I don't want to have any more children. I don't want to have any children with you.'

Joe walked by himself over Battersea Bridge practising saying these two sentences out loud. However he said it, they both sounded equally cruel and final. He wasn't sure which one would sound worse to Catherine, and he wasn't even sure which one was more true. Not that it mattered which he chose: either would be devastating for her and would certainly mark the collapse of their relationship as soon as the words were out. There would simply be nowhere for them to go on to from there. He tried lightening the words with kindness, consideration – a list of mitigating circumstances to make her (and himself) feel better about it. It wouldn't be fair, he would explain to her, to deprive her of the chance to create a family with someone else. It wouldn't be fair to continue the relationship knowing that that was how he felt and knowing that she, with her thermometer and charts and babywear catalogues, felt exactly the opposite. He would tell her all that, make sure she knew it was *her* he was thinking of as much as, no, *more than*, himself. She was such a beautiful girl, talented, clever – everything a trophy wife, he caught himself thinking disloyally, could be. She'd make some lucky rich old bastard a terrific consort. But not him. Later in life than most, he'd finally grown out of girls. He'd have to get used to living alone.

Wallowing in the prospect of eternal solitude, he imagined himself over years ahead, becoming one of those old men with a collection of pastel cardigans, each one just lightly stained with trickled blobs of beige dinner-for-one. He couldn't think of anything more depressing. Perhaps one day, out of sheer loneliness, he'd team up with a calm widow and they'd have an Afghan hound just like Genghis which he'd walk in the Brompton Cemetery and remember the unappreciated glorious days when his daughters were little, life's possibilities seemed endless and Nina hadn't yet despaired of him.

I'm learning everything backwards, he thought; there should be evening classes in how to avoid regret. But then, who'd go to them? Whoever would admit they weren't going to have it all sussed by this time next week?

Paul was making Nina nervous. He'd called in with Sam 'just to be neighbourly' well before 6p.m. She'd sympathized that after several hours of small-child company he'd been in need of a grown-up to talk to and had given him a glass of wine, he'd drunk it and had a refill and was now pacing her kitchen restlessly. Any other visitor, even Henry, would have gone off home by now unless she'd specifically invited him for supper. Paul didn't seem to know the rules and she wanted to listen to the end of *Just a Minute* while she prepared supper for the girls. Nina kept looking at the clock, wondering at what point she could reasonably chuck him out so that she could go and get ready for meeting Mick later.

'The curse of the self-employed,' he was saying as he paced, 'is having too much choice about how to allocate one's time. We all do it, we're all experts at displacement activity.'

Nina, chopping garlic into the herbs and olive oil for lamb cutlets, privately thought that he could use some of his 'displaced' time to be stopping his small son from stamping on snails in her garden.

'Is Sam all right out there?' she asked pointedly. 'He seems to be massacring the entire wildlife population.'

Paul laughed gently. 'Well you see, that's typical boy stuff,' he told her, rather patronizingly.

Nina stabbed viciously at the garlic. 'Actually, it's just typical *cruel* stuff. If you won't, then I'm going to tell him to stop.' She put the knife down and went to the door. 'Sam, please don't kill the snails,' she asked him, trying a polite request before resorting to outrage.

'Why?' He stopped and looked at her, genuinely amazed.

'Because they're little living things,' she explained, wondering why his father wasn't there as back-up. 'They have a right to be here too, sharing the world. You're hurting them but they're not hurting anyone.'

'Unless you count munching all your bedding plants,' Paul drawled from the kitchen behind her. 'What's the difference? Sam's foot or your poisoned pellets?'

Sam was for the moment diverted by Lucy appearing at the entrance to the treehouse. 'Come up and see the hamster,' she invited kindly.

Nina returned to the supper preparation. Paul was holding the Sabatier knife she'd been using and running his thumb along the blade. 'Jolly sharp,' he said approvingly, handing it back. 'Most people keep such uselessly blunt ones.'

'The difference isn't so much for the snails,' Nina told him, refusing to be distracted and taking the knife

243

from his hand, 'it's for Sam. Surely you don't want him to move on to setting fire to cats' tails and dismantling butterflies?'

'Oh he'll know the difference. They all do, deep down,' he said casually.

'Well I think they need to be reminded now and then.' Nina put the wine bottle back in the fridge in the hope that he'd get the message and go home.

'Right I must go,' he suddenly announced and Nina felt perverse guilt which she did her best to quash. 'I've promised Sam we'll go to Pizza Express and actually eat there for once, no take-out this time. Thanks for the drink. Come over to me, any time.'

He went out through the back door, collected Sam from the treehouse ladder and made for the side gate.

'Sorry, that one's locked and bolted,' Nina told him. 'It's quicker to go the front door way than to unfasten it all. Henry's idea, because of the man on the Common.'

'OK, no problem. Though you shouldn't worry too much. Whoever it is is obviously an open air freak, not very likely to sneak into domestic premises.' Coming back into the kitchen he gave her a sly smile. 'By the way, how's that brother of yours? Still living with your mum?'

Nina looked at him carefully, calculating what he was getting at and if he really expected a reply. It seemed that he didn't, that it had simply been a flip, throwaway comment and he gathered up Sam for a piggy-back, the two of them laughing and jostling. Nina went to the sink and finished chopping the vegetables and then, without really being able or willing to work out why, she collected all the sharp knives off the wall-rack and stashed them away carefully at the back of the tea-towel drawer.

'Was that the man from across the road? I haven't

even met him yet, not to talk to.' Emily wandered into the kitchen and started picking at pieces of raw carrot that Nina had just scraped. 'What did he want? Did he happen to mention he might want a babysitter for Sam while he goes out and gets drunk?'

'No he didn't. I think he just wanted company,' Nina told her. She remembered what it had been like when Emily was small, those endless days alone taking care of one small child, Joe working every possible hour, taking on any job that came his way on the basis that half the projects would come to nothing so you had to accept every one, just to get by. Sometimes they all worked out and he'd spent twenty hours a day working, shut away in the hot little upstairs studio, trying out melodies, or setting finished sound to video on the U-Matic. The house was eerily quiet without him, even after so many months, and she wished the girls would play the piano more, just to remind her of how it used to be.

When the doorbell rang, just as Nina was putting potatoes into the oven, her first thought was that this was the worst possible time for anyone with half a brain to choose to visit.

'Mum! Gran's here!' Emily roared down the stairs to her.

'*Grandmama*, please!' Nina heard Monica firmly correcting Emily on the stairs.

'Mother! Hello! What brings you here?' Nina asked, wishing immediately that she hadn't said that in case she was the one who'd forgotten a supper invitation. Monica would be terribly hurt if she had. She did some brisk calculating. There were plenty of potatoes and salad if she wanted to stay and eat with the girls, and perhaps the chops would just be enough unless Lucy suddenly decided she was on a growth spurt.

'And how did you get here? Is Graham with you?'

Monica took off her jacket, put her large beige handbag (plenty of room for a toothbrush, nightie and next day's knickers, Nina calculated, beginning to feel uneasy) on the table and sat down heavily.

'I took a bus,' Monica announced grandly. 'But I didn't have my pass with me and the driver wouldn't let me pay. Isn't that nice? There are still some gentlemen, you see.'

'Yes, that was kind. Are you all right?' Nina went to the cupboard and pulled out the sherry bottle. She wondered if Monica actually remembered why she had come. The calendar on the kitchen wall said nothing about a visit. It was quite possible she'd taken to wandering – she'd heard that an accident like a fall could start off bouts of alarming age-symptoms. Henry had had a grandmother, he'd once told her, who'd started spending whole days travelling London's tube network because she couldn't quite recall where she was supposed to get off. It had been useless trying to persuade her that she had no need to get on a train in the first place.

'I was right,' Monica announced abruptly. 'I knew I would be.'

'What about?' Nina asked, putting a rather miserly half-glass of sherry in front of her mother, on the basis that if she was already confused, alcohol probably wouldn't improve things.

'Graham of course,' Monica said. 'Whoever did you think? He's seeing a woman. Not a girl, mind. A *woman*.' She sipped her drink quickly. 'Nothing of the girl about Jennifer. You should see her. Strapping. That's the right word.'

'Heavens! This is a surprise! You've met her, then? What's she like? It must be pretty serious.' It must be *very* serious, Nina thought, if Graham had summoned the nerve to bring her home to meet Monica. He must have had full and thorough confidence that Monica's opinion would make no difference to his relationship with . . . with Jennifer.

'She's wonderful,' Monica stated with a broad smile. 'That teal suit from Harrods will be just the thing for the wedding. I've come out to give them time to themselves. So I thought I could have supper with you and you could run me home a bit later.' She chuckled slyly. 'Let them play house for a bit. See how they like it.'

Nina wasn't sure how to take that. Did Monica *want* them to enjoy domesticity, or to discover its potential dreariness before it was too late?

'She could be the answer to all my prayers,' Monica continued to enthuse. She leaned forward and pointed her glass towards Nina. 'And she's a *nurse*. Now isn't that just perfectly timely?'

Nina felt puzzled. 'I don't know. Is it?'

Monica got up and went to the sherry bottle, helping herself generously and slopping a good bit onto the worktop. She dabbed her finger in the spilt puddle and sucked at it.

'Well of course it is! It means when I lose my faculties I won't have to go into a dreadful old folks' home called Final Solution or something! And when I finally pop off it means Graham will have someone to take care of him! She was sent by the gods, believe me. They could have that big bedroom at the front, and Graham can keep his old room for his hobbies. Frankly, she's probably a little bit older than him, which is lucky so I don't think she'll be having babies. They could get a cat of their own though, if they wanted to. Oh I can just see it, so exciting!'

Nina felt depressingly pessimistic. A long list of 'But what ifs . . .' immediately came into her head. One of them was 'What if Jennifer starts wondering what's in this for her?' That wouldn't occur to Monica. What was in it for Jennifer was Graham, which his doting mother would consider nothing short of life's first prize. Monica had always been like that, always assumed that the thing she decided should happen, *would* happen, whoever else was involved. Once she'd made a decision, she'd always felt there was no need for anyone else to burden themselves with deciding otherwise. It had been exactly the same with childhood holidays. Nina remembered coming home from school and her mother waiting to greet her, thrilled and bursting with news: 'It's all arranged! We're going off to Scotland, I've rented a mountain cottage. All that hillwalking. Won't that be wonderful?' It didn't matter that her husband suffered acute vertigo, or that Graham had just been to Scotland on a school trip and all they'd talked about was beaches and seaside for the past three months. To thwart her was to be guilty of inflicting such severe disappointment that it was simply not worth the effort. Nina feared for the Graham-and-Jennifer pairing. It would need to be stronger than titanium. As far as Monica was concerned, the rest of her life and theirs was settled, to the absolute contentment of all concerned.

Nina turned the chops in their marinade, imagining the two of them, at that very moment, sitting in Monica's kitchen eating risotto and discussing the little house they could buy between them, how they might decorate it, where it might be.

'Are you here for supper, Gran? Sorry, *Grandmama*?' Lucy came clattering in from the garden.

'Yes darling, I am. And your mother and I are going

to have a nice chat afterwards about your Uncle Graham and his new friend.'

'Er . . . well actually, Mother, I'm going out tonight. Sorry. You're very welcome to stay and eat with the girls but I'm off at 7.30.' She turned and looked into the oven, keeping Monica's inevitable face of exaggerated disappointment firmly out of view.

'Oh, oh that's a shame. Somewhere nice? Some*one* nice?' Monica hesitated just the smallest fraction of a second for fast thought (no dimming of these faculties) and said 'A man?', giving the word at least three rising syllables with her eyebrows zooming upwards to match.

Nina grinned at her. 'A man, yes but just a friend, that's all. We're just going to an Italian for a bit of pasta. Nothing to get excited about.' She crossed her fingers to wipe out the severe economy of truth: Mick had managed to get a table at the River Café.

'If you say so dear,' Monica said. 'Though if he's at all passable, you know, don't be too, oh what's the word, *remote*, yes that word will do. They need a lot of encouragement. And you don't want to spend the rest of your days alone like me, do you. Now a drop more sherry I think . . .'

Graham was wary of his mother's plans for him. He knew she was up to something, excited and secretive, and he was terrified she would take over Jennifer in some way. It was confusing because, whatever he'd said to reassure Jennifer that his mother would like her, he'd anticipated, almost counted on, her disapproval. He knew he could deal with that: he and Jennifer would then have been even closer in the face of opposition. They'd have had to have secret meetings, they might have had to resort to fast coupling at work, in the laundry store. Now he wasn't sure, in the face of Monica's enthusiasm ('When's she coming again? Would she like to pop in for breakfast after the night shift?') quite what she had in mind. It was impossible, now, to go back to how things were: the sexy furtiveness of having a secret, the sneaking out to pretend to go owl-watching or whole-day plane-spotting. If he said now that he was off to Fairford to watch a dozen US B-1s on a NATO exercise she simply wouldn't believe him. It would be 'Oh you don't fool me, I know what you're up to' and lots of knowing looks. He hated it. Jennifer loved it. Jennifer was now seriously fond of his mother and thinking about taking up bridge. She'd phoned to ask Monica's advice about windowboxes while he was at work. He decided that was something to do with the choking incident, bonded together by the saving of life.

'This is a lovely kitchen. It's such a change, not feeling cramped while you cook. In the flat, you don't have to take a single step to be able to reach everything,' Jennifer commented as she pulled the lamb casserole out of the oven and gave it a stir. 'I've always fancied a dishwasher.' She opened a few drawers at random. 'Now where's the knives and forks,' she murmured. Graham took plates down from the dresser and put them on the table.

'Oh, don't you use that lovely dining room?' Jennifer asked in surprise. 'Shame to slum it in the kitchen, however wonderful, if you've got a room like that.'

'I can't remember when it was last used,' Graham admitted. 'We always eat in here.' He put the plates down, took cutlery from her hand and arranged it on the table. Playing house was one thing, playing bossy wives was something else. He liked the kitchen. It was comfortable, informal, homey. Surely not everything in his life had to change, not all at once anyway.

'To be honest, I was a bit surprised you agreed to come out.' Mick was playing with his watch strap and looking peculiarly nervous. They were at a window table, sipping coffee and watching the inky Thames flow by.

'Whyever wouldn't I? Did you imagine I have such an outrageously thrilling life that I'd actually be bored by the thought of dinner at the best Italian restaurant in the country?' Nina teased him.

'In the *world*, so I've heard it claimed,' he corrected her.

'Well wherever it's the best of, it was all completely delicious. I don't know when I last managed to eat so much.'

Mick looked up and down her body. 'Not as if you have a weight problem, is it? Some women are a pleasure to feed. You're definitely one of them.'

'Thank you. I'm glad I could do the bill justice. Feed a lot of women, do you?' she asked, amused.

'One or two,' he shrugged. 'It's a lonely old life sometimes. I like meeting new people, hearing how they pass the years between growing up and passing on. I like taking people home, showing them my . . .'

'Oh God, please not etchings!'

Mick laughed, 'Hell no, it's books, that's what I like. First editions. I've got some rare ones – Coleridge, Keats, that sort of thing. And, don't laugh . . .' he looked sheepish for a moment, attractively vulnerable, it occurred to Nina.

'Go on, tell me,' she encouraged him.

'Enid Blyton. I've been collecting first editions of Famous Five books for years. They're rare in good condition because when a child had one, they'd read it over and over again and weren't exactly over-careful about bending the spine. I used to be terrible, myself. Used to fill in all the "o's" with a red pen. So if you get a well-cared-for one, it's just terrific.'

Nina gazed at him, struck silent. 'What's the matter?' he asked. 'Is it just too naff for you?'

'No! No, not at all. It's just that, well from the way you look and everything I would have imagined you were about to confess to the ultimate collection of Mod artefacts or something. A pristine Vespa that you ride to rallies in Brighton or mint condition Small Faces albums. The sort of thing Joe . . . oh sorry, my ex-*that-we-don't-mention* would like.'

'Tell you what, you should come and have a look. Not too late, is it? You don't have to rush back?' Mick looked at his watch and summoned the bill, which he'd already insisted he was to pay. 'My place is only a couple of streets away, I'll get us a cab.' And he was up, wandering to the doorman with his request. At the back of Nina's head, Sally's voice was telling her not even to think about it. She wanted to go, though, wanted to be in someone's house who wasn't a safe neighbour or long-time friend. He was attractive too, all that soft brown hair and wit-filled eyes. Sally's voice came back again, changing its mind saying, *Go on, you're single now, take a chance.'*

Nina had had a vague idea that Mick would live in a block of apartments: something large, newly built and with a residents' gym and pool in the basement. It would be full of single people who didn't really know each other. Either that, or perhaps something run-down and rambling that was part builders' yard. It threw her when the cab drew up in a typical tree-lined Fulham street of terraced family-sized Edwardian houses, all with converted attic rooms, smart pale curtains and lavender-edged front gardens gouged out for extra parking space.

'I'd better just phone home, make sure my dotty old mother managed to get home all right,' Nina said as they went into the house. There was a child's bike in the hall, and a pair of Siamese cats hurtled down the stairs to greet Mick.

'OK, the phone's in the kitchen. Come through and I'll get us both a brandy.'

'Oh, not for me, actually,' Nina said, determined to keep her head reasonably straight. 'I've had enough with all that wine.'

Dialling, she quickly took in her surroundings. The kitchen was bachelor-clean but family-equipped. It wasn't the vast amount of cooking implements that hung from every spare piece of wall, but the knick-knacks of day to day living that gave it away. On the wall hung a school term calendar, a noticeboard full of holiday photos, dating back, Nina could see from the ages of the two blond and beaming children, several years. There was a pair of very small Nike trainers by the back door and a selection of frog-face Wellingtons on a rack. A muddy football sat under the large pine table and a school homework diary was abandoned on the top of it.

'Little bugger won't know what he's supposed to be doing. Typical.' Mick flicked through the book, smiling at its contents. 'Maths, page 48 numbers 1 to 6, leaving out no 5. I bet he doesn't give it a thought!' He laughed, 'Are yours like that? Minds like sieves?'

'Sometimes. Lucy's quite good, pretty organized I'd say.' She was still taking in what was becoming obvious: that Mick must have custody of his children. Presumably it was his ex-wife's turn to have them.

'I poured you one anyway, leave it if you don't want it.' Mick handed Nina a glass of brandy as she put down the phone. She hoped Emily really had written down the number she'd given her, not just pretended there was a pen conveniently handy. Mick's hand had brushed against hers as he handed her the drink. 'Come on through, let's get more comfortable,' he suggested, leading the way to a sitting room the colours of toffee and banana. Behind glass doors were the collection of books. 'Sit there on the sofa beside the lamp and I'll show you *Five Go to Smuggler's Top*,' he said with a grin. And then he was sitting beside her, very close, close enough for her to smell how clean he was. His arm was round her shoulder, pulling her close so she could see the book. As she was wondering if she would be able to get away with no more than an experimental kiss, just to check out what it was like with someone who wasn't Joe, Nina's eyes caught sight of the collection of photos on the desk by the window.

'Oh. You've kept all your wedding photos out,' she said, more or less involuntarily.

'What? Oh yes, they're always there I think.'

'Didn't your wife want them? Or did you have loads more as well? Sorry, perhaps I shouldn't ask, that must come into the forbidden talking-about-the-ex category.'

Mick laughed, 'No, actually "ex" doesn't quite apply here. Carol's in Hampshire at the cottage with the children. She often takes them for weekends, it's so good for them to be out of London. All that riding and running in the woods.' Nina looked puzzled. 'Don't worry,' he murmured, stroking her shoulder hard with his thumb, 'we're quite safe. She won't be back till Sunday night.'

Nina's brain was unravelling what he was saying.

'You're not actually divorced, then? Or even separated?'

'God no! Not likely to be either. Why bother? We have what you might call an arrangement. She asks no questions and I tell no lies. Very modern.'

'Not really,' Nina told him. 'Didn't that sort of thing go out with the Sixties?' She stood up and put her drink down on the glass-topped table in front of her. 'So what were you doing at a Knights Out singles dinner?' she demanded. 'Isn't it against the rules?'

Mick was lying back comfortably, cockily Nina rather thought, arms behind his head and legs stretched out. 'What rules? It's a great place to meet people. Believe it or not I've got some of my best building contracts from women I've met at those events.' He chuckled. 'It's just another way of networking.' He stretched out an arm and pulled her hand. 'And you meet the nicest people. Come on, come and sit with me and let's get back to being cosy. You can't chill out on me now, not after I've bought you that wonderful dinner.'

'Hang on a sec,' Nina told him. She went back to the kitchen, retrieved her handbag and took out her purse. 'Here, sixty-five quid. Probably just about covers my share. Then you can't complain you haven't had your money's worth.'

She scattered notes over his body, noted how satisfactorily astonished he looked, and was out of the door and halfway down the street before she'd even gathered her thoughts. Bloody men, she thought in the taxi, and then laughed to herself. Joe would love it, she could hardly wait to tell him.

Monica had come home in a minicab, ringing the doorbell instead of using her key. Her tactfulness embarrassed Graham and he'd started fidgeting to take Jennifer home soon after. The two women were having a complicated discussion about the best plants for hanging baskets and whether or not a bright multi-coloured display was superior to something more subtle. Eventually, just as Graham was putting on his jacket and wondering if he'd have to sit in the car revving the engine before she'd get the hint, Jennifer decided she was ready.

'That was a lovely evening. We don't have to end it yet, you know,' Jennifer said to him as the car pulled up outside her block. She was looking at him with the same nervous seductiveness that had been there that night when he'd first come to her flat. He was tempted, but there was Mother at home, totting up the time he was spending out, working out what he'd have time to get up to. He felt uncomfortable, but he also wanted Jennifer. He wanted to claim her back from Monica, have her tending to just him, him and the needs that were nothing to do with his mother. 'I'll tell her I was out watching the owls,' he said, grinning.

Later, back home and parking in the driveway, he looked up at Monica's window and saw the light still on. He didn't want to go in yet and be someone's son again. He was feeling powerful, heady with the satis-faction of good sex, a long way from the need to sleep. He checked in his pocket for his ancient balaclava and headed for the Common. In the distance, far ahead where the stringy thickets and older beeches were, he could hear a barn owl – a blood-chilling noise, he always thought, like a small child being murdered. He sensed the direction it was travelling, then heard it screech high above as it settled on a branch. Things that fly were calming, made you feel that God put more effort into the winged creatures than he had into man.

He'd given them a privilege and grace that earthbound animals didn't have. His own privilege was to have the gift of enough stealth and silence to be able to get close and watch them.

They would never know he was there.

Chapter Seventeen

There were people on the Common, out from the road-side edge where the blackness was dense and inky. Graham could sense them before he could hear them properly. The bushes were snuffling and stirring with more than just breeze and there would be no low-slung foxes crossing his path tonight. Other times, he'd chanced upon couples with nowhere more comfortable to go, risking spearing their bodies with blades of twig growing through the bracken and taking home great weals of nettle-rash. Once he'd seen two men in leather and vests against a tree and dashed away, embarrassed, before they could think he was looking on purpose.

The hand on his arm startled more than frightened him.

Graham was in a bit of a dream, listening for the birds and thinking about future things, wondering if it was possible that Jennifer and he really could be more than just two people who lived not very far apart and liked each other's company. Some of Mother's bridge set had man-friends like that: men to go for theatre outings with and to show off with at the bowls club annual dinner. He wondered what he and Jennifer were *called*: they were too old to be boy and girlfriend. Perhaps they should be classed as lovers – they surely qualified, though he couldn't imagine his mother actually using the word to the bridge club. He tried it, out loud, 'My son's lover, Jennifer.' The word gave him a tingle, so sensuous and unfamiliar. The tingle was peaking just as the hand fell heavily on his arm.

'OK. Come with me please, sir.' The voice wasn't expecting there to be any disagreement about this, in spite of the veneer of politeness.

Suddenly there were a lot of them, looming shapes and thick footsteps and torches dazzling into Graham's face. There were crackling walkie-talkie sounds like on TV, and phrases from *The Bill* like 'IT One male' whatever that was supposed to mean. Graham broke into a nervous laugh, supremely relieved that he was not about to be beaten up but was in a protective circle of police. Something must have happened. He must have been about to walk into a crime.

'Sorry if I'm in the way, I'll just go home now if you like, back the way I came,' he said, eager to be helpful.

A stern face was looking into his. This man was in jeans and a heavy jacket like the council bin-men but there was no mistaking his profession. He was brick-shaped, chunky. His hair was wild and wiry and his face had a bitter sneer. 'I think not, at this stage, don't you *sir*?' He was too close to Graham's face. Graham could smell chewing gum on his breath, the same sugar-free type that he liked. Ridiculously, he found himself staring down at the man's stomach, trying to gauge if it protruded enough to be the reason for sugar avoidance, or if like him he was being careful for his teeth. Graham shivered. He was starting to feel nervous. Perhaps they weren't really police at all, just people dressed up and dangerous. They might have robbed one of the vast houses on the Common edge and be distributing the spoils. He took off the balaclava and tried to shove it in his pocket.

'I'll take that. Come on, let's get going,' the detective

said, pulling it sharply out of his hand.

'If I don't go home Mother will be worried,' Graham found himself saying as he was marched back towards the road by some of the uniformed retinue. Others, when he looked back, could be seen with torches weaving, like children with sparklers on Bonfire Night. 'Live with your mum, do you? Yeah well that figures.' The one with the sneer gave a short, knowing laugh.

'What do you mean?' Graham was becoming even more mystified, if that was possible. It was as if they knew stuff about him that he hadn't been told about. He remembered when the boys at junior school had sniggered about how babies were made and he hadn't known what on earth they were talking about and then they'd laughed at his ignorance. *'Ask Mummy!'* they'd jeered. There wasn't going to be any laughing here though, he felt sure.

'Shut it, tosser.' The man pushed his shoulder hard, sending him stumbling on the bracken. One of the dark shapes laughed. He was really frightened now. Something awful was happening and he had no idea what or why. He knew there might be evil people out there, he'd read the papers, but he wasn't one of them. If that was what they thought, they'd made a mistake and he'd say so if any of them were up for listening.

It was very late in the night when Graham was allowed to phone Nina. She was asleep, dreaming that she was about to give birth but couldn't find a safe place to do it. It wasn't a biblical thing, like Mary looking for a room. She was more like a cat fretting to find some-where that wasn't public, where no-one knew her. She was walking on a busy midnight road, then in a res-taurant full of men in shining green suits, then in a library that had no chairs, no carpet, no sympathy.

When the phone rang she reached across to grab it and felt her stomach with her other hand, strangely disappointed to find it as soft and flat as ever.

'Nina it's me. I've been arrested. Can you come?'

Graham as ever was not wasting words. Nina sat up abruptly, which made her head spin. 'What have you done? Have you been charged?'

There was a wobbly sigh from Graham's end. 'I haven't done anything. It's a mistake. But they won't let me out because they think I'm . . .' his voice went soft and he seemed to be having trouble with organizing how to put the words. Nina held her breath. 'They think I've done something horrible on the Common,' he said eventually, all of a rush. 'You know, like that man in the local paper.'

Nina choked back a dreadful laugh which she recognized as nervous relief. It was all a mistake. 'Oh, well they've obviously got that wrong. What about Mother? Does she know?'

'That's the thing, why I'm ringing. She'll be worried. Can you think of something to tell her?'

'The truth?'

'I don't think so,' he said quickly. 'She might think . . .'

'No she wouldn't,' Nina reassured him. Though she might, of course. One thing was sure: Monica had never been known to settle to sleep until Graham was safely home. Even when he worked on the night shift she liked to say that she never closed her eyes when he wasn't there, though whether that was actually true or not . . . Right now, she was probably lying in bed with the lamp still on, dozing over a book, the cat kneading its big paws on her legs.

Nina got dressed quickly and padded up the stairs to Emily's room. She would have to go to Monica and tell her what had happened and leave Emily in charge of the house and Lucy.

'Em? Can you wake up a bit?' Emily stirred and grunted. Teenage sleep wasn't like baby sleep with its milky soapy smell. Teenage sleep had a scent of cigarettes and slightly greasy hair, of make-up not well enough removed and the astringent tang of optimistic spot-treatment.

'Emily? Please wake up!' Nina shook her arm gently and Emily at last opened her eyes. 'What?' she demanded.

'I have to go out to the police station and to see Grandma. Graham's been arrested.'

'You're kidding?' Nina now had Emily's full attention. 'What's he done, broken into a secret air base?'

Nina thought for a moment then decided the truth was the simplest. 'The police think he's the man on the Common.'

'You're joking. They're so wrong. Do they think I wouldn't know my own uncle?' Emily was wide awake now, climbing out of bed and reaching for her underwear. 'I'm coming with you. It *wasn't him*. The real one smokes, something strong and horrible. And uses fancy aftershave, I smelt him, I told them. They wrote it down.'

Emily was hurling on clothes faster than Nina had ever seen her. She felt touched that the girl was so angry on behalf of her strange, vague uncle. Shy Graham had hardly said a dozen words to Emily since she'd hit stroppy teenagerhood and gone beyond his field of comprehension. When she was little, though, he'd patiently taught her how to identify the planes that flew out of Heathrow across the Common, taken her to Farnborough Air Show on a special enthusiasts' outing and helped her to build her own Airfix Harrier

Jump Jet, when she'd said she liked them best because they looked like big naughty flies.

'Ready. Let's go, then.' Emily was at the door looking back at Nina.

'But what about Lucy? We can't just leave Lucy, and I really don't think we should take her,' Nina said, thinking fast. 'I'll call Joe. He'll have to come. I hope he will. Or there's Henry. Yes, I'll call him.'

'Henry's gone to that all-night darts-and-piss-up thing in Southampton,' Emily reminded her. 'Get Dad. Graham's a grown-up, *and* he didn't do it, so he can wait another hour.'

Joe felt absurdly pleased to have been summoned. It felt like such an awful long time since he had been of any real use to anyone. It had been lonely, not being needed, as if he'd lost his place in the world's scheme. Catherine didn't need him, not really, not unless he counted her impregnation plans, with which he was absolutely not going to co-operate.

'Where are you going? What's happening?' she murmured sleepily as he stumbled around the hated floral bedroom, trying to find his shoes.

'Nina's. She's got to go out and she needs me there for Lucy,' he explained.

'I need you here,' Catherine whined. Her hand stretched out and got hold of his arm. Her silver-polished nails gleamed on his skin.

'No you don't,' he told her firmly. He would tell her a whole lot more in the morning, he decided. It was time.

Nina drove fast to Monica's house. It was after two and no-one was around. Cats darted into hedges as she approached and as she drove past the Common she could sense the activity of night creatures out there beyond the trees going about their hunting and mating. It was no place for people, in the dark. They, with their pathetic limited eyesight and clumsy crushing tread, could only be intruders.

'She might be asleep, not worrying at all,' Emily suddenly said as they turned the last corner into Monica's road.

'No, I don't think so. You know what she's like about Graham,' Nina said. 'If anything, she's probably already been on to the police by now.'

'Then she really will be worried,' Emily pointed out.

'No. She'll know it was a mistake. She shouldn't be on her own, but we'll have to go on to get Graham out, if they'll let him go. God they'll have to . . .'

'*Will* Gran know it's a mistake? They're always someone's son or husband or boyfriend. She might think they're right. I'm the only one who knows for sure that they've got it wrong.'

As they pulled up outside Monica's house, Nina could see immediately that she'd been right about her mother. Lights blazed at every window, a sure sign of emergency for Monica was habitually thrifty, and the front door stood open to the cold night air as if Graham was really just a lost kitten who she hoped would simply wander back in.

Nina and Emily walked cautiously up the path and into the hall. 'Mother? Are you there?' Nina called tentatively, suddenly nervous that these signs of activity might just be one enormous coincidence and that she might be interrupting a ruthless burglary. Or perhaps the police were already swarming everywhere, upturning beds, rifling through Graham's collection of plane magazines in search of damning pornography and a stash of girlish knickers.

'Nina is that you?' Monica in her pink satin dressing gown emerged from the kitchen. Her face was alight with anxiety and a certain triumphant excitement. 'Jennifer's here with me,' she announced importantly, 'so I'm all right.'

Nina looked past her into the kitchen and saw a stout brisk woman bustling with cups and saucers and the kettle. So this was Graham's new friend. She looked capable, motherly, *happy*. She seemed to know her way around the kitchen, opening and closing drawers with practised confidence. Her body, Nina thought, resembled a very large pair of scones stacked one on top of the other. Her cream Aran cardigan was having difficulty staying fastened across her large breasts.

'Hello Nina,' Jennifer said with a bright smile and no sign of real anxiety. 'Sorry to be meeting you in such dreadful circumstances. Would you like some tea?' Jennifer was clearly in charge and Monica looked as calm as was possible. The pair of women were already a unit, bonded by their concern for this all-important male who shared their lives. Nina felt oddly depressed. Jennifer wasn't going to represent an invigorating escape from smother-love for Graham, just an extension of it. It was simply life as he knew it, what presumably made him happy or at least contented.

'He didn't do it, you know,' Monica stated firmly. 'I wanted to go straight down there and tell them but Jennifer says no, not yet, because they'll have to let him out in the end. So we're just going to wait.' Monica sat down at the kitchen table and took a biscuit from the selection on a plate in front of her. Nina thought the whole scene looked as if Jennifer was setting up a snug midnight tea party. It hadn't occurred to either woman, clearly, that Graham might really be about to be charged with a horrendous sexual offence and that he might have trouble extricating himself.

'How did you know where he was?' Nina asked.

'Well his car came back, and then he didn't,' Monica explained. 'And then an hour later he still didn't come back so I started to worry. And then . . .' she looked rather guilty, 'I, er, I looked up Jennifer's number in his address book up in his room. I don't think he'll mind, just this once, do you?'

'No, I'm sure he won't,' Nina said, stifling a smile. Monica wouldn't have had to look up the number; she'd have done it ages ago, as soon as she'd started wondering where he was off to at night. She'd always claimed personal privacy was a devious affront to family life. 'The truth will out!' she used to declare when teenage Nina was less than accurate about where she was spending a night and Monica had weaselled out the truth somehow. The only bit of DIY that Graham had been known to do was to attach a bolt to the door of the downstairs loo when he was twelve years old.

'Haven't you got school tomorrow, dear? It's awfully late,' Jennifer addressed Emily anxiously.

Emily looked startled. 'So? Don't you want me to get Graham off this thing?' she challenged. Nina held her breath, waiting for Emily to start asking what business it was of hers and so on.

'Oh yes, of course dear, if you think you can help.'

'You don't know about what happened to me, do you?' Emily suddenly said. Monica looked puzzled.

'Well I'll tell you. Some fucking tosser flashed at me out on the Common by the bit where the horses go and it was, well . . . So I know it wasn't Graham.' Emily shuddered and folded her hands round the hot mug of tea for comfort.

'We didn't want to worry you,' Nina explained into the silence.

'Well I'm not surprised,' Jennifer contributed.

'She didn't mean you,' Emily said rudely, glaring.

'She knows that,' Nina said gently. 'Just stay calm.'

'Don't you worry about your mother, Nina,' Jennifer said, resting a claiming hand on Monica's arm. 'I'll stay here for the night and take care of her. And of course Graham will be back soon and I expect he'll be hungry.' She got up and went to look in the fridge. 'Yes, bacon and eggs. I expect he'd like that. And lots of tea, for the shock of being in that dreadful place . . .'

'She's even worse than Gran, fussing over Graham,' Emily commented as she and Nina climbed back into the car. Nina didn't reply. She was feeling horribly sick again. It had come over her at the mention of bacon and eggs, a combination that made her think about lakes of grease and the smell of stale frying. She started the car and swallowed hard, then reached across and fidgeted in the glove compartment for mints. There was just one dusty one, unwrapped in a corner under the *A to Z*. She shoved it in her mouth and prayed it would pacify her troubled stomach. It was either nerves or – the weird dream she'd had earlier flashed across her mind. It would have to be thought about properly later. Jennifer still stood in the doorway, waiting to watch her drive away. 'You're right,' Nina told Emily when she could trust herself to speak. 'Jennifer's either the best or the worst thing for Graham. I just can't tell. I do hope it's the best.'

'Well he's old enough to decide.'

'You'd think so,' Nina said doubtfully. She didn't really think Graham doing any real 'deciding' was going to come into it.

* * *

The bed was still just about warm. Joe snuggled up to the side where Nina slept and inhaled the familiar scent of her body. She was still using Eternity perfume, he could tell, and the usual fabric conditioner could just be identified in the white linen pillowcase. He felt like a small boy, home at last from his first everlasting school trip. There were changes, but not many, not yet. Nothing of his was still in the bathroom – no abandoned recharge flexes from the many electric razors he'd got through, and there was none of his favourite vanilla-scented shower gel left over in the cupboard. But the feel of his bare feet on the nubbly carpet, the way the street lamp up the road caught the top left corner of the mirror by the window, these were familiar.

Lucy hadn't woken up when he'd arrived, hadn't stirred when he'd looked in just to see her sweet sleeping face in the room he hadn't seen her in for almost a year. She looked just the same as when he'd left. Not enough time had passed yet for her to look different from how he went to sleep at the flat imagining her. When she stayed those weekends with him, she was so much more of a visitor than family should be. He wondered, now, lying snugly in his old bed, if he'd ever get used to being apart from his home, his family. He wished, more than he ever had before that he didn't have to.

They didn't believe him. Whatever he said, however he said it, they didn't believe him. Graham didn't know how to say it any other way. There was no point: they weren't listening.

He'd told the truth, first to the one who was being matey and had offered him cigarettes and then to the woman who'd crossed her legs and showed her thighs and then glared at him because he couldn't help but look. He was supposed to, he could tell. She'd hitched her skirt up on purpose, not accidentally. And then he could tell that he shouldn't have looked. He hadn't wanted the cigarette either, which had made the friendly one smile a lot less. He knew from television that they liked you to have one, it showed nervousness and weakness and then you had to be grateful and say thank you. But he didn't smoke, unlike most of the people working up at the hospital who didn't seem to learn anything from all the coughing and dying they saw. He wasn't going to start now just to make a policeman's day. Or night.

He sat alone in the room, wondering if his mother was all right. Jennifer would be asleep by now, in the bed that wasn't really big enough for two people, with a mattress that dipped in the middle. It made you roll into the hollow together. He wished he was there now with Jennifer's breasts pressed against him and her cool clever hands taking charge of his body. She'd been married once, she'd told him. But he'd died. He got one of the cancers that had a long name, the sort that doctors at the hospital sometimes mentioned casually in front of the patients as a possible diagnosis, professionally sure that the patient wouldn't know enough to translate it into a death sentence. He hated it when they did that, as if they were so certain that people outside their sacred building knew nothing. Right now he felt as if he too knew nothing. Certainly he knew nothing about the workings of the communal mind of the Metropolitan Police. No-one had been really horrible to him yet, but it was surely the next step, seeing as he wasn't about to change his story. And even if he did, just to please them, even if he told them they were right, he'd done those awful things on the Common, how much worse than horrible would they be then? He couldn't win. No wonder so many people confessed to things they hadn't done. You could see why.

'You can go now. Just don't leave the fucking country.' Graham took his head out of his hands and stared at the sergeant who'd appeared by the door. 'Go on then. Piss off.'

'Is that it?' Graham asked, still not getting up.

'*Yes*. That's it. Don't think you're quite off the list, not yet. Just go before we change our minds.'

'They had to check the witness statements. We made them,' Emily told him in the car as Nina drove Graham home. Graham was still confused and dazed. So Emily had been attacked by some man on the Common, and then so had someone else and they'd thought it might be him because he liked to watch owls and go out in the dark. Emily's man had been in the day. 'And you wear a Barbour but this man had one of those big long Drizabone riding mac things. And he smoked. You don't.'

'Oh. Right.' Graham was dreadfully tired. His head lolled against the car window and when Nina turned corners he was jerked awake, thinking each time he opened his eyes that the street lamps were the harsh police strip-lights and that the woman with the legs was going to slam her fist down hard on the desk in front of him, or smash it in his face with her diamond cluster ring puncturing his skin.

At the house, all the lights were still switched on as if Graham needed some kind of beacon to find his way back. Lights had been left on when their father had finally gone missing for good, he remembered. It was as if worry and grief overwhelmed the need to be frugal about the burning of electricity, as if it became suddenly a frivolous and irreverent thing to think of.

'Are you coming in?' Graham asked, looking with dread at his blazing home.

'No. We must get back. You've got Mother *and* Jennifer waiting for the prodigal's return,' Nina teased gently.

'Oh. Right,' Graham said again, climbing slowly out of the car. 'Good night then.' He waited awkwardly, shuffling his feet. 'And thanks.'

Nina wasn't surprised to find Joe in her bed. Where else would he be, she thought. She could hardly expect a man she'd lived with for nineteen years *and* had fairly recent sex with to find a spare duvet and try to get comfortable on the sofa. He was only half asleep, and when she climbed into the bed his arm reached round and pulled her towards him, warm and comforting. She was too tired for any prim pretence of pulling away. There was no point, especially as she was absurdly pleased he was there.

'Was it awful? Is it sorted?' he murmured into her ear. She could smell faint whisky on his breath. He must have helped himself to the Glenfiddich down in the kitchen, she thought, which made her feel happy that he'd felt at home enough to do it. Or, she reasoned, he could just have been drinking it at home. His home. With Catherine, who might sip virtuous fruit juice and take a sneaky folic acid tablet in preparation for that perfect baby . . .

'Its sorted. Emily was brilliant, quite stroppy and demanding. They probably just thought she was being kind, trying to get her uncle off.'

Joe chortled. 'Stupid buggers. Doesn't it occur to them that if he'd really done it, she might want him sent down *because* he was her uncle?'

'Probably not. That would take logic.' Nina wriggled

slightly to get more comfortable. She and Joe were fitted together like spoons, the way they used to fall asleep when they first met. Between them was only the thin silk of her nightdress. Joe, as ever, had got into bed naked. She could feel him crushed against her, hardening.

'I met Graham's woman, girlfriend, whatever,' she murmured.

'Really? What's she like?' Joe propped himself up on his elbow and she turned to look at him. He was still interested, then, in her family business.

'Well she's . . .' Nina hesitated. 'She's just like my mother, I think. A bit older than Graham, and she's been rather pretty, still is I suppose – used to be blonde and she's got very wide open brown eyes like an eager little girl. Graham seems to be all-important, it never occurred to her for a single moment that he could be guilty, and she's got a body like dough. I don't know her yet. It isn't fair, is it, to say anything till I do.'

Joe chuckled, 'No I suppose it isn't. When you say "dough", do you mean sort of cosy-shaped like those farmers' wives in Enid Blyton who were always described as looking like cottage loaves?'

Nina shivered. 'I'm off Enid Blyton,' she said, giggling. 'And I'll tell you why. I met a man . . .' And she told Joe the awful saga of her date with Mick.

'I really shouldn't laugh,' Joe said when she'd finished, ending with the showering of cash over Mick's supine body. Joe was giggling like a schoolboy and Nina felt ludicrously content. He stopped laughing suddenly and she could see him looking down at her in the dark, strangely intent.

'If he hadn't been married . . . would you have slept with him?' he suddenly asked. 'I shouldn't ask,' he immediately conceded.

'No you shouldn't,' Nina said, smiling in what she hoped was an enigmatic manner. 'I don't ask you what you get up to with Catherine.'

Joe sighed, nuzzling her neck comfortably. 'Nothing. I don't want to do anything with Catherine, not any more.'

'Are you sure? What if she said she'd stay with you and just manage to give up on wanting to be pregnant?' Unrealistic, she told herself, as soon as the words were out; how could a woman with an intense craving to breed suddenly cave in and say, 'Oh, all right then, if you don't want one . . .' as if they were talking about a puppy or a wide-screen TV? Joe was breathing warm and damply into her ear. She could feel him thinking with every soft breath.

'No, it's no good, there's no Catherine without the baby thing. It's become all she is just now,' he said. 'I've got to find a way of telling her it's not what I want.'

'Just *her* babies or anyone's?' Nina asked.

'Any babies, her babies, does it make a difference?' he asked.

Nina hesitated. 'I suppose not,' she said. 'Well, not to Catherine anyway.'

Chapter Eighteen

'Of course I didn't know. No-one tells me anything,' Emily said to Simon over the school telephone. 'When did she move out?'

'On the same day he told her about not wanting kids. Monday. No point in hanging around.'

Emily sighed. Simon wasn't being very communicative. Dad had spent a night, That Night, all snuggled up in bed with Mum just as if they'd never split in the first place and now Catherine and her dad had broken up. One might have led to the other; one probably *had*, and no-one was saying. No-one had done any explaining at home, as if Dad dropping in and being in the kitchen drinking coffee in his old dressing gown was just not worth a comment. Simon knew all about the Catherine thing and she didn't, so she'd have liked more details, proper ones, the way another girl would have told it. There was all the important who said what to whom, all the whys and what went wrongs. There was a sulking silence down the phone. Simon was waiting for her to tell him why she'd called, just as if she was some stranger ringing up on the off-chance to sell him something. She thought she shouldn't have to tell him, they should be on much more advanced terms by now, but things had changed.

'So. Where did Catherine move on to?' she asked eventually.

'Here.' That *did* change things, she supposed.

'Oh. Right.' She pictured Catherine surrounded by peachy pigskin luggage, sitting on Simon's unmade bed, tearful with a box of floral tissues and a mirror, mopping mascara.

'So you see, it's not a good time . . .' Simon began, businesslike as if she'd interrupted a deal-clinching meeting and trusting, manlike, that Emily would do the decent thing and fill in the rest of the sentence. Fuck it, Emily seethed to herself, he means *piss off, kid*.

Behind her at the phone booth a bustling queue of small noisy second-years had formed, all waiting to call their mums and tell them there was an extra pre-contest gym club practice. They pressed close to her and she could smell greasy lunchtime burger and chips. She turned her back on them, leaning out slightly and nudging the first one further back with her hip. There was a scuffling sound as they dominoed into each other and started squealing.

'Shut *up*!' she hissed at them and then turned back to the phone.

'Why isn't it a good time? When will it be?' she persisted. She could hear the tone of her voice rising, an unattractive desperation.

'I don't know.' She could hear his apathy. He might as well be flicking through the car-sales pages of *Loot* at the same time. Bastard Simon, he was supposed to be blitzed with adoration for her by now. He must be blaming her as well as her dad for the Catherine thing. How juvenile to take sides.

'Oh forget it,' she said. 'Call me when you're more grown up than I am, if ever,' and she slammed down the phone. There was a chorus of mocking *Ooohs*! from the queue and she stormed off back to the sixth-form common room where she knew, she just knew, Nick and Chloe would be in a giggling, tickling heap on the battered old sofa and Nick would be mentally counting his condoms.

It was Friday afternoon and she'd now got nothing to do at the weekend except a few hours' babysitting. Simon was supposed to have asked her out to impress her with a proper adult dinner – Saturday night at the Pont de la Tour or somewhere else that people his age and income went to. Or he should have surprised her with tickets (and Access All Areas passes of course) for Radiohead at the Brixton Academy. She was supposed to be going into the common room now to show off her luck to anyone who'd listen. Now all she wanted to do was crawl onto that sofa and squeeze in between Chloe and Nick and be comforted by both of them. Then, as a last resort, when Chloe was in the Politics class, she could just mention to Nick that she'd be babysitting that night, just across the road from home and that it would be lonely on her own.

She opened the door. The common room was unusually empty. How sleazy and scruffy it looked with no-one in. Posters were torn and hanging, with blu-tack missing from corners. Chairs were sloppily scattered about, their cushions crushed. The bin overflowed and reeked of stale cigarettes. You could almost hear the mould growing in abandoned coffee cups. The sofa was pulled away from the wall and all the cushions were missing. She crept inside, wondering where everyone was. Then she heard the scuffling noise and a low throaty giggle from the far side of the room. She recognized the laugh. Nick had got someone on the floor behind the sofa and whatever they were doing (at *school* – couldn't they just wait?) they'd obviously managed to persuade the rest of the sixth form that afternoon classes were starting early.

'Shit,' Emily muttered, leaving the room and slamming the door. In the far corner she'd just caught sight of Chloe's big purple bag. 'He's not worth it. None of them are bloody worth it,' Emily told herself as she stamped down the corridor towards the careers office. Inside, hardly knowing what she was doing but feeling the need not to go to the French lit. class, she picked up brochures and read their titles without interest till she came across one about gap year students and foreign travel. For the first time she could see herself free and travelling like the people in the cover photograph with a backpack somewhere hot and dusty, sharing beer and sun and fun with fellow world citizens. She'd know no-one but make friends. Selling underwear and snaring unwilling men seemed a dismally tame alternative.

'Yeah, Australia, Goa, Africa, anywhere far, far away,' she decided.

Joe didn't know what to do with himself. Now that Catherine had gone the flat felt like an anonymous place where he was simply staying temporarily, not properly living, waiting for the next thing to happen. He wished he knew what it was, this next thing, so he could just go and get on with it. It was affecting his work, not being able to make proper decisions and give it his full attention. Every time he sat at the piano he needed to get up and pick up a guitar instead. Then he'd play a few chords and move across to the phone to check out what the girls were doing. Lucy was always thrilled, always 'Dad! Are you coming to see us? Can we come over to you?' but Emily was moody, wary, he assumed, that his revived interest in them was just a between-women phase, that he'd be back to the alternate weekends kind of fathering just as soon as a new Catherine moved in.

It was after one of these one-sided conversations with Emily ('How's Wordsworth?' 'Boring') that he walked out of the flat and got a taxi straight to Art and Soul. Nina didn't like surprises, he knew that because he'd given her plenty of bad ones during their marriage. Right now she might be lunching with the Enid Blyton man, or simply not want to see him when it wasn't His Day. In the past, following his instinct had been wayward and had taken him to illicit meetings far away from home and family. Now instinct was taking him back – and the risks were all his.

Joe was hovering awkwardly in the gallery, picking up bits of jewellery and putting them down again without really looking, flicking through the pile of artsy recipe books, choosing and looking through the same one twice and not noticing.

'You seem very nervous. What's wrong?' Nina asked. He looked strangely lost, she thought, like a child whose new bike's been stolen.

Joe grinned, rather sadly. 'I don't know. I suppose I don't know what to do with myself next.'

'What about work? Nothing on right now?' There were customers browsing and she had to push down an urge to hug him, be comforting.

'Oh, work, well yes plenty of that, luckily. Title track for a new sitcom series.' He laughed. 'You wouldn't believe the brief: "Not too larky, more knicker dropping than farcey trouser loss." I think that's what it said. They want modern but not alienating, whatever that means.'

'I suppose it means a hummable tune, uplifting but not . . . oh I don't know.'

'Not anthemic. I suppose I'll have to come up with

something that's a cross between *Game On* and *Terry and June*,' Joe supplied. He knocked a papier mâché dish off the counter, bent to pick it up and apologized. 'Look, do you get time for lunch? Is Sally coming in?'

'She might be, who wants me?' Sally bustled her large self in through the gallery door and kicked it shut with her gold sandal. 'Oh Joe! Hello stranger!' She leapt forward and kissed him.

'Hi Sal. How are you and er . . . goodness I don't even know who you're with any more. Out of touch or what?'

'I'm with Weight Watchers, sweetie. That's my most regular date just now. Men are far less reliable than our group leader. She is constant and loyal in her care and attention, sees a positive side to every lapse with the choccy cake and has my best interests always at heart. What more can a woman ask?' she said. 'Were you saying something about lunch, because if you two want to go out, I'll hang on here for an hour or two.'

The restaurant was just opposite the gallery, with most of its tables occupied by pairs of women. Nina imagined they were the employers of all those bored au pairs, keeping out of the way while the girls read *Marie Claire* and fed mush to babies.

'We drank champagne in here, remember, the day Art and Soul opened,' Joe mused as they looked at the menu. Everything on it seemed to be fish. He didn't much like fish.

'Of course I remember,' Nina told him rather sharply. He was in a peculiar mood, mentally not quite there. He must be missing Catherine, she concluded, just not admitting it. Regret must be creeping in. Typical man, making a decision like that and then wanting everyone to feel sorry for him because he's now all alone-eo. She wondered if he'd been like that when he'd left *her*, but then recalled that it had been very much her decision, a kind of freedom-or-me wing-clipping gesture with not a lot of real choice about it, not for him, not by then. If he now wanted to come home again, he wasn't giving the impression that he was about to ask.

'Actually,' she said, putting down the menu, 'I'm not very hungry but I do want to thank you.'

'What for?' He looked mystified.

'That night last week, the Graham thing. Not just for coming to the house to be there for Lucy but the way it never actually occurred to you that they might have got the right bloke.'

'Oh, well . . . Graham. He's gentle, thoughtful. Just because he's a bit of a loner doesn't mean he has to be that dodgy. There's room in the world for all sorts.'

Nina looked hard at him, thinking before she spoke. 'It could have been him, you know.'

'But Emily said . . . and she'd know.'

'No, I'm sure she was right. But we don't know for sure that he didn't do the other attacks. There might be more than one person. He fits the description – wandering about on the Common in a balaclava is definitely a bit odd, and, well there's all that profiling business you hear about. It's just something Paul across the road said about all those murderers who live with their mums.' She fiddled with the salt dish, arranging a row of the fat grains along the blade of her knife. 'God what am I saying? My own brother. I hope the people he works with don't know anything about the arrest. If *I* manage to think in a no-smoke-without-fire sort of way, imagine what others would think. Sorry, I'm wittering on.'

Joe reached across and took her hand. 'No, it's OK. I'm glad you can talk to me about it. I still think you're wrong, though.'

'Yes. Thanks, Joe.' She squeezed his hand and didn't let go. Their fingers threaded themselves together. 'So do I really. I think. Oh I don't know, I keep feeling so sick and I'm sure it's just the worry. You won't believe it, but Henry even suggested I might be pregnant!'

'Oh Henry, he hasn't a clue about anything!' Joe laughed. 'He thinks Arsenal will win the FA Cup before the year 3000.' Nina looked at him speculatively. He hadn't even given the idea a second's credence, just dismissed it without thought. He was frowning now and silent, staring past the menu at the pattern on the green tablecloth. Sally would say you could hear his brain whirring like stubborn old clockwork, counting and calculating. 'I don't suppose,' he started saying, 'I don't suppose it's, well . . .'

'Possible?' she said, trying to sound lightly amused. 'What can I say? I know how you feel about the idea because of Catherine, so don't . . .'

'Don't what?' he said quickly, clutching her hand tightly. 'Get my hopes up?'

'But would they be hopes?'

'Yes. Yes they would.'

When Nina got back to the gallery, she found her mother and Jennifer, heads together, inspecting a set of hand-blown wine glasses. In the moments before they caught sight of her they looked intent and serious, like health officials checking out a dubious café's kitchen. Sally was making eagerly enquiring eyes at her behind Monica's back and she had to suppress a giggle.

'Oh hi. Looking for a present?' Nina greeted them. The two women looked strangely similar, perhaps bonded by their vigil, each with a large black oblong handbag, the rigid type that when she'd been a child Nina had thought resembled a coffin for a kitten. They both wore navy blue jackets and heavy silk scarves tied loosely at the throat. Jennifer had strangely jaunty ankle-strap black shoes, the sort that Monica used to sniff at as 'flighty'. An awful vision of Graham strangling them both in turn on Monica's sitting room floor came into her head. She wished she hadn't eaten the artichoke. The lemon butter had been far too rich and was sitting like an oily lake on top of her stomach.

'We just came to see you, actually. I wanted to show Jennifer where you worked.'

'I'll make coffee, shall I?' Sally suggested brightly, escaping to the little kitchen at the back.

'I wanted her to get to know more about us all, you see,' Monica explained. 'So she knows what I'm talking about and can picture what we all do.'

Nina wondered why Jennifer would want to. Or were Nina and her mother soon to be marched to the hospital and given a special tour of the orthopaedic wards so that reciprocal imaginings could be done? Monica might need warning, it occurred to her, that she should leave well alone and let Jennifer and Graham get on with their love life by themselves.

'Yes I do like to get the full story,' Jennifer chipped in. 'If Graham and I are chatting about you and what you do, I'll know what he's on about, won't I?' Nina felt uncomfortable. She was being inspected for gossip-fodder. She wondered if she should make their day and tell them that Joe and Catherine had separated. Monica would then probably take Jennifer straight off to Chelsea to point out Joe's apartment, like a tour guide doing the rounds of family landmarks. They'd kick themselves if they knew they'd just missed him climbing into a cab right across the road.

'Well, what do you think of our stock?' Nina asked instead. 'Anything take your fancy?'

'Oh yes,' Jennifer enthused. 'There's a lot here would make lovely wedding presents.' Nina's mouth fell open. This was exactly the kind of remark of blatant tactlessness she would have expected Monica to make, but it was Jennifer who'd said it. 'Jolly expensive. Place must be a little goldmine,' she was now muttering, picking up a vase and checking the price label on the bottom.

'Oh who's getting married?' Sally asked cheerfully, emerging from the kitchen with a tray of coffee in gallery stock mugs.

Nina, behind Jennifer, shrugged and grinned at Sally. 'I do like weddings,' Sally commented comfortably, winking at her and offering sugar. 'Well I liked mine, both of them. It's the marriage afterwards that's the problem. You have to live with them you know, after the big day. Ghastly,' she shuddered, mock-confiding.

Jennifer and Monica tittered. They would talk about Sally afterwards with great satisfaction, Nina knew. They would describe her as A Character and not even begin to imagine that she'd been anything but joking.

'Right, well, for me it's time to get off to work. Nice to have seen you again,' Jennifer said to Nina. 'Perhaps I'll come back and actually buy something one day,' she added.

'Oh feel free. Any time,' Sally told her, opening the gallery door and ushering the pair out. Nina waved as they left, feeling like a child left at school.

'Strange,' she commented to Sally. 'Whatever is my mother up to? Is she giving Jennifer a one-day crash course in how this family functions?'

'Exactly that, I'd say,' Sally agreed. 'And I hope you were up to standard or Jennifer will mark you all down as a big Fail and go back to the usual nurse hobby of pursuing Dr Right.'

'I think she's had one of those before. She's been married anyway.'

Sally shuddered. 'And she thinks it's a good idea to do it again? Mad.'

'Well no-one's mentioned marriage. I don't suppose Graham has anyway.'

Sally gave a loud laugh. 'Graham? What's he got to do with it? He'll be the last to know, trust me.'

Emily felt about as depressed as it was possible to be.

'Come to the pub,' Chloe was trying to persuade her down the phone. 'Honestly, everyone'll be there and Nick's being a pathetic lost soul without you. He keeps talking about you, I'm sick of the sound of your name!'

Why were you on the common room floor with him then? Emily's mind demanded. She didn't want Chloe to know she knew. Something said couldn't be unsaid.

'I would come, but I promised to babysit for the bloke across the road. You know, the one I told you about whose bratty little girl got Lucy's Barbados modelling job. Lucy made her some suntan lotion out of real cream so that she'd put it on and stink the beach out.'

'Nice one, Lucy,' Chloe giggled 'Revenge is sweet.'

'Mmm, probably is though the smell won't be. Anyway, so I can't come out. He's going to the airport to meet them – not the sort of thing you can cancel.'

'Shall we come to you?'

'Depends who "we" is . . .'

'Well me and Nick and Alex and Mel and Miranda and whoever's there. We could bring drink.'

Emily considered. There'd be Nick, giving her a chance either to show he was With Chloe or Wasn't With Chloe. She was feeling a bit too emotionally fragile to be able to take a With Chloe scenario.

'Nah, leave it. I'll end up having to clean their house if everyone comes, they'll spill beer on the sofa and stuff. They always do. I'll come out tomorrow and get pissed with you.'

All the same, Emily spent a lot longer in front of her make-up mirror later than a lonely babysitting job would normally require on the basis that you never knew who or what would turn up. She was wearing a new, tight black T-shirt and her favourite cream floppy trousers. Nick might miss her at the pub, take a good long look at Chloe, realize he'd got the wrong one and slope off to find her. She'd be ready, even if it was only to tell him to get lost. Or Simon might have second thoughts. He might want someone fun to be with and look around the flat and out of the window at pairs of people wandering about and realize he was stuck for the evening (or even for *years*) with his boring sister droning on about her miseries.

'Are you going somewhere else later?' Lucy asked looking wistful. 'I wish I was old enough to go out. I never go anywhere. No-one's even letting me go modelling any more. How am I going to get famous if I don't even get looked at?'

Emily applied a second layer of mascara, concentrating hard and unable to reply. 'And why does your mouth drop open when you put eye make-up on?' Lucy went on. 'Let me see if mine does.' She made a grab for a pot of eye shadow and sent the whole make-up bag tumbling to the floor. Coloured powdery flecks settled onto Emily's trousers. 'Sorry!' Lucy said quickly, flapping her hands at the marks.

'Get off! You're making it worse!' Emily shoved at Lucy and pushed her out of the bathroom. 'You're a complete pain, Lucy, these were just back from the cleaners!'

'I said I'm sorry!' Lucy wailed from the other side of the door.

'What difference does that make? I can't wear these now!' Emily yelled back.

'What's going on? You sound like a pair of three-year-olds!' Nina dashed up the stairs to see what was going on.

'Look what she's done!' Emily came out and showed her the damage.

'Is that all? Just sponge it off, it'll be all right.'

'I said sorry.' Lucy scowled at Emily. 'And she's *still* cross.'

'No she's not,' Nina reassured her. 'Are you, Emily? And to prove it she's going to take you babysitting with her and you're going to be nice to each other and *not fight.*'

'Why? Why've I got to take her with me?' Emily fumed.

'Because I'm going out for a while. I'm going down to the pub with Henry for a quiet drink and to thrash him at darts. I won't be long, and I'll collect Lucy on the way back.'

'Do I get paid? I'll be doing two lots of babysitting at once.'

'I do two lots of parenting at once. No-one pays me double,' Nina replied.

Nina walked slowly along the Crescent towards Henry's house and gazed into other people's windows. She wondered if their lives were as orderly as the rooms she was seeing. Not a cushion looked out of place, not a painting askew, not an ornament carelessly positioned. Perhaps these were people who never made mistakes about who they lived with and who they didn't. Probably they never dithered over what to wear for lunch with their ex's just because they still cared enough to want to look good for them. Now and then she could see the backs of heads watching flickering televisions. At one she peered in and was surprised when an elderly male head bobbed up next to her from a flowerbed, and gave her a wary 'Good evening' as if worried that the simple words might lead to unsuitable personal revelations, a discussion about Jehovah or even a mugging. She walked quickly past the alleyway that led to the Common, wondering who was out there doing what unspeakable things.

'You're early,' Henry greeted her as she rang his bell.

'I'll go away again if you like then,' she said, turning round and starting back down the path. She turned back and grinned at him. He was already closing the front door and coming to join her.

'Earlier the better as far as I'm concerned. Time for an extra drink.'

'I think I only fancy a Coke,' Nina said. 'Alcohol's too depressing.'

'Oh God, I wanted a jolly night out,' Henry said, putting an arm round her shoulder. 'Don't tell me you're going to cry all over me.'

'I might just do that. I've just realized two things. The most important one is that I wish, I really wish Joe was living with us again.'

Henry laughed. 'Took you long enough to work that one out, didn't it? I suppose the other thing you've realized is that you never want to learn to play darts.'

'I don't need to. You're just assuming,' Nina said. 'I was captain of the college darts team. We beat everyone over three counties.'

'Sam doesn't want to go to bed yet, do you Sam? He's extra excited because his mum's coming home.' Sam and Emily glared at each other but he gave Lucy a big smile. 'So I said he could play with you for a while.' Paul patted Emily on the shoulder in a matey sort of way and reached across her to get his jacket from the hook.

Emily gave Sam a look of hostile suspicion. She'd heard about the snail-treading incident. She'd seen Megan applauding his every tantrum, squealing 'oh he's a real boy!' as he smashed up Sophie's Lego castle with his wooden hammer. Here was a small child who might think it was fun to sneak up behind the sofa and pull her hair out, strand by strand. Or he might, while playing angelically quietly, pour Fairy Liquid all down the stair carpet.

'What time does he go to bed?' Emily asked, hoping the answer would be 'soon'.

'When he's tired,' Paul shrugged. 'Isn't that when you go?' His hand was now on the door latch.

'Yes but I'm not five,' Emily snarled under her breath.

'We won't be too late, unless the plane's delayed, so have fun all of you. There's Coke in the fridge and biscuits in the jar.'

'Thank you very much Mr Brocklehurst. We'll take good care of Sam.' Lucy smiled up at him.

'Creep,' Emily said when he'd gone. 'You're only hoping you'll get paid extra.'

'Well *you* don't deserve to get paid at all. You're horrid to Sam.'

'I'm here aren't I? That's babysitting. You sit, they're babies, end of story.' Sam was standing by the front door, looking bereft and as if he was in two minds whether crying might bring back a parent or not.

'I'll play with him, just for a bit, then it's your turn,' Lucy volunteered, feeling sorry for him and worried for herself. Sophie would have to be faced in a couple of hours, Sophie and her mum who had had two weeks to work out exactly how horrible Lucy had been, giving her that disgusting suntan lotion concoction. If she played with Sam, Emily might be persuaded to be on her side later.

'Thanks.' Emily relented and grinned at her. 'And I'll split the money, just this once. Just give me half an hour's television peace.'

She went into the sitting room, flopped onto the sofa and picked up the remote control. Lucy took Sam up the stairs and for nearly ten minutes there was blissful quiet, broken only by the occasional burst of Lucy's donkey-laugh.

'That's not fair!' Emily heard Sam shriek. His voice, for one so young, carried right through the whole fabric of the house. Emily was sure she could feel his fury vibrating in the sofa. She sighed, giving up any hope that this would be any kind of successful or even restful evening. Sam was simply too indulged and pampered to be anything but a hundred per cent demanding.

'What's wrong?' she said to Sam who sat huddled and brooding halfway down the stairs. He was dressed in a green beret, a khaki sweater with elbow patches and his face was smeared with brown and grey eye make-up. Glittery flecks lay on his cheeks like Christmas dust. He carried a plastic hand grenade.

'She won't play war. Sophie plays war with me. *She* likes it.'

'I don't,' Lucy insisted. 'Well not much. That's Sophie's thing, not really mine. I only played it with Sophie because I was being nice then.'

'Can't you be nice now?' Emily asked.

'No. I'll play cars and I'll play doing gym or

289

something but I'm not wearing Sophie's smelly old army clothes. And I'm definitely not putting that stuff on my face. I might get allergic. Sophie can play all that with him tomorrow. *If* she's not too jet-lagged.'

She stamped off into the sitting room and dropped onto the sofa, immediately engrossed in a TV ad for shampoo. Emily watched her running her fingers through her long hair, copying the actress. Sam looked up at Emily, large brown eyes appealing like Genghis when he could smell food. Emily softened. The poor child's mother had been away for ages. It must seem half a lifetime to him. It wasn't his fault that he was so cherished and spoilt. Perhaps, left alone like this, he deserved to be. His daddy could at least have taken him to the airport. She used to love going there with Graham when she was little.

'OK Sam, what do we do?' Sam leapt up and ran back up the stairs. Emily followed. In Sophie's room (SAS posters, army leaf-camouflage netting draped over the top of a junior four-poster bed), Sam opened a cupboard and started pulling out clothes.

'Are you allowed to do this?'

He looked back at her, wondering at the sense of the question, and didn't reply. 'You wear some of this,' he instructed. Emily climbed into the only pair of trousers that looked big enough for her. Goodness only knew how Sophie managed to wear them, they seemed big enough for a full-sized man. 'And this,' Sam said, pulling out a toy gun-belt complete with silver Lone Star gun. 'And then we kill each other.' He grinned.

'OK,' Emily groaned, trying to fit the gun-belt round her waist.

'And you can wear this.' Sam handed her a black knitted object. 'You put it on your head. It's special,' he told her.

Emily pulled the black balaclava over her head, praying that Nick (or even Simon) wouldn't choose this moment to come and visit. It was hot under the wool, and there was a smell. She started feeling sick and sat down on Sophie's bed. Slowly, deliberately, she inhaled, letting her senses do sorting and recalling.

'Come *on*, let's *play*.' Sam was tugging at her arm. Emily felt limp. It was *the* smell. It was the smell of those cigarettes and that aftershave. She could almost feel the man pressed against her, shoving at her body, forcing her against the tree. She could feel the bark again digging into her back. She'd been right, it could be any man, from any family.

Chapter Nineteen

'So where is Joe tonight and what's he doing now he's all on his own?' Henry asked.

Nina threw her second dart, which hit the edge ring of the five and bounced uselessly to the floor. This 'all on his own' thing kept coming up now that people knew Catherine had gone. It was just like all those months ago when she and Joe had first separated and everyone assumed he, turfed out of the family nest, was suddenly a lost soul. *She'd* been all on her own too for the past year, if anyone had noticed. Apart from Henry, who had spent just as much time in her kitchen when Joe was living in the house as he did now, there hadn't exactly been a queue for the comforting.

'Is it only selfish women who chuck out their men?' she asked Henry.

Henry shrugged. 'And misunderstood men who chuck out their women? I don't know. The usual mixture I suppose. Badly treated women don't chuck their men out often enough, and badly treated men . . .' he laughed. 'They pay alimony.' Nina grinned at him and threw her third dart.

'Double ten. Not bad when I'm out of practice.' She took a sip of her bitter lemon and thought for a moment. 'I don't know where Joe is tonight. And you didn't really think I would, you're just being conversational. Actually, he's probably out in some restaurant with a new young thing,' she giggled. 'Either that or he's stripping flowered wallpaper from their bedroom at the flat. Really Henry, you should see it. Swagged, dragged and smothered. The rest of the flat is just like Joe, uncluttered, casual and probably more expensive than you'd think.'

'You've been inspecting the premises then?'

'Mmm. Briefly. I hope she's taken her art deco lamps with her. We've got some lovely spiralled steel ones in the gallery. Perhaps I'll take one round as a Catherine-moving-out present.' She pulled the darts out of the board, handed them to Henry and smiled. 'Your go. You need fifty-six. Ten, six and double top?'

'If I smile inscrutably and say "possibly" you'll never know whether I missed on purpose or not, will you?'

'I don't think you'd miss on purpose Henry, not unless you'd got the urge for our relationship to be on a totally different level.'

Henry pouted, mocking. 'Even if I did, there'd be no way of convincing you I was more worthy of your life-long devotion than Joe is.'

'Don't be daft, Henry,' she told him, pushing him towards the dartboard. 'There's no point spoiling things.'

Henry picked up the darts and threw them with casual negligence. 'My game, your round. Look how talented I can be when you make me cross. Kiss for the winner? Just a between-friends one for no hard feelings?' Henry leaned across and kissed her gently just on her jawbone. It tickled, nothing more.

'Sorry to interrupt. Emily said to come and get you.' Cool air swept through the door and Joe was standing in front of Nina, his hair awry and the collar of his jacket twisted. He was frowning, worried enough to be rude, ignoring Henry.

'What's happened? Where are the girls?' Nina's insides lurched. Like all mothers, within milliseconds she'd imagined them burnt to ashy flakes in Megan and Paul's house, huddled with little Sam under a locked bedroom window, firemen in tears carrying bodies.

'They're fine. But . . .' Joe said, taking Nina's arm and pulling her firmly out of the pub door. Focusing hard on Joe's face for clues, she could only just make out Henry, trailing and wondering what could possibly have happened that needed to be explained out on the pavement.

'Emily says she knows who the man who attacked her was. She's babysitting for him. She called me and I told her I'd find you, go back there and we'll talk to the police. She can't leave the child or Lucy, she says. That's why she rang me.'

'But she's babysitting for neighbours, for . . . for Paul across the road. But she can't mean . . . he's . . .' Nina felt confused, waiting for some kind of information to take hold. 'I don't like him that much, but surely . . .' her voice trailed away. Surely what? Surely not a nice nuclear-family man with a gorgeous wife, all the desirable trappings that made up middle-class life. There was nothing 'surely' about it. After all, she'd even briefly suspected her own brother, ignoring the 'surely it's not him' that was instinctive, protective.

'How does she know?' Henry asked as they walked towards Joe's car. Nina, held between them, felt like an injured footballer being led off the pitch by concerned team-mates.

'Something to do with the smell of Sophie's hat,' Joe said. 'At least that's what she said on the phone. I didn't much understand, but I believed her.'

'If she says it's him, then it's him,' Nina said, climbing into the Audi. She was feeling nauseous again and put it down to the bitter lemon – and also to the shock of another proven instinct, this time one she'd ignored: her kitchen knives were still in the tea-towel drawer after Paul's visit, and yet she'd let her children babysit for him.

'Exactly,' Joe said, switching on the engine.

Emily felt strangely calm as soon as she'd put the phone down. Dad would fix it, just like when she was little. She didn't tell Lucy. Lucy might panic, get theatrical and upset Sam. And then Sam would cry and be frightened and everything would be chaos and no control. They were upstairs, tired, thumbs in their mouths, lying on Paul and Megan's high brass bed watching a film of dreadful violence.

Emily sat on the sofa and waited. The balaclava was in her bag, safely stashed in a self-seal freezer bag. The police would be pleased about that. The coat he'd been wearing that day was hanging in the hallway, just as if it was any old real coat. She couldn't touch that.

Breathing quietly and concentrating on not looking at the clock, Emily calculated how long it would take for Paul and Megan and Sophie to get from Gatwick if the plane and the customs and baggage had no delays. She imagined them, as her nervousness started to cut through the calm, bursting in through the door and shouting 'We're home! Record time!' They'd be all smiles and family life because Paul wouldn't be an evil violent creep all the time. When the doorbell actually rang, and she knew that her parents had got there first, she almost flung herself into the hallway. But the shapes through the window were not theirs.

'Hi. Thought you might want some company!' Chloe and Nick were standing on the doorstep looking eager.

Emily laughed, a disjointed shriek, mildly hysterical at the shock of it being *them.*

'I mean, sorry, if you want us to go away, that's cool, but—'

'No! No come in. The more the better!' It sounded sarcastic, even to Emily's ears, but she didn't bother to apologize. She didn't mean it to sound like that but they'd have to understand. They would if they were real friends.

'We brought you some drink. Ready mixed, Archer's and lemonade.' Chloe was holding out a Perrier bottle full of clear, fizzy liquid. 'You'd never know, would you?' she said, making herself comfortable on the sofa, 'just what that innocent little bottle contained.'

'You're so right,' Emily murmured vaguely. Nick was standing with his hands in his pockets, eyeing her tits. She pulled her T-shirt away from her body, making it baggy and giving herself more air next to her skin. Nick looked down at the floor, going pink.

'My parents are on their way,' Emily told them very quickly. 'And then the police will come because the man I'm babysitting for is the man who grabbed me that day on the Common.' She said it calmly enough, but she kept looking at the window, willing Joe's Audi to pull up outside, now, right now. 'So if you're carry-ing anything you shouldn't be, like the odd spliff . . .' she glanced at Nick and shrugged, her hands stuffed in her pockets, as if none of what she'd said mattered really, it was just one of those things to be dealt with.

'Shit! Are you sure? I mean are you *really* sure?' Chloe said, her eyes wide and amazed.

'Well of course I'm sure. Stay if you want, then you'll see. I already called the police station and spoke to that nice woman officer that they gave me that time. You get one allocated, sex crime victims. She said to call again after he's come back and she'd do some checking while we wait. I think I'm supposed to just get paid for the babysitting, be like nothing's different and go home. Except that I called Dad.'

'You're very, well, businesslike about it,' Chloe commented. She didn't, Emily thought, looking particularly approving.

'What do you want me to do, scream and yell? Bit late for that. Nothing's going to happen to me now.' She picked up a wedding photo of Megan and Paul, all smiles and confetti. 'It's going to happen to *him*.'

'You'd better be really, really sure. Surer than you've ever been about anything,' Nick said in a slow, considered way. His voice sounded discordantly male, as if, right now, it had no real business being heard. The doorbell rang before she could even think of a reply.

'Em! Are you all right? Are they back yet?' Nina hugged Emily and peered beyond her.

'What's happening, why are you here, Mum? And Dad?' Lucy appeared on the stairs. Nina looked at her over Emily's shoulder. She shouldn't be there, she thought, and neither should Sam, but she wanted Joe with them all.

'I'll take them to my place, shall I?' Henry suggested.

'Oh Henry, thanks. That would be great.'

Lucy stepped backwards up the stairs, sensing she was to miss a drama. 'Why? Why can't we be here? Megan will be really cross if Sam's not home.'

'Tough,' Joe said. 'Lucy my love, we'll explain later. Just go with Henry for now.'

'Fish and chips?' Henry said, opening the door and ushering Lucy and a quite amiable Sam out onto the path.

'It might be an idea if you left, too,' Joe said to Chloe and Nick. The two of them looked at each other and then at Emily. She could tell they wanted to stay, but that they also knew they'd wish they hadn't.

'Tell us about it at school,' Chloe said, hugging Emily. 'Or call me in the morning.' Nick said nothing. Emily watched him from the window, walking down the path and waiting till the gate was almost shut before he put his arm round Chloe. Australia, Emily thought with longing. New people.

There was nothing like the urgent nee-nawing of police sirens for linking a community. Doors edged open as the cars stopped, lights flashing, outside number 26 and eager nosy onlookers gathered in small speculating groups on the pavement at the shortest distance they could consider discreet. Even posh Penelope, still shoving her arms into a jacket, indulged her curiosity quite shamelessly and bustled along the Crescent to see what was going on. 'Look at that,' Joe commented to Nina. 'She's not even got the dog with her so she can be pretending to be just passing on her way to the Common.' Far more accustomed to being the victims of burglary than perpetrators of anything more criminal than a dodgy tax return, the residents clung together in outrage and shock as the truth emerged. 'But he's so . . . Paul's just . . .' Penelope waffled to one of the policemen. 'So what, love? So like everyone else? Like you and me? They all are.'

Megan blamed Nina. 'Why couldn't you just leave things alone?' she hissed at her over the luggage still cluttering the hallway. 'He only did it because of *this*. He'd have been all right when I'd finished being pregnant, he was before.' She clutched the baby-bulge that had clearly grown in the Caribbean sun.

Nina was close to feeling sorry for her: she imagined the twins cuddled safely together under the stretched skin, innocently growing their limbs, their hair and their beautiful baby faces. Megan's own face was frantic with anger and terror and she looked from Sam to Sophie and back to Nina with furious desperation.

'What about them? You didn't think, did you? Their lives will be ruined, don't you realize?'

'What about his victims' lives?' Nina asked her quietly. 'If you knew he was doing this, why didn't you ask *him* to think about *them*?'

'You can never tell, with men,' Monica stated ominously when she heard about Paul's arrest from Nina. 'I suppose, all things considered, it's just as well that you've let Joe move back in again.' Her tone was somewhat grudging, Nina thought with amusement and rather implied that he shouldn't even have been considered for another chance if Genghis had been more use as a guard dog.

'What will he do with that flat of his?' Monica continued. 'Keep it on?'

'To instal a mistress in for afternoon fun?' Nina teased. 'No, he'd only rented it. He's brought all his studio equipment back, and that battered old sofa. Everything else he bought has gone into storage for now, till we decide just what to do with it.'

'Graham could do with a new bed,' Monica told her with a very intense look. 'I'm going to have to buy a hat, to go with that blue suit we got in Harrods. He and Jennifer are about to name the day.'

Many months later, Nina thought again about Megan and wondered how she was coping. She thought of her living alone with Sam and Sophie and her fast-growing twins, and wondering how on earth she was going to tell them, when they asked, that their father wasn't around for the birth because he was locked away on remand. Some people joked about prison, called it being a guest of Her Majesty. For what Paul had been doing there wouldn't be any element of being a guest about it.

The first time Paul had been caught, years before, during Megan's pregnancy with Sam, there'd been a fine and a mention in the local paper and a swift, embarrassed change of area for living in. It didn't seem likely that Megan would play the understanding wife this time, not now there would be a prison term to live down and the realization that her husband had actually committed real sex crimes, not some joky little misdemeanour that had simply got a bit out of hand. Now number 26 was up for sale again, but then so was number 23.

Nina and Joe were taking their last Sunday walk on the Common. Neither of them would miss it. They would still see Henry. He and posh Penelope, who had got together in the post-arrest excitement and discovered a shared taste for gossip, the Post-Impressionists and good Burgundy, had promised to be frequent visitors and to keep them supplied with decent wines and delicacies that London people always assume simply aren't to be found beyond the M25. Down in Dorset there would be the long empty beach to walk on and Genghis, at last, would be able to run free. Emily, on her postcard from Ayers Rock, had simply said she didn't mind where they moved to as long as absolutely nothing of hers got thrown away in the packing except her copy of *Man-Date*.

Lucy was holding Genghis's lead, skipping ahead. Another Sunday afternoon, another arm-wrenching run for the dog with Lucy imagining she had control. Her chilled breath billowed under the trees as she ran and panted, shrieking and laughing at the dog and telling him, hopelessly, to slow down.

'Look how free she thinks she is. No sense of danger. That must be bliss,' Nina was saying to Joe. 'Emily might never have that again. No woman does, not really. Wherever we go, there's always that back of the mind feeling about someone like Paul, stalking and creeping and watching.'

'Men get that too, you know,' he told her. 'We don't all go through life feeling like Superman. If we're not scared for ourselves, there's always someone we care about.'

Nina looked down into the pram Joe was pushing. Their new baby, milk-full and secure, was sleeping. 'The sleep of the innocent,' Monica had said when she'd first seen him at the hospital. Nina, in a post-natal mental blur, hadn't been listening properly and had misheard it as the *slaughter* of the innocents. Her eyes had filled with new-mother easy tears and she'd crushed her new son to her in automatic protection. Later, she thought carefully about that, analysing her reaction. She'd have felt the same about the girls. She had done at the time, when they were that tiny, she was certain. It really wasn't that this one was a boy. The girls had been just as treasured and adored and had turned out fine. You didn't get them for long, that was the trouble. She would bring this boy up the same way as the girls, she was sure of it. Really, she was absolutely sure.

Chapter Twenty

Graham was out on the Common again early in the evening, long after the wintry sun had disappeared. It was chill and bleak, the stiff, freezing branches of the trees motionless as if the slightest stir would snap them and give them pain like broken bones. Soon it would be time to go back. The women would worry. They would be making supper, busy together in their kitchen harmony. Monica still, after all these months, would be telling Jennifer just how much chilli was right for him and double-checking that the parsnips had been put in the oven at the right time to roast with the potatoes. They didn't mind him sloping off out, as long as he told them more or less where he was going and when he'd be back.

'Men do that,' Jennifer had conceded, as soon as they were back from the San Francisco honeymoon (Edwards air base in time for the open day and then Miramar – sitting at the end of the runway watching the F-18s, pretending to be Tom Cruise). 'I know they like to go to the pub.' Sometimes he drank a can of lager he'd brought out with him just so she could imagine that was where he'd been. Occasionally he even lit a cigarette and let it burn down, wafting smoke over his clothes so he'd smell of lounge bar. If it made them happy.

The scuffling in the dry frozen undergrowth startled him from his musings. It was too small to be a mammal, too early in the year to be a bird fallen from a nest. He went to investigate, treading fearfully across the crackling twigs. It was a thrush, broken winged and terrified, limping and dragging beneath the trees. He picked it up, gently in his soft gloves. He could kill it, should kill it and put it out of its misery. The thought both sickened and attracted him. Killing it would be power, would be *doing something about it.* He didn't get many opportunities for positive action, not on his own. The little bird squawked in his hand and its eyes were full of panic.

Carefully, he put it back on the ground. There would be starving foxes later, or an owl. He would leave it. Nature was cruel enough – she didn't need any help from him.

THE END

A SELECTED LIST OF FINE WRITING AVAILABLE FROM BLACK SWAN

THE PRICES SHOWN BELOW WERE CORRECT AT THE TIME OF GOING TO PRESS. HOWEVER TRANSWORLD PUBLISHERS RESERVE THE RIGHT TO SHOW NEW RETAIL PRICES ON COVERS WHICH MAY DIFFER FROM THOSE PREVIOUSLY ADVERTISED IN THE TEXT OR ELSEWHERE.

99564 9	JUST FOR THE SUMMER	*Judy Astley*	£6.99
99565 7	PLEASANT VICES	*Judy Astley*	£6.99
99629 7	SEVEN FOR A SECRET	*Judy Astley*	£5.99
99630 0	MUDDY WATERS	*Judy Astley*	£6.99
99618 1	BEHIND THE SCENES AT THE MUSEUM	*Kate Atkinson*	£6.99
99722 6	THE PULL OF THE MOON	*Elizabeth Berg*	£6.99
99687 4	THE PURVEYOR OF ENCHANTMENT	*Marika Cobbold*	£6.99
99624 6	THE COUNTER-TENOR'S DAUGHTER	*Elizabeth Falconer*	£6.99
99657 2	PERFECT MERINGUES	*Laurie Graham*	£5.99
99611 4	THE COURTYARD IN AUGUST	*Janette Griffiths*	£6.99
99685 8	THE BOOK OF RUTH	*Jane Hamilton*	£6.99
99754 4	CLOUD MUSIC	*Karen Hayes*	£6.99
99771 4	MALLINGFORD	*Alison Love*	£6.99
99689 3	WATERWINGS	*Joan Marysmith*	£6.99
99649 1	WAITING TO EXHALE	*Terry McMillan*	£5.99
99701 3	EVERMORE	*Penny Perrick*	£6.99
99696 3	THE VISITATION	*Sue Reidy*	£5.99
99732 3	A PRIZE FOR SISTER CATHERINE	*Kathleen Rowntree*	£6.99
99671 8	THAT AWKWARD AGE	*Mary Selby*	£6.99
99753 6	AN ACCIDENTAL LIFE	*Titia Sutherland*	£6.99
99700 5	NEXT OF KIN	*Joanna Trollope*	£6.99
99655 6	GOLDENGROVE UNLEAVING	*Jill Paton Walsh*	£6.99
99673 4	DINA'S BOOK	*Herbjørg Wassmo*	£6.99
99592 4	AN IMAGINATIVE EXPERIENCE	*Mary Wesley*	£5.99
99642 4	SWIMMING POOL SUNDAY	*Madeleine Wickham*	£6.99
99591 6	A MISLAID MAGIC	*Joyce Windsor*	£4.99

All Transworld titles are available by post from:

Book Services By Post, P.O. Box 29, Douglas, Isle of Man IM99 1BQ

Credit cards accepted. Please telephone 01624 675137,
fax 01624 670923 or Internet http://www.bookpost.co.uk.
or e-mail: bookshop@enterprise.net for details

Free postage and packing in the UK. Overseas customers: allow
£1 per book (paperbacks) and £3 per book (hardbacks).